Mystery Woman

☆

I sat down, shut the door, and as I leaned back I smelt violets and I heard someone give a deep, trembling sigh in the darkness beside me.

The car began to move, and as we passed the first lamppost I looked into the dark corner beyond me and saw what I thought was a woman with her head bent and her face hidden in her hands. I wondered where on earth they were taking me.

We drove for the better part of an hour. We had not met another car for perhaps a quarter of an hour, when we slowed down and stopped. The driver got down, opened my door, and stood by whilst I got out.

"This way," said the driver. He had a torch in his hand and set the light dancing down a grassy path to the right.

When I said, "The Lady?" he answered me with an effect of surprise.

"What lady?" His voice was thick and indistinct.

"In the car."

And at that he turned the light and let it shine upon the back seat. It was empty.

☆

BEGGAR'S CHOICE

Also by Patricia Wentworth

THE CASE IS CLOSED
THE CLOCK STRIKES TWELVE *Jown*
THE FINGERPRINT *Jown*
GREY MASK
LONESOME ROAD
PILGRIM'S REST
THE WATERSPLASH
WICKED UNCLE
DEAD OR ALIVE *Jown*
NOTHING VENTURE *I've read*
OUTRAGEOUS FORTUNE
RUN!
MR. ZERO *Jown*
THE LISTENING EYE

Published by
WARNER BOOKS

PATRICIA WENTWORTH

BEGGAR'S CHOICE

WARNER BOOKS

A Warner Communications Company

I

From Carthew Fairfax's diary:

September 14*th* 1929—I SUPPOSE I'VE TOUCHED BOTTOM to-day. I'm going to write about it because it's something to do, and because of the odd thing that happened. The more I think about it, the odder it seems, so I think I'll just write everything down whilst I can be sure I'm remembering and not imagining. They say you get to imagine things when you're alone a lot. Extraordinary to think that one used to come up to town to have a good time and see one's pals. Now it's not town any more; it's London—a grimy, gritty loneliness—and if I saw a pal, I'd make tracks in the opposite direction. I thrashed that out with myself when I dropped past the middle of the ladder and began going down, rung by rung, to the bottom. I suppose I haven't quite got there yet, but I must be pretty near it.

And now I'm going to write down what happened to-day.

I started out bright and early to answer an advertisement for a secretary. The extraordinary thing was that I really felt most awfully bucked. I suppose I'm hopeful by nature, because when I'm job-hunting I generally feel exhilarated and sure I'm going to get something this time. I remember feeling particularly hopeful just before I took on with that beast Craddock, and I only stayed a week, and left in a hurry because I was afraid I'd murder him if I didn't get out—and whatever the luck's like, I'd rather keep clear of the gallows, if it was only for Fay's sake.

Well, I started out and stayed hopeful until the bloke who interviewed me turned me down. He was a smug brute, with black bottle-brush eyebrows and indecently new clothes. He turned me down. I saw him look at my boots, and I went out boiling with rage. I suppose three years of losing cheap jobs and hunting cheaper ones ought to have broken me in—but I boiled. I wanted to round on him and say, "I don't write with my boots, fathead, and anyhow I'd eat them raw before I'd take your damned job!"

I was still boiling ten minutes later, though I'd begun to call myself a fool. I took a good look at my boots in the open daylight. It was a muggy day, with the sun struggling to get through the clouds and not quite bringing it off; but even without the sun to show them up, I'm bound to say those boots gave me a sick, discouraged sort of feeling; because when your boots go, it's all up with you as far as job-hunting's concerned. I knew the soles were pretty far gone. Soles don't matter so long as the uppers hold. Well, mine weren't going to hold much longer. I've always been hard on a left shoe, and I could feel the brute giving as I walked. It will be through by to-morrow.

I thought about that pretty soberly. To-morrow began to look like being a small private edition of the end of the world as far as I was concerned. I owe three weeks' rent, and three is Mrs. Bell's limit. It would be "pay or go"; and I certainly couldn't pay.

I turned the corner, and came face to face with Isobel Tarrant.

I don't think I've ever had such a shock. I'd got pretty far down amongst cheery visions of what was likely to happen if I didn't get a job in the next few hours. And then to see Isobel like that! I don't think I can explain how I felt, but Isobel hadn't any business to be within a thousand miles of the things I was thinking about. I felt as if I'd met her in some beastly slum, and as if it was my fault that she was there; and I felt as if I didn't care whether it was a slum or not, or how much she oughtn't to be there, so long as I was seeing her again. It's three years since I've seen Isobel— and I saw her this morning. What's the good of pretending? I'm not writing all this down because something rather odd happened afterwards; I'm writing because I want to write about Isobel—because I've been starving for her, and pretending to myself that I've forgotten.

Well, I saw her. I've forgotten her just as much as a man who's dying of thirst has forgotten water—he's forgotten what it tastes like, and he can't get it, and he's dying without it, and then some one shows it to him—shows him a pool with the sun on it and the water coming up in a clear spring. There was a pool like that at Linwood, and it always reminded me of Isobel. The trees stood round it so close that the water had the look of being extraordinarily deep. And first of all you'd think it was as still as glass, but if you watched, you'd see the spring of the water moving in it a long way down, and if you knew the right place, you could stand and see the sky in the water; and, once in a way when the sun was just right, you could look down, and down, and down. I used to think there was something hidden in the pool, and make up stories about it. And afterwards, when I met Isobel, I thought about the pool at once. I suppose at first it was her eyes—because they have the same look that very deep water has. And then I loved her so much that she reminded me of all the beautiful things I had ever seen. The Linwood pool is very beautiful.

I've got a long way from meeting Isobel. I came round the corner, and she was only about half a yard away. If there had been any earthly way of avoiding her, I'd have taken it—but there wasn't any way, so I took my hat off. And she said "Car!" and stopped dead and said "Car!" again. And before I knew what I was doing we were shaking hands. I don't see that I could have helped it—I couldn't have cut her dead. And when I wanted to take my hand away, she held on to it, and she said, "Oh, *Car!*"

I don't know what I said—I dare say I didn't say anything—I didn't want to say anything—I wanted to look at her. She had on a blue dress, and at first I thought she was pale—frightfully pale—and my heart gave a sort of jerk of pure funk because I was afraid she was ill. And then when she said "Oh, *Car!*" the color came into her face and she looked so beautiful that I could have gone down on my knees and kissed the ground she was walking on—I didn't, of course; I stood like a stockfish and looked at her. And then she said, "Oh, Car, where have you been?" and I came to my senses and got my hand away.

"Oh, all over the place," I said.

"And what are you doing?"

"A job of work—when I can get one."

She said, "Have you got one now?" She has such a soft voice. She was sorry for me. I don't mind as long as it doesn't hurt her. She didn't look at my boots, and at all the rest of my shabbiness, but of course she could see exactly where I'd come to, and her voice wasn't quite steady. She's got a soft heart as well as a soft voice.

I told myself just what sort of a cad I should be if I traded on it, and I laughed a little and said,

"I'm on the trail. Wish me good hunting!"

She ought to have taken my cue, wished me good luck, and let me go. Instead, she looked at me with a sort of heavenly hurt look in her eyes.

"Why did you disappear?" Her voice was so soft I could hardly hear what she said.

"My dear," I said, " 'disappear' sounds like a detective story. I've merely been dull and respectable—a little work, a little play, and so on."

"And no friends?" she asked. Then, before I could answer, "You *did* disappear. You didn't give your friends a chance. It wasn't fair."

I'd more or less got hold of myself by this time, and this was something I'd got an answer for.

"Look here, Isobel, what do you mean by 'not fair'?"

"You didn't give your friends a chance at all."

"How could they have helped me? Lent me fivers until they began to say to each other, 'I say, here's Car—I'm off!'?"

She made a little sharp sound as if I'd hurt her.

"No, of course I didn't mean that."

"Perhaps you meant that I might have asked them to go round touting for a job for me—'I say, you know, there's poor old Car—absolutely down and out—had to send in his papers because his father didn't leave him a sou—took on with Lymington and got let in for the great Lymington smash——'"

She stopped me.

"Car—don't!"

"Well, that's what they'd have had to say—isn't it? The Lymington smash takes a bit of living down, my dear. Lymington's secretary wasn't exactly in demand. One man told me that if I wasn't a knave, I must be about the biggest fool in the British Empire, and whichever I was, he hadn't any use for me."

She made a sound without any words. I knew I'd hurt her, but I was feeling savage and I wanted to hurt. In a way, it brought her nearer. For three years she'd been as far away as if I'd been dead. It made me feel alive again when she showed that I'd hurt her.

"You see I wasn't a very marketable article," I said. "Shorthand nil—typing nil—languages English public school—in fact, commercially speaking, a wash-out. You can't walk into a man's office and say, 'I'm a decent shot, and fair to average at polo and racquets' "——I broke off with a laugh—"and that was about the best my best pal could have said for me. I can type now, and I grind out shorthand, but any bright lad from a secondary school has probably got me beat at both."

"You didn't give any of us a chance," she said. "I'm not talking about jobs—I'm talking about being friends. When I'm——" She hesitated, and then said, "*down*—I want my friends all the more."

I looked at her for a moment because I couldn't help it.

Then I was afraid to go on looking. There was such a beautiful eager kindness in her eyes, and I thought I saw her lip tremble. That was when I was afraid to go on looking.

"People soon get over wanting you when you're down in the world," I said.

"That's pride," said Isobel steadily.

I laughed again.

"No, my dear—experience. Do you remember Jimmy Buckley? No, you wouldn't—he was before your time. Well, it's a very instructive story. Jimmy went smash, and all Jimmy's pals rallied round, and pressed fivers into his hand, and hunted jobs for him. And when Jimmy didn't keep the jobs, they hunted more, but not quite so enthusiastically, and they stopped pressing fivers on him. And when they stopped, Jimmy started asking, and the last I heard of him was that he'd settled down to a permanent job of writing begging letters—very systematic and regular. He'd work through all his relations, and then get on to his pals—only by that time they weren't pals any more, and he was 'that damned fellow Buckley,' or 'Jimmy, poor devil.' And that's that. Jimmy, my dear, is an awful WARNING. See?"

"There might be something between sponging on your friends and cutting them dead."

"*Facilis descensus!*" I said.

She put out her hand, but I stepped back from it.

"There's your uncle, Car—why wouldn't you let him help you? I know he wanted to—he said so—he said he'd offered you the agency."

I laughed.

"With conditions! Did he tell you what they were?"

She said "No," quickly and as if I'd hurt her again. I supposed I spoke roughly, for she looked timid, and I felt a brute.

"You couldn't accept the conditions?" she said in a soft, hesitating way.

I shook my head. I wonder what she would have said if I'd told her that one of the conditions was marriage. What a fool I am! It wouldn't be anything to her one way or another—it wouldn't ever have been anything. If I had come to heel, licked my uncle's hand, taken his bone, and married Anna Lang, she'd have sent me a wedding present and wished me joy. It's an odd world. Anna wanted me, and I wanted Isobel, and so here I am in the gutter. Why, I never even liked Anna. I remember telling her so at a franker age. I suppose I was about fourteen, and she the same—all bones and eyes. I remember I told her straight out how jolly glad I was that she was only Uncle John's niece and not my cousin, and how she argued that if she was his niece, she was bound to be my cousin. And she finished up by flying into a most almighty rage and scratching my face. I told Uncle John the cat had done it, and the little spitfire burst into tears of pure rage and said, no, she'd done it herself because I didn't love her, and she'd do it again—and again—until I did.

All this went through my head in a sort of confusion. I think I tried to stop myself saying anything. When I found I couldn't, I said good-by, but I'm afraid my voice gave me away.

I said good-by, and Isobel said,

"Will you come and see me, Car?"

And I said, "No, my dear, I won't," and I lifted my hat and walked on.

I walked as far as I could, and I didn't take very much notice of where I was going, but after a bit I got hold of myself and started to go home. I ought to have been thinking what I was going to do next, and what I was going to say to Mrs. Bell, and what I was going to tell Fay, but I couldn't think of anything or any one but Isobel. I was blundering along pretty fast, and I'd got within half a dozen blocks of the house, when some one pushed something into my hand. This is where the queer thing begins, and I want to put everything down very exactly. If I hadn't been wool-gathering, I should have seen the man's face as he came up to me. As it was, I just came out of the clouds to find a paper in my hand, and the man who had shoved it there shooting across the road diagonally with his back towards me and no more to be seen of him than a shabby suit of clothes, a greasy bowler hat, and a sheaf of handbills under his arm.

I looked down at the paper in my hand. It was the size of a handbill. But it wasn't a handbill; it was a blank sheet of paper with what looked like a newspaper cutting pasted on to the middle of it. I should have dropped a handbill in the gutter. When you're job-hunting, newspaper cuttings rather rivet your attention. I read this one. And here it is, word for word:

> Do you want £500? If you do, and are willing to earn it, write to Box Z. 10, International Employment Exchange, 187 Falcon Street, N.W.

I looked up from the paper and saw the man with the greasy bowler on the other side of the road. He thrust a handbill upon a girl in a sleeveless cotton frock and turned the corner. I hesitated for a moment, and then made after him at a good pace. When I reached the corner, he wasn't anywhere in sight. There are one or two shops, and about fifty yards down there's a public house. From the look of him he might have turned in there. I certainly hadn't any intention of following him. As I stood there, I saw one of his handbills lying half on the curb, where some one must have thrown it down—that is, I saw what at first sight I took to be one of his handbills. After a second glance I picked the paper up. It was of the same size and shape as my own, but instead of being a blank sheet with a newspaper cutting stuck on to it, it had typed across it the words, "Eat More Fruit and Encourage the Empire."

I threw the paper down again and retraced my steps. There was a second handbill lying on the pavement a yard or two from where I had seen the man give one to the girl with the bare arms. I couldn't swear that it was the paper she had taken and then dropped, but there it lay, quite clean, and therefore newly dropped by some one; and, like the one

I had picked up round the corner, it bore a typed exhortation to "Eat More Fruit and Encourage the Empire."

I stood with the thing in my hand, and then after a bit I came back here and tried to think what it might mean. You see, it's odd—whatever way you look at it, it's odd. Here's a fellow distributing handbills about Eating More Fruit and Encouraging the Empire, and right in the middle of these blameless tracts he's got a newspaper cutting stuck on a blank sheet, and he shoves it off on me. Why me? That's what I want to know. Is it because it's me, or just because the thing was there by accident and some one was bound to get it? And if me—why? Of course you may say it's obvious that I could do with £500. Why, a fiver would be a godsend.

II

ISOBEL TARRANT STOOD QUITE STILL. SHE LOOKED AFTER Car Fairfax, but she didn't see him, because her eyes were full of hot, blinding tears. She had met him again after three years, and he was going—going, and in a moment he would be gone, and it might be three years, or it might be thirty, before she saw him again. Or never. The word knocked hard upon her heart—never, never, never, *never*. Never to know where he was, or what he was doing, or whether he was ill or well, or whether any one cared for him or looked after him, or even whether he was in the same world at all.

"I can't bear it," she said under her breath. "Oh, I can't!"

And then, like a horrible echo, something said, "You've got to."

With every bit of her strength Isobel said, "I *won't*!" She shook away two tears, and saw Car turn the corner with his old swing of the shoulders. The next moment she was beckoning a taxi.

"I want you to go round that corner slowly. I want you to follow a gentleman who has just gone round it—in a blue serge suit—a tall gentleman. I want you to follow him—but don't let him know."

Isobel was rather breathless, and her cheeks burned. She sat back in the corner and wondered what the man must think. She didn't care, but she couldn't help wondering.

They turned the corner. She could see Car striding along with his head up. She leaned out of the window and said, "There—there!" and the man said, "All right, miss."

She was late for lunch. Not that that mattered, as Aunt Willy was later still. Miss Williamina Tarrant had never been in time for anything in her life. In her own house meals occurred when she was hungry. At the moment, she and Isobel were on a visit to Aunt Carrie. Though Carrie Lester and Willy Tarrant had been sisters for sixty odd years, time never staled the infinite number of ways in which they annoyed one another.

Mrs. Lester was in the hall when Isobel came in. She had been drifting in and out of it for the last ten minutes like a small reproachful ghost, her pretty lined features quite puckered up with fretful disapproval.

"I'm so sorry, Aunt Carrie."

"My dear," said Mrs. Lester, "it's no use your being sorry, or my being sorry, or any one else being sorry. Your Aunt Willy gets more and more unpunctual, and why she can't be in to meals like other people I shall never understand. And Eliza is in one of her tempers—and I'm sure I don't wonder, because if I was a cook and had everything dished up and then had to put it all back again and go on keeping it hot—and then in the end your Aunt Willy will either not come home at all, or as likely as not she'll bring some one back with her—and though I hope I'm not inhospitable, one does have to consider one's servants a *little*, and I must say that I think Eliza has grounds for complaint—though of course your Aunt Willy thinks I spoil her—but, as I always say, I'd rather have one spoilt cook and keep her than have thirteen cooks in a year like your Aunt Willy.''

Mrs. Lester took a small lace-edged handkerchief out of a large gray silk bag and rubbed the tip of her nose with it until it was quite pink. Then she put the handkerchief back and shut the bag with a snap.

Aunt Carrie always reminded Isobel of a white rabbit—her pretty white hair; her tendency to get pink about the eyes and nose; her air of timid antagonism. As she went upstairs with Isobel, she looked like a rabbit at bay over its last lettuce leaf.

Just as they reached the top, the hall door burst open and Miss Willy Tarrant burst in. There was more to it than that, because actually a latchkey was introduced and withdrawn; but the effect was the effect invariably produced by Miss Willy's arrival. She burst in accompanied by several other people, and her voice, deep, full, and resonant, instantly filled the small house.

''Parker—I'm in. Where's Mrs. Lester? Oh, and Parker—three more to lunch—perhaps you'd better tell Eliza.'' She surged towards the stairs. ''Come along, Janet. Carrie! Car*rie!* Here we are. I've brought Janet to lunch. And I don't believe you know the Markhams—two of the very best. Bobby, this is my sister, though you wouldn't think it—and this is my niece, Isobel, who lives with me. Cis, where have you got to?''

Mrs. Lester remembered that she was a lady. She trembled with passion, but she shook hands with Janet Wimpole, who was a connection, with the fat bald-headed man who, most unsuitably, was Bobby, and with the thin dowdy girl, who appeared to be Cis.

Miss Willy filled the drawing-room with her deep voice, her presence, and her overpowering self-possession. She was tall and stout, but she seemed to be taller and stouter than she really was. She was tightly molded into a bright black satin garment relieved with pink. Her face was red and sunburned above the pale pink of a tulle scarf. Her black hair crisped and waved like a wig and was only lightly touched with gray. She had removed a pink felt hat as she came in, and it lay, where she had tossed it, on a table devoted to framed photographs of Mrs. Lester's grandchildren and a bowl of *potpourri*.

The gong sounded, and they went down to the dining-room. Each guest received about a tablespoonful of soup, after which Parker set down in front of her mistress a Sheffield entrée dish containing the six small cutlets which had been intended for the three ladies. "And not another bite, nor drop, nor bit, nor sup goes out of this kitchen," Eliza had declared as she dished them up.

Miss Willy burst out laughing.

"I told you it would be pot luck—you can't say I didn't! But there's a ham. Parker, where's the ham? Bring up the ham, and we shan't starve."

Parker looked at her mistress.

"The ham will do nicely," said Mrs. Lester in a small pinched voice.

Parker coughed and drew nearer.

"If you please, ma'am, Eliza didn't think the ham was fit to send up."

Mrs. Lester blenched visibly. She had lived for fifteen yeas with Eliza, and she recognized an ultimatum.

Miss Willy sprang to her feet.

"Oh, nonsense—nonsense! I'll go and see Eliza myself. It was a very good ham, and plenty of it. Help the cutlets, Carrie—I shan't be a moment—you and I and Isobel will have ham. You needn't come, Parker—I'll just go and speak to Eliza."

Janet Wimpole wanted to laugh. She was a fair, lovable creature, a childless widow of thirty-five, at the beck and call of every one who wanted a child looked after, a girl chaperoned, or an invalid amused. She looked at Isobel and wondered why she was so pale. And then Miss Willy came back in triumph with the ham on a lordly dish.

It was when every one had been helped, to the accompaniment of loud-voiced instructions from Miss Willy, that Car's name suddenly emerged from a buzz of talk. Janet was not quite sure how it came up. Bobby Markham, and the girl called Cis, and Miss Willy were all talking at once, whilst she herself was leaning across Isobel to try and catch a twice repeated remark of Carrie Lester's. It was Bobby Markham, she thought, who said "Fairfax," and as he said the word, Janet felt Isobel's arm move against her own with a wincing movement as if she had been suddenly hurt. Miss Willy caught up the name and, turning, flung it at Isobel.

"Car Fairfax—I was going to tell you—the most extraordinary thing—Bobby came across Car the other day. You know, we've always wondered what on earth had become of him."

"Oh, I hope he's getting on," said Janet. She leaned forward, screening Isobel.

"Now, my dear Janet, was he likely to get on, after having to leave his regiment and being mixed up with that atrocious Lymington man, who was nothing but a common swindler—and if I hadn't had the gumption to get my money out of his clutches just in the very nick of time, wouldn't Isobel and I be in the workhouse this very minute?"

"I hope not. But, Willy, you mustn't say he had to leave his regiment like that—it sounds——"

"Well, he did have to leave it," said Miss Willy bluntly.

"Only because he hadn't enough money to stay in it. It wasn't his fault that his father had been living above his income for years and left nothing but debts."

Miss Willy tossed her head.

"Pride goes before a fall. Bobby met him in his brother's office, standing in a queue on the chance of being taken on as twentieth clerk or something of that sort. Rather a come-down for Car Fairfax!" She laughed angrily and looked at Isobel. "He didn't even get the job," she added, with malice in her voice. "But there, it wouldn't have helped him if he had. You can't help people who won't take help. He's gone under, and he's got his deserts."

"I thought Carthew Fairfax a very pleasant young man," said Carrie Lester. "And a friend of Isobel's—wasn't he, my dear?"

There was no color in Isobel's cheeks. She smiled at Aunt Carrie with her eyes and said,

"Yes, a very great friend."

"He wouldn't be helped," repeated Miss Willy. "John Carthew would have helped him—That's his uncle, his mother's brother," she explained to the Markhams.

Bobby Markham nodded.

"I know—*rolling*. I wish I'd an uncle who wanted to help me. Little Bobby's not proud!"

"Car Fairfax is a fool," said Miss Willy. "He offended John, and now, apparently, he's gone to the dogs, and serve him right."

"It isn't actually disreputable to be poor, is it, Willy?" said Janet in her charming voice.

"Who's talking about being poor? You're poor—I'm poor—everybody's poor. But Car's gone under. First he had to leave his regiment, and then he went as secretary to that dreadful swindling Lymington man——"

"Who had been at school with his father," said Janet Wimpole firmly.

Miss Willy's bright, hard color rose.

"And a pretty pair, I must say! Not a penny to choose between them really, though I suppose it's better to swindle your own family than to ruin total strangers by the thousand— No, Isobel, don't contradict me! I don't care what any one says, a man who pretends to be rich, puts his son into an expensive regiment, spends money like water and lives like a prince, and then dies and doesn't leave twopence halfpenny is a swindler. And as for that Lymington wretch, nobody knows how many people he ruined by going smash and blowing his brains out."

"What happened to the son?" said Bobby Markham.

She stared at him.

"Car Fairfax?"

"No—Peter Lymington."

"He went abroad, I believe. You really can't expect me to take any interest in what happened to him, but I do say this—if Carthew Fairfax had had an ounce of self-respect, he'd have gone too. I'm sure no one wanted him here."

"His mother did," said Isobel. Her voice was quick and clear. "She was very ill, and he wouldn't leave her——"

"And she died at least two years ago. Why didn't he go then?"

"Why not ask him, Willy?" said Janet.

Miss Willy rapped the table.

"Because I don't need to ask any one—I *know*. He's mixed up in a discreditable entanglement, and he doesn't want to. I forget who she is. Wasn't it you who told me about it, Bobby?... No? Then it was Kitty Mason—no, Joan Connell—no, it wasn't—but it doesn't matter—some one told me. And if John Carthew wasn't an old fool, he'd stop hankering after the boy and let him go his own way."

"Does he hanker?" asked Janet quickly.

"More than Anna Lang cares about—his wife's niece, you know. She lives with him, and I should say she'd take pretty good care it didn't get beyond hankering."

Parker came in. She had a scarlet spot on either cheek. She placed a microscopic tart at one end of the table and half a plum cake at the other. Lunch proceeded.

Isobel's head ached more and more. Her heart ached too. When the others went upstairs, Janet kept her back.

"Let them go on, and then we'll go up to your room. I want to talk to you."

The little chintzy room was deliciously peaceful. Isobel took off her hat, smoothed her dark hair, and drew a breath of relief. She had very soft black hair, the white skin that does not burn, and eyes that were the color of dark blue water. Just now the waters were shadowed. Car told her once that her eyes were full of secrets. As he said it, he was wondering whether she would ever tell him her secrets.

"What is it?" said Janet.

"Car," said Isobel, simply.

"My darling child, you mustn't mind what Willy says—it doesn't mean much."

"I know—but——"

"What?"

"Oh, Jan, I saw him!"

"Car?"

"Yes."

"Where?"

"In the street. Oh, Jan, he looks——" She put a finger up to her lips because they trembled.

"How?"

Isobel lifted her pretty chin.

"Not what she said. He's just the same—just Car, but—*thin*. Oh, Jan, he's so dreadfully thin and so——" Her voice sank away. She couldn't tell anyone that Car—*Car*—was so shabby that it hurt.

Janet walked to the dressing-table and stood fingering some of the pretty trifles that lay there—pretty ivory things with Isobel's golden I on them. Everything in the room was delicately pretty. She wanted to comfort Isobel; but it might be cruel comfort to encourage her in an attachment to Car Fairfax, who had gone under. She wondered how much Willy guessed, and whether it was love for Isobel that had put the angry color into her cheeks and the edge on to her tongue when she spoke of Car.

She said, "My dear——" in a puzzled, distressed voice; and then the door was bounced open and Miss Willy came in. She wore an air of triumph, and she fanned herself with the pink felt hat.

"I've just been giving Eliza notice. Carrie would never dare, and she ought to be thankful she's got some one to do it for her. You can't think how impertinent she was when I went down for the ham."

III

CAR FAIRFAX GOT UP WITH A SIGH, STRETCHED HIS HAND, which was cramped with writing, and went down the narrow stairs to the next landing. He had heard Fay come in an hour ago, and he supposed he had better go and tell her that he hadn't got the job, and that in all probability Mrs. Bell would be pushing him out to-morrow. Fay had been hipped for days, but it wasn't much use not telling her. There really wasn't any reason why she should mind particularly, except that she was used to having him handy.

He knocked at the door and went in in response to an irritable "Oh, come in—come *in!*" The room was cloudy with cigarette smoke. A half made dress of bright green lace lay across the bed, and snippets and cotton ends littered the worn red carpet. Fay's little black hat with the diamond dagger was thrown down by the door.

Fay herself, in a short black frock, was lying back in the shapeless armchair smoking. She was a little creature, with the air of being so fragile that a touch might break her. She had reminded Car at first sight of one of those little transparent birds made of spun glass which you sometimes see in the window of a curiosity shop—small, artificial, delicate—a miniature bird of paradise, whose plumage would dissolve at the lightest touch. She had a transparent skin, large pale blue eyes, tiny hands and feet, and hair of the true spun glass texture and hue—the very pale straw-yellow which never darkens. It is possible that her lashes would have been of the same shade if they had been left to nature, but not since her fifteen year had nature been allowed its tactless way. The lashes were now as dark as Car's own.

Car Fairfax shut the door and almost trod on the hat. Fay looked up with a jerk.

"Oh Lord, Car, do keep your clumsy feet off something!" She flung her cigarette across the room, and said "Damn!" when he went to pick it up.

"It's scorched your green lace. You'll burn the house down one of these days."

"I'd like to," she said. Then she laughed. "I'd *love* to burn the house down and go up in a puff of smoke! Wouldn't you?"

"Don't be an ass, Fay! I say, what's up?"

"Up? Nothing's up—everything's down," she said. "Down—down—down—*down*—DOWN!" Her voice went up into a sort of scream.

Then she sat up, took out another cigarette and started to light it, spoilt three matches, and flung the box at the door. It hit the middle panel and bounced back.

Fay jumped up.

"How much money have you got, Car?"

"Why, none."

"You must have some. Every one's got *some*." She came up close to him. "Car, how much money *have* you?"

Car Fairfax laughed.

"Four and sixpence halfpenny—or four and seven-pence halfpenny. Do you want me to count?"

A curious flickering something showed in her eyes. It was there, and it was gone. He couldn't have described it—it was too fleeting.

Fay looked at him a little bleakly.

"I'm quite serious."

"So am I. Money's a very serious thing—especially when you haven't got any."

He was still holding the cigarette end which he had picked up. A faint wraith of smoke curled up between them. Car frowned, but before he could speak her hand was on his arm.

"You don't mean that you've really only got a few shillings?" Then, as he nodded, "But you could get some more—I mean there must be some way—I mean—Car, don't look like that!"

"I'm not looking like anything," said Car rather gravely. "My dear girl, you've always known I hadn't a bean."

"I know—but"—she had drawn back a little, but now she pressed close to him—"you could ask some one—you could borrow—you could ask your uncle."

Car disengaged himself.

"You're talking nonsense. What's the matter? What have you been up to? Getting into a mess?"

"I suppose you'd say so."

"What sort of a mess?" He lifted the cigarette end to his nose, sniffed it, and tossed it into the fireplace. His eyes dwelt on her consideringly. "Where do you get those beastly things?"

The flicker came again. It was fear—quite naked and unmistakable this time.

"Have I got to account to you for every cigarette I smoke?"

"That one was doped," said Car.

"It wasn't."

"It was—it is. Where did you get it? It'll save a lot of time if you tell me at once."

Fay went back to her chair, sat down, produced another cigarette, struck a match, and bent to light it—all with her shoulder turned to Car. He watched her, and saw the match shake in a shaking hand.

"It's a mug's game," he said as she leaned back and sent up a little puff of smoke.

"I wish I could blow rings," said Fay. "I wish you'd teach me."

"It's a mug's game, Fay."

"Write and tell Peter," said Fay. Then, as he didn't answer, "That's what you'll do if I don't go down on my knees and promise to be good—isn't it?"

"No," said Car.

He came over to the fireplace and stood with his back to the narrow gimcrack mantelpiece.

"What will you do?"

"I don't know. Who's been giving you doped cigarettes, Fay?"

She blew a puff of smoke at him.

"They're not!"

He stood up without another word and went to the door.

"Car—you're not going?"

"Yes, I think so."

"Why?"

"What's the good of my staying?"

Fay dropped the cigarette and jumped up.

"Car, come back! I told you—I told you I was in a mess—and I am—and if you won't help me, I'm done." She caught him by the arm and pulled him round. "Done—done—*done*! Do you hear? *Finished!* You don't care—do you?"

"I wish you'd talk sense. Of course I care!"

"Because of me—or because of Peter?"

"Because of both of you."

Fay pushed herself away from him and sprang back a yard.

"And if there weren't any Peter—if there were only me—you wouldn't care a damn what happened—would you?"

Car stood against the door and looked bored, but behind the boredom there wad distress and distaste. It didn't suit with his friendship with Peter to be having this sort of scene with Peter's wife. On the other hand, if she'd got herself into a hole, it was naturally up to him to get her out of it, since Peter Lymington, in New York, was too far away to take a hand. He frowned his heaviest frown, the one that deepened every line with which the last three years had marked him, and said, almost roughly,

"Would you mind telling me what you've done?"

There was a pause, Fay looking at him, blue pale eyes in a pale face, lips pale too and parted in a trembling curve, eyelids just a-quiver, hands hard clenched at her sides.

"All right then, I'm going." But as he moved she flung

round, went over to the hearth at a stumbling run, caught the mantelpiece with both hands, and so stood, swaying.

Car turned back and came across to her.

"Why don't you tell me what's the matter?"

"You don't care."

"I told you I cared," he said wearily.

"Not enough to help."

"What do you want?"

"I want five hundred pounds," said Fay, looking up suddenly.

The sheer, bright daring of her glance was like light flashing on water—blue shallow water. It flickered across his face, dwelt a moment, and was gone.

"Five hundred pounds?" said Car.

This time he got a nod, quite cool and steady.

"What for?"

"To pick up the bits."

"What bits?"

Fay put her forehead against the edge of the mantelpiece. She spoke down into the dusty grate.

"I told you I'd got into a hole. It'll take five hundred pounds to get me out of it. That's all."

"Oh, that's all?"

"Yes. Car, what a *beast* you are!"

"I don't mean to be a beast—but you've got to do the talking. What have you been doing?"

Fay was silent; and when she was silent, the whole room was silent too. She and Car might have been dead; or she might have been dead, and Car as far away as Peter. She wondered with a curious prick of anger whether Car would care if she were dead, and in a moment the anger mounted and loosened her tongue.

"All right, I'll talk. But you won't like it." She flung up her head and looked straight in front of her. "I took some money."

There was a pause before Car said, "Yes? Who from?"

"My beastly shop, of course. Delphine *asks* for it, she's so careless. She leaves checks lying about for days. Days?

Weeks—months is more like it. Well, I took one and cashed it. They know me at the bank, and it wasn't crossed—some of her customers are as careless as she is. And then, as luck would have it, there was a row, and I only just got off by the skin of my teeth."

Car's hand came down on her shoulder.

"What are you talking about? You're not—in earnest?"

She pulled away from him with a jerk.

"Of course I am. You don't suppose I think this is amusing, do you? I was very nearly for it, and I've never been less amused in my life."

His hand fell to his side.

"And you've got to find the money—five hundred pounds?"

"Not exactly. That's only the beginning of it."

"Oh—that's only the beginning?"

She stamped her foot.

"I said so! Don't look at me like that!"

Car didn't want to look at her at all. He said,

"Go on."

"I got the money all right."

"May I ask how?"

"Yes—that's the point—I got it from a man."

"What sort of man?"

"A man called Fosicker. I—met him——"

Car raised his eyebrows. He said with cold conviction,

"You met him. You mean you picked him up?"

Just for a moment Fay looked around at him. He wondered if she was going to strike him, but the look was all the blow he got. Then, as she turned away, he heard her say in a confused, choking voice,

"You never—took me—out."

He felt utterly bewildered. What did she mean? They were talking about money. . . . He got back to it with a determined effort.

"This man lent you money?"

"He gave it to me"—with a toss of the head.

"For nothing?" said Car with bitter irony.

"No—of course not. I'm not a fool. I didn't expect him to. But I can look after myself. It wasn't what you think."

"What was it?" said Car gravely. This was Peter's wife.

"It was a business arrangement." Fay's tone had hardened. The worst was over. She let go of the mantelpiece and began to light another cigarette. The bit about the check was the worst. Men fussed so about things like that, and Car——

Car was speaking:

"Will you go on?"

"Well, he let me have the money, and I said—that is I—agreed—I—it's rather difficult to explain."

"It seems to be. But I think you'd better try."

"Well, he had a business. He wanted me to be a sort of agent—*you know*."

"I don't yet."

"How dull of you!"

"Yes. What was the business?"

Fay blew out a cloud of smoke. It hung in the air like a shifting veil. She could have wished it thicker, because Car's eyes——

"Well, that's just it." She laughed, not very successfully. "That's just it, you see—because I suppose it's a *sort* of smuggling."

"What sort?"

"I can't see why people shouldn't have those things if they want them and like to pay for them," said Fay airily.

"What things?"

"Oh, Car, for the Lord's sake stop saying 'What'!"

"I will when I get an answer. What things?"

"Drugs," said Fay in a sullen whisper.

IV

HALF AN HOUR LATER CAR FELT AS IF HE WAS STILL
playing blindman's buff in the crowd of Fay's evasions—
shifting, half caught, but never plainly grasped. If she made
a statement, it was only to qualify it with the next breath. If
he thought he had touched fact, it slipped from him and was
gone. From standing over her, he had taken to pacing the
room as a relief to his impatience. He had come to anchor
now astride of a chair, his arms across its back, and in the
silence that had fallen he tried to sort her story, or stories,
out.

She had taken money from Delphine and replaced it with
what Fosicker had given her. But she could only have
replaced it partially, since she spoke of Delphine's finding
her out. Or perhaps she had replaced it all, and had again
found it convenient to "borrow." When pressed, she slid
away. Fosicker frightened her. "If he gets his knife into
you, you're *done*—every one says so. There was a girl—"
And then Fay's bitten lip, and the jerk of the head which
sent a shower of ash all over her bare neck. One thing
emerged with the utmost clearness—Fay was frightened,
and the farther they got with this game of blindman's buff,
the more plainly did it appear that she had reason.

As far as he could piece it together, Fosicker carried on a
lucrative business selling forbidden drugs. But Fosicker
took care to run no risks himself. Why should he when he
could get fools like Fay to take them for him? And if they

kicked, they could be threatened with exposure to Delphine. Yes, that was how it was worked.

He looked over the top of Fay's head rather grimly. It was a pity the great Lymington smash hadn't happened just one week earlier. Car's cynicism decided that Fay Everitt would probably not have entered into matrimony with the son of a ruined man. It seemed to him that Peter was likely to pay pretty dear for his secret marriage. Meanwhile Peter was in America and Fay was his wife, and some one had got to get her out of this beastly mess.

"I think you might say something," said Fay.

"I don't know what to say. You've pretty well torn it, haven't you?"

"If I had five hundred pounds——"

"Yes—what would you do with it?"

"Square things up and get out of the country."

"You owe Delphine five hundred pounds?" The euphemism left a bitter flavor in his mouth. Owe? Good Lord, she'd stolen the money! But five hundred—even in the most careless establishment!

"No, of course not!" Her tone was virtuously surprised.

"What do you—owe?"

"Oh, I don't know. Fosicker gave me fifty last week, and that—let me see——" She plunged into calculations. "It's awfully hard to say exactly—but not more than three hundred or three-fifty."

"Oh, not more than that!"

"No, I don't think so. You see it all goes through my hands, and sometimes I'm nearly square, and then sometimes I'm a good bit down."

"I see."

The irony of his voice drew a jerk of the shoulder.

"I see," said Car again. "Well, you'll square up—and then?"

"I thought I might go out to Peter," said Fay with a quick sidelong glance. "Suppose it took four hundred to clear everything right off—that would leave a hundred to get my passage and anything I really had to take with me."

Car got up.

"And what do you propose to tell Peter?"

Fay's lids lifted; her eyes, palely blue, looked straight at him with an effect of innocent surprise.

"There wouldn't be anything to tell him—I should be all square," she said.

"The clean slate! Well?" He laughed harshly. "Where's the money coming from?"

"Car!"

The fear in her voice was not put on. Yes, Fay's fear was the one thing that stood out plain. She was unmistakably afraid.

"Car—Peter said he'd have my passage money saved by October. If you cabled to him and said I must have it now—"

"It wouldn't be five hundred pounds."

"No. But if I got out of the country—if I got clear—do you think they would try and get me back?"

"Yes—they might." He was considering. "Yes, I think they would—if you'd gone off with four hundred pounds."

"I *haven't*! I wish you wouldn't say things like that. They couldn't bring me back because I'd borrowed some money— I'm sure they couldn't."

Car got his hand on the door.

"Oh, stop talking about borrowing! Call things by their proper names if you want me to help you." He steadied his temper with an effort. "Look here, Fay, I'll help you if I can."

"For Peter's sake?"

"Yes," said Car.

"Not for mine?" Her lashes were low over the watching blue of her eyes. He had the feeling that something was waiting for his answer, something that he didn't understand.

He opened the door.

"I'll do what I can," he said roughly, and went out of the room.

When the door shut, Fay was staring at it, her eyes wide open now. They were angry, bright, and daring. But the door was shut.

The door was shut, and Car's steps going away. She jumped up and ran to the door, but he was gone. What was the good of calling him back? He only cared about Peter. He didn't care for her. If she was Peter's wife, he would know that she existed; but if she was only Fay Everitt, he wouldn't even know that. Her face went white and hard. Why should he care about Peter like that—stupid, fat, blundering Peter? If he was only going to help her for Peter's sake, he could leave it alone. No—no—no—she'd got to be helped. Fear came again like a stabbing pain.

She walked to the bed and stared through swimming tears at the green lace dress which lay across it. Then suddenly, passionately, she threw herself down and broke into a flood of unrestrained weeping.

V

Carthew Fairfax's diary:

September 14*th.*—I'VE HAD A SCENE WITH FAY. SHE SEEMS to have got herself into a perfectly beastly hole. I was losing my temper, so I came away. It looks as if some money has got to be found somehow. She talked as if you could pick it up in the street. I'm writing this to-night because odd things keep happening and I want to write them down. It's simply ages since anything happened at all and now it's just one damn thing after another. I'm not going to write about the scene with Fay—it riles me too much, and she's got into the sort of mess that's better not written about. It's bad luck on Peter. She says he's pretty well got her passage money saved. He didn't say anything about it in his last to me—but then, come to think of it, I can about count on my fingers the times he's ever mentioned Fay at all. He did ask me to look after her, but he left it to her to tell me so and that they were married. I'm afraid he won't think I've looked after her very well.

I hope I got away without losing my temper—I don't know whether I did or not. I got back to my room, and the first thing I saw was that paper that was shoved into my hand in the street, and staring at me in big print at the top of the cutting that was pasted on to it: "Do you want five hundred pounds?" Do I want five hundred pounds? I thought it was a pretty odd coincidence. As far as I can make out, Fay's got to get five hundred pounds or else—well, I won't go into that, but she's scared stiff. She can't speak the truth if she tries—she don't try of course—but she's scared all right, and I don't think she's scared easily.

I read the newspaper cutting all through again: "Do you want £500? If you do, and are willing to earn it, write to Box Z.10, International Employment Exchange, 187 Falcon Street, N. W."

Do I want—I looked at the thing, and I thought it was a bit of a coincidence. I'm still no end puzzled as to why I should have had "Do you want £500?" shoved into my hand, when everybody else was getting "Eat more Fruit." Anyhow, I wrote to Box Z.10 and said I'd like particulars, and then I thought I'd walk out to Falcon Street and have a look at the International Employment Exchange. I should save a stamp, but I suppose I should take more than a penny-halfpennyworth out of my boots. You're pretty near the bottom when you have to consider pennorths of shoeleather— but if your boots go, you're done.

I was just getting up to go, when I heard Mrs. Bell come puffing up the stairs. You can't mistake her. She sounds exactly like a steam-roller. Well, she knocked and burst in. I don't know why she knocks—you can't stop her anyhow. She came in, very red in the face and very short of breath, and pushed a letter at me, and then stood fairly bulging with curiosity.

"District messenger," she said; and then, "Perhaps there's an answer."

I looked down and saw Isobel's writing—Carthew Fairfax Esq, and the address. Now how in the name of all that's wonderful did Isobel find out my address? It doesn't matter of course, because I probably shan't be here to-morrow unless Box Z.10 sends me that five hundred pounds by return.

"Perhaps there's an answer," said Mrs. Bell. She looked at me as hard as if I was something in a circus.

"I don't think so," I said.

And then she started fanning herself and telling me how she once got a proposal by post—"*registered*, if you'll believe me, and me thinking as how me aunt in Dorset had sent me half a sovereign in a postal order, which she did once in a way when she done well with her chicken. But no such thing, and I give you my word when I see what it was you could ha' knocked me down fair and square with a burnt match. 'Herbert Hopkins!' I says out loud, and never so much as turned my head to see if the other girl was listening. It was when I was in service with Mrs. Murgatroyd, and if ever I come across a nasty, jealous, spiteful, two-faced toad, it was that girl Maud Jones, and well I knew she'd been a-laying for Herbert herself—and welcome to him as far as I was concerned, for I wouldn't have touched him with the kitchen tongs, and so I told the two of them!"

I did get rid of her in the end, and then when I'd heard her clump down off the stairs on to the landing, I opened Isobel's letter. She said:

Oh, Car, why did you go off like that? I had such heaps and heaps to say—three years of things all bottled up—and you went off like a flash of lightning before I'd said more than about two and a half of them. Please, Car, don't hide from me. I won't tell any one if you don't want me to. But I must see you—I want to tell you things you ought to know. There *are* things, but I can't put them in a letter. I really must see you. If you knew what I want to tell you, you'd come at once.

No, that sounds silly and Irish. But, Car, *do* come. Write to me at Linwood and say where we can meet. I thought we were staying with Aunt Carrie for another week, but she and Aunt Willy have just had the most terrible row, so we're catching the four-thirty. They'll be all right in a day or two, but for the moment they're simply not safe, so I'm taking mine away and leaving Janet Wimpole to soothe Aunt Carrie. Aunt Willy sacked the cook, and Aunt Carrie *turned*. Family scenes sound amusing, but they're not. I feel like a sparrow on a housetop, and I want to cry.

ISOBEL

Please, Car, don't hide.

I made a fool of myself over Isobel's letter. How she stands Miss Willy I never could make out. Any one else would have stopped trying to stand her years ago. I made a fool of myself because I daren't see Isobel again—I can't answer for myself. She must just think me a low brute who hasn't the manners to answer her. Of course I might write and tell her—No, you don't, you fool! If I wrote a single line to her, I should give myself away. I put her letter away. I meant to destroy it presently. I really did mean to destroy it—but not just at once—not till I'd got it by heart.

And then I took my letter for Box Z.10 and went out to look for Falcon Street.

It was a longish walk, and I had plenty to think about. Part of the time I thought about Fay, and what a knock-down blow it would be for Peter if she got run in—because he felt old Lymington's crash a good deal more than he let on, even to me, and if he were to get another facer over Fay, it might knock him out altogether. What fools women can be! Peter doesn't talk about things, but he feels them a lot. He doesn't write about Fay. I don't think he's mentioned her more than two or three times since he went out, but to my mind that only shows what he feels about her goes too deep down to talk about. Well, I thought about Fay and Peter, and I thought about Isobel's letter, and I wondered what she wanted to say to me. And I thought about my boots and how on earth I was going to get another pair, and I wondered whether Mrs. Bell would let me stay on for a week, and whether the advertisement about the five hundred was a take in. I thought there was bound to be a snag, but even if it only ran to five hundred pence, it would be worth having a shot at it. And then I thought a lot more about Isobel.

I hadn't any idea how to find Falcon Street. People who hadn't any more idea than I had told me to turn to the left and then to the right and keep straight on for half a mile and turn sharp to the left by the policeman. When you ask a man the way, he never says he doesn't know. I went a good bit out of my way after listening for about five minutes to an old gentleman with a beard and a string bag full of lettuce.

When I found Falcon Street, I didn't like the look of it very much. The houses were shabby, and most of them had dirty curtains in the upper windows. One end of the street had a sprinkling of brass plates, but most of the houses looked like cheap lodgings. At the other end were the sort of shops that serve that sort of street—a butcher, whose shop was pretty good propaganda for vegetarianism; a baker, with a window full of flies and wasps; and, bang on the corner, a flourishing looking public house.

The baker was 186, and the butcher 184, so I crossed over, and found the numbers on the other side all muddled up in the crazy way you sometimes find in a London street. The first I struck were 1, 2, 3; and I found that they were, properly, part of Falcon Crescent, which started round the corner. I worked back to 1, and next to it were 203 and 204—and goodness knows what they belonged to. Then I struck 186A, which was a little mixed sweet-shop, very grubby. And next to it there was a tobacconist with no number at all. Tobacconists always know everything, so I thought I'd go in and ask for 187 and the International Employment Exchange.

The shop was very dark and stiflingly hot, and thick with the smell of tobacco *cum* fish and chips. I should say at a guess that about six people had been eating fish and chips and drinking beer in some windowless lair opening off the shop. There were seven or eight men banked up between me and the counter, and a girl in a scarlet blouse and a lot of pearls was behind it. I got into a corner out of the way of the door and waited. As I hadn't come to buy, I thought I had better wait until the crowd cleared off. The bother was that it didn't seem to clear. Three of the men were young fellows, lads of the local village, and they were chaffing the girl and getting back rather better than they gave. Then there was a beery old man who said he hadn't got his right change, and a pal of his who was trying to persuade him that he had, and a very large man with a very soft voice who was trying to get the girl to listen whilst he told her what sort of pipe he wanted. The place was like an oven.

I had got out my handkerchief, and had begun to mop my face, when another man came in. He was a fat man in City clothes. He went through the crowd and up to the counter as if the place belonged to him. Perhaps it does. Anyhow the lads rather melted away, and the girl stopped giggling and went out through a door at the back of the shop. There was an appalling influx of fish and chips—so I was right about the lair. And then she came back with a little sallow greasy man with a diamond ring on his little finger and hair oil that I could smell through all the other things.

I worked round nearer the counter so as to try and catch the girl when the large man who wanted a pipe had said his piece. And as I stood waiting, I heard the fat City man ask, "Any news?"

The other man said, "Not yet." And then he said, "There hasn't been time—is there?"

I couldn't help taking notice of what they said, because the fat man looked so out of place in that beastly hole, and besides, I thought I knew his voice. He had his back to me, so I couldn't see his face. He turned his shoulder, leaned on the counter, and said,

"No, there hasn't been time—to-morrow would be the earliest—but did Benno . . ." His voice went away into a mumble and I lost the rest.

Fortunately the girl with the red blouse had stopped giggling. The large man was choosing his pipe as slowly and carefully as if his life depended on it. She was most awfully bored, and only said "Yes" and "No" between yawns.

The little man with the hair oil spread out his hands in an eager sort of way.

"Benno give it him—oh yes, he give it him nice—he shove it right into his hand—and there he stand and read it with all his eyes. Five hundred pounds! Something to read about—isn't it?"

He laughed, and I took out my handkerchief and began to mop my face again, and as I mopped it I edged backwards into the dark corner by the door. I didn't think I'd got to go any farther to find No. 187 and the International Employment Exchange. It seemed to me that I'd landed right in the middle of it, and I wanted pretty badly to hear some more about Benno and what he'd been up to. I got into the darkest place I could find and kept my handkerchief handy. And all the time I was puzzling about where I'd heard the fat man's voice, and whilst I was puzzling he took off his bowler and had a mop at his head with a silk handkerchief, and the top of his head was bald. That ought to have been a help, but for the life of me. I couldn't place him. I listened all the harder.

"Bound to rise—he's absolutely on his uppers. Now look here—it's just possible he may come in here. He's at a loose end, and he may get it into his head to come nosing around. If he does, you don't know anything—naturally."

The little man spread out his hands again, and the diamond on his finger twinkled.

"Not a word. How do I know? If he come, I say nothing—I know nothing—I speak nothing—isn't it?"

The fat man put on his bowler and nodded. Then he beat with his hand on the counter.

"Now look here—that isn't all. If he does come, I want to know what he's looking like and how he speaks. I want you to be sharp. Get him into talk about anything you like and watch him a bit. I want to know how keen he is. You understand?"

The hands went out again.

"Yes, yes, yes—if he come, I see how he look. Hungry?" He threw an abominable cunning into his voice and looked knowingly out of screwed up eyes. "Yes, he will be hungry. Five hundred pounds is a good dinner! He will be hungry to swallow it—isn't it? Oh, my, my, my, my, my!" He began to laugh. "And not a word to the other—no, no, no!"

The man in the bowler lifted the flap of the counter and walked through.

"I want a word with you about that," he said, and they went out through the door at the back of the shop, and as soon as they were gone I nipped out into the street and got round the corner.

I thought I had found the International Employment Exchange, and I thought I would post my letter even if it did cost me a penny halfpenny; for I had no manner of doubt that I had heard Hair-oil told to size me up, and I thought I wouldn't give him the chance.

VI

September 15th—SOMETHING HAS HAPPENED WHICH I CAN'T understand at all. I was too wild to write about it last night, but I'm going to put everything down to-day.

I posted my letter to the International Employment Exchange and came back to my room, where I made quite a decent supper of bread and cheese. I was just about ready for it, as I hadn't had anything since breakfast. I'm getting quite good at knowing how long one can go without it's being uneconomic in the long run. I suppose one really used to eat a great deal too much.

When I had finished my supper I opened the drawer where I had put Isobel's letter—and it wasn't there. That sounds awfully bald, but that's how I felt. It wasn't there. I felt as if I'd tried to take a step that wasn't there to take. You know how that brings you up short. I took everything out of the drawer—there wasn't much to take—but the letter wasn't there. Then I went through the other drawers, and every minute I was getting angrier because, although I felt bound to go on looking, I knew that the letter was gone, and that meant that some one had come into my room and taken it. I turned out everything I'd got, and I went through my pockets. But the letter was gone.

I went downstairs in a rage and tackled Mrs. Bell. At first she was as angry as I was, and said no one hadn't ever accused her of *thieving*. But after a bit she sobered down and was pretty decent about it in a sentimental sympathizing sort of way, so I had to beg her pardon, though I really preferred her being angry. I don't know why she should have thought it was a girl's letter, because of course I took care to say it was about business. She told me a long story about a letter she'd had from her husband before they were engaged, and how there was mischief made—"And you couldn't believe the artfulness, nor the perseveringness of that girl Maud. All was fish that came to her net, whether it was her own young gentleman or some one else's—and a bad end was what she did ought to have come to, instead of marrying the greengrocer and riding in her Morris car like a lady. Some folks have all the luck. And don't you never trust a red-haired girl, Mr. Fairfax. Sandy eyelashes too, she had."

She's not a bad old thing. Just as I was going out, she called me back.

"What about that rent, Mr. Fairfax?" she said in a hesitating sort of voice.

I felt an awful brute.

"I haven't got it, Mrs. Bell."

"Well, you'd give it me if you had—I know that."

I thought I had better know the worst, so I asked her if she wanted me to go, but she flared up all over again, and said she wasn't a bloodsucker *nor* a thief, and folks that misjudged other folks would live to be sorry for it. And then she began to cry and talk about her son that was killed at Mons, and I patted her on the shoulder, and she said I was his living image—which I hope to goodness I'm not, because the photograph she's so proud of is pretty awful. And then she got to calling me "my dear," and I escaped. She's an awfully good old soul.

On the way upstairs I met Fay. Her door opened just as I passed. She had on the green lace frock she was making yesterday, and I should think she'd used the best part of a box of make-up on her face. I can't think why. Her skin's good enough when she leaves it alone. She came out looking at me as if she wanted me to flirt with her. It didn't improve my temper. Women always seem to think they've only to look at you through their eyelashes, to get anything out of you that they want. It makes me wild. So I was going on; but then I thought of something, so I turned back.

"Did you come up to my room for anything whilst I was out?"

She began to put a sort of scarf thing over her head.

"Why should I?"

"I don't know. Did you?"

She looked over her shoulder.

"Would you have been sorry if you'd missed me?"

I suppose it was rude of me, but I said "No." Fay wants whipping.

She whirled round in a rage.

"Thank you! How polite you are! Do you really flatter yourself that I should come running after you into your beastly attic?"

I said, "I wish you wouldn't talk nonsense. I can't think why you can't answer a plain question. I've lost an important letter, and if you'd been up to my room—"

She stamped her foot.

"Why should I come up to your room?"

"You might have wanted me—and you might have noticed the letter if I'd left it on the table." Of course I knew I hadn't left Isobel's letter on the table. I knew I had put it in the right-hand top drawer of the chest of drawers.

Fay dropped being angry.

"Would you like me to come and pay you a visit?"

"No, I shouldn't."

"Perhaps I will some day."

It's no good talking to her when she's in that mood. I turned my back and went upstairs, and when I was about half way up I heard her run down into the hall so fast that I was afraid she'd break her neck. She didn't. She went out and banged the door as hard as she could.

I went back to my room, and when I opened the door something rustled. I bent down to look. There was a scrap of paper dragging along with the door—I could just see the edge of it. I got it out with a match and looked at it under the gas. It was a scrap of writing-paper with one word on it. The word was, "hide." Isobel had written it. The piece of paper had been torn from her letter. I looked everywhere, but there were no more pieces. Some one had come into my room whilst I was out and torn up Isobel's letter. I didn't believe it was Mrs. Bell.

VII

September 17th; morning—I'VE GOT A LOT TO WRITE, BUT I'll begin at the beginning.

I got an answer from Box Z.10 by the first post. It was typed, and there was no address at the top of the paper, only Box Z.10, and underneath that: "Your letter received. Ring up Victoria 00087 and ask for Mr. Smith between eleven and eleven-fifteen.'' There was no signature.

I thought that was an odd way of doing business, and I began to feel sure that there was something fishy about the whole thing—no address, no signature, only Mr. Smith and a telephone number. I pretty soon found out that the number belonged to a shop. The name was Levens, and it was a stationer's. Lots of shops of that sort have a telephone that their customers can use, and I thought that Mr. Z.10 Smith was going to stroll in at eleven o'clock and take my call. It would be the easiest thing in the world—he'd go in and say he was expecting to be rung up, and it would be no odds to anybody so long as he was willing to pay for his use of the telephone; and if any one came along and asked questions, I was ready to bet that nobody in the shop would know anything about him. What I thought the fishiest part was having his letters sent to one place, and getting himself rung up at another. Falcon Road is N. W., and Victoria 00087 is S. W. I thought it was damned fishy.

I waited till five minutes past eleven, and then I rang up. A woman answered me at first. She had one of those die-away voices that you can't really hear. I kept on saying ''Mr. Smith—I want to speak to Mr. Smith''; and she kept blowing into the telephone and making sounds like a swooning mosquito. And then, just as I was wondering whether the whole thing was a plant, she faded out altogether, and I heard a door shut. Then somebody else said ''Hullo!'' and I said ''Hullo!'' And then he—I thought it was a man—said, ''Mr. Smith speaking. Who are you?'' And I said, ''Carthew Fairfax.'' The voice had called itself Mr. Smith, but I couldn't have been sure that it was a man who was speaking.

As soon as I had said my name he said,

''I'm here in answer to your letter.''

I said, ''Yes?''

''Am I to understand you wish to proceed?''

''I would like to have particulars—I said so in my letter.''

''Yes—certainly—but this is a confidential matter.''

''You're either prepared to tell me what you want, or else I don't see how I can be of any use to you.''

''Yes,'' said Mr. Smith—''exactly. But the matter is confidential, and my client would wish to be assured of your discretion.''

''Your client?''

''I am acting for a client.''

I wondered if he was. I said,

''I don't see how you can be assured of my discretion. In fact, I'm not prepared to give any assurances. I want to know what it's all about.''

''Yes, yes,'' said Mr. Smith—''*exactly*. Will you be outside the corner house of Churt Row and Olding Crescent to-night at ten o'clock?''

I wondered whether I would. I waited for a moment, and Mr. Smith said,

''Will you be there?''

''I don't know.''

He didn't let his voice get eager, but I could tell he was keeping himself in. He said,

''You don't know whether you want the money?''

I didn't want him to think I was suspicious, so I rose to the bait. I said I'd come. He sounded quite chirpy after that, and began to boss me.

''Mind you're not late. And please remember to bring the advertisement with you, together with the letter you received this morning. These will be your credentials, and it will be useless to present yourself without them. Good-morning.'' He rang off.

I walked home in two minds whether I would go or not. If it hadn't been for Fay, I don't think I'd have touched it. No—I don't know whether that's true—the mere fact of the thing being so fishy intrigued me—I wanted to know why I had been picked out to have a spoof advertisement palmed on me, and why Mr. Smith was being so careful to cover his tracks. Letters to Falcon Street, N. W. An accommodation telephone somewhere in Victoria. A rendezvous somewhere else. I hadn't the remotest idea where Churt Row and

Olding Crescent might be. And, most unpleasantly suspicious of all, I was to bring my "credentials." I wasn't under any illusion as to what that meant. Mr. Smith was going to make sure that neither the advertisement nor his careful typewritten letter remained in my hands. When I had presented my "credentials" they would vanish—at least that's what I thought. And just because I thought all that, I wanted to go. I believe the worst part of the sort of life I've been living for the last three years is its dull, grinding monotony. You go on and on, just keeping alive. You get jobs, and you lose them. If you don't get them, you go under. Nothing happens.

I'd a bit of trouble finding out where Churt Row and Olding Crescent were—no one ever seemed to have heard of either of them. I had to go down to Mrs. Bell's cousin, who keeps a little newspaper shop, and ask him to let me have a look at a tape map—he sells that sort of thing as a side line. I found I should have a longish walk. Churt Row was in Putney, and there was something that might have been Olding Crescent running out of it, but there was a worn place where the map had been folded, and I couldn't be sure of the name. I thought it was good enough.

It was a darkish evening and warm. I allowed plenty of time and meant to get there early, but after I crossed the bridge I took the wrong turning and it got dark suddenly. There was some heavy clouds about, and I wondered if it was going to rain at last. I found Churt Row, a little quiet street with trees on either side and houses with pocket-handkerchief gardens in front of them. Olding Crescent ran out of one end. The houses were bigger and only ran along one side of it; on the other there was the high brick wall of some big garden.

I began to walk up and down and wonder whether Mr. Smith was going to keep me waiting. I heard ten o'clock strike on a church clock, and before the air was quiet again a car drew up at the curb—a Morris four-seater with the hood up. The driver put out his head.

"Mr. Fairfax?" he said; and then, "Get in behind, please."

There wasn't much light. There was no lamp-post at the corner. It went through my head that he must have known about that. The nearest lamp was fifty yards away. The headlights made everything behind them look inky black. I groped for the handle and got in, not knowing whether there was any one else in the car or not. I sat down, shut the door, and as I leaned back I smelt violets and I heard some one give a deep, trembling sigh in the darkness beside me. I don't know what I had been expecting—but not this. I couldn't see a thing except the driver's head straight in front of me and the bare outline of the closed side-screens.

The car began to move, and as we passed the first lamp-post I looked into the dark corner beyond me and saw what I thought was a woman with her head bent and her face hidden in her hands. The hands were bare, and she wore a ring, for the yellow light touched the facet of some bright stone. I don't know whether she moved, or if it was just a trick of light, but I thought a quiver went over her. After that she didn't move at all, and neither she nor the driver spoke a word. I wondered where on earth they were taking me.

We drove for the best part of an hour. For a time we followed the Kingston by-pass, but after we passed Esher I lost myself hopelessly. The road lay amongst trees, and there were no lights but our own. We had not met another car for perhaps a quarter of an hour, when we slowed down and stopped. The driver got down, opened my door, and stood by whilst I got out. I turned instinctively, but no one moved behind me in the car.

"This way," said the driver. He had a torch in his hand and set the light dancing down a grassy path to the right.

When I said "The lady?" he answered me with an effect of surprise.

"What lady?" His voice was thick and indistinct.

"In the car."

And at that he turned the light and let it shine upon the back seat. It was empty. I thought the far door hung open, but the light just flashed and came back. She must have been both quick and silent to have got out without my hearing anything. I wondered if she was standing on the other side of the car laughing to herself or sighing.

He switched off the headlights, and we went along the grassy path.

VIII

THE PATH TURNED ALMOST AT ONCE. IT WAS JUST WIDE enough to take two people abreast. We walked along, and neither of us spoke. There was a dense undergrowth on either side.

The driver swung his torch carelessly. Now that I had him walking beside me, I could be sure that he was not the fat man whom I had seen in the tobacconist's—he wasn't nearly fat enough. For all I could see, he was exactly like any other taxidriver. He had spoken three times, and only a word or two each time. He seemed to have a cold—his voice sounded thick. I thought he might have been Benno, but I couldn't be sure. The fat man's voice still bothered me. I knew it, and I didn't.

We took another turn, and the light flickered on to a rough hut or shelter. The door stood open, and as I stepped across the threshold, I knew that I was not the first arrival. The driver had switched off his light, and the place was in pitchy darkness, until a match spurted. A man's hand came round it, sheltering it and keeping the light down. I could only see the hand, part of the arm, and a black hump of head and shoulder.

The hand moved, and I saw a lantern—an old-fashioned

affair with a tallow candle and a dark slide. The match caught the wick, and in a moment the light was turned in my direction, and the dark slide came down with a jerk. I saw four bare walls, a wooden table, one chair, and a rough bench. Between the bench and the table, the black bulk of a man, with a hat well pulled down over his face and a coat turned up about his chin. He had some sort of scarf too, and the whole effect was of a large shapelessness.

I thought it was the fat man, but I couldn't have sworn to him. He sat down on the bench, and as the chair was on my side of the table, I reached out for it and sat down too. The candlelight shone straight into my face. As far as I could see, we were alone. The driver certainly hadn't come into the hut.

I reached back and shut the rickety door.

"Well?" I said.

"Mr. Fairfax?"

I nodded.

"Mr. Carthew Fairfax?"

I nodded again. If it was the fat man, he was disguising his voice. I thought he was disguising it. One voice sounds very much like another if you get it down to a sort of flat whisper, and that's what he was doing. It was very tiresome to listen to.

"Well, Mr. Fairfax," he said, "I'm sorry to have brought you such a long way, but my client's interests—you see, the matter is confidential."

"Yes—you said so on the telephone."

He made a little pause at that. I thought he didn't like being identified with Mr. Smith and his telephone conversation. I began to feel sure that he was Mr. Smith, but not so sure of his being the fat man at the tobacconist's. He went on in a moment.

"It probably occurred to you when you saw the advertisement. Five hundred pounds is a large sum of money."

I didn't say anything. I thought he seemed vexed as he went on:

"My client is willing to pay this large sum, but he wishes to be assured in advance of your absolute discretion."

"What does he want me to do?"

"He would like to have your word of honor that you will treat the whole of this interview as confidential, whether you accept his offer or not."

I thought for a moment. Suppose they were planning murder. . . . Well, I didn't really suppose it, but the thing certainly had the air of being on the wrong side of the law.

I said, "I can't give an absolute undertaking. I want to know a lot more before I can do that."

"That's very difficult."

"Why is it difficult? You say your man is offering five hundred pounds, and I want to know what he's offering it for. If it's too confidential for you to tell me, the thing's off so far as I'm concerned."

He put up his hand and then began to fidget with the lantern, pushing it a little nearer me and fiddling with the slide. Then he went on in that embarrassed whisper.

"My client—" He jerked the lantern back. "My client—" And there he stuck.

I wondered if it *was* murder.

"Well," I said, "he's either done something shady, or else he wants me to do something shady for him. Which is it?"

I thought perhaps that would clear the air a bit, and it did.

"Neither—that is—let me explain——"

"I should be glad if you would."

He got it out this time.

"My client has been unfortunate enough to become liable to a term of imprisonment——"

"Yes?" I said, and I tried to make my voice as encouraging as possible.

"He doesn't wish to go to prison."

"Naturally."

"He is willing to pay five hundred pounds for a substitute."

So that was it. I had thought of several things, but I wasn't expecting that. There was a nasty drab, penal sound about it. A feeling that even the Embankment was preferable as a place of residence to the shelter of one of His Majesty's prisons came over me pretty strongly. Besides, I didn't see how they were going to work a thing like that. I hoped I wasn't going to be told I was the double of a criminal who hadn't even the courage of his crimes.

"Well, Mr. Fairfax?"

"What has your man done?" said I.

He hummed and hawed a bit, as I thought he would, and I felt my temper getting up. It always riles me when people won't come to the point. If a man doesn't mind doing a dirty job, he oughtn't to mind talking about it. The fellow turned my stomach with his humming and hawing.

"What is it?" I said sharply. "Murder?"

That rattled him. He drew back.

"Murder? No! What are you thinking of?"

I laughed.

"You're not very communicative, you know. If I'm to have committed a crime, I shall want to know what it is. It seems to me that that is only reasonable. You see, there are some crimes that aren't just in my line."

I suppose it was stupid of me to be sarcastic—it always puts a man's back up worse than anything. He got back on me all right when he said,

"You can afford to be particular?" And then after a moment, "You were Lymington's secretary, weren't you?"

I nodded. That beastly candle shone full in my face, and I was afraid I had flushed.

He leaned forward with a change of manner.

"Look here, Fairfax, are you in a position to refuse five hundred pounds? You could get away abroad and start fresh."

"After I came out of prison?"

He waved that away. There was something familiar in the gesture. I was sure he was the man I had seen in the tobacconist's, and I was sure that that wasn't the first time I had seen him, but I couldn't place him yet. He wasn't any one I knew, but I had certainly seen him and heard his voice. He talked about his "client," but he seemed too blundering to be a lawyer.

"You'd get off with three years if you'd any luck."

That got my goat. Three years! I could have driven my fist into his fat face.

"I've not had much luck so far," I said, "so I don't think I'll count on it now."

Then it came over me that they were offering me under two hundred a year to go to prison, and it made me mad to be reckoned so cheap. I suppose he saw something in my face, for he pushed back the bench and stood up. I think his feet were cold, and seeing him afraid like that made me think that the driver was out of earshot. And then next minute I thought I was mistaken, for I heard the door behind me open softly. I looked over my shoulder and saw about an inch of black night showing between the door and the jamb. I couldn't see anything else. The door didn't move; but I thought that some one was standing there listening.

I turned back again. It didn't matter to me who listened.

"Well?" I said. "What's my crime? You haven't told me yet."

"You agree?" said he with a show of eagerness.

"I don't agree or disagree till I know where I am."

He sat down again.

"Well, just suppose a case. Let us suppose that a person— who we needn't name—has anticipated a sum of money which would in all probability have passed to him legally within a year or two."

"All right," I said, "he anticipated some money. In other words he pinched it."

He waved again. I thought the door moved behind me.

"Do you mind telling me how?" I proceeded.

"There was a matter of a check," said he.

"Forgery runs to more than three years," said I—and I thought the door moved again.

I looked back, but it was still just ajar. The smell of violets came in out of the dark outside. There are no violets in a Surrey wood in September; but there had been a scent of violets in the car. I did not think that it was the driver who had opened the door. I thought that there was a woman standing there listening, and I wondered who she was.

The fat man spread out his hands.

"A first offense—it would be that, I suppose."

"I really don't know. You haven't told me who your forger is."

"That," he said, "is not necessary."

"Or how you propose to persuade a jury to accept your—substitute."

He had an answer ready for that. I suppose he had prepared it.

"Let us put it this way. Money has been withdrawn from a certain account—let us call it Mr. A's account, and Mr. A's suspicions have become aroused. He knows that a check has been forged. He is determined to find out who forged it and to prosecute. His suspicions will inevitably lead him to the right person unless they are diverted to a substitute——"
He talked like a man who has learnt a thing by heart. Every now and then he slid a paper into the light and looked at it.

"And how do you propose they should be diverted?"

"If a second check were presented—a second forgery—in circumstances which plainly indicated the—substitute, Mr. A would naturally conclude that his suspicions had been groundless, and that the two checks were the work of the same hand."

I put my fist on the table and looked at it.

"My hand?"

He nodded and sat back with the air of having got the thing off his chest.

"Thanks," I said. "I think not." And I got up to go.

"Five hundred pounds," he said, and rapped the table.

Like an echo I heard Fay say, "Five hundred pounds—I must have five hundred pounds."

It was a relief to get the light out of my eyes. Standing, it didn't worry me. I looked over the top of the lantern, but I couldn't see his face. He had both hands on the table and was leaning over them. I saw his hat, his bulky shoulders, and his stubby hands, and I stood there, pulled this way and that. He said five hundred pounds, and Fay said five hundred pounds. He was offering it, and she was going to everlasting smash if she didn't get it. Then prison—three years of it—a perfectly damnable thought. And then . . . Not much use being free to starve. I was pulled this way and that.

I opened my mouth to speak. The thing I was going to say never got said. All at once I knew I couldn't do it.

I said "No," and turned on my heel and went out.

IX

THE BLOOD WAS POUNDING IN MY EARS, AND I FELT AS IF I had just pulled myself back on the edge of something frightful. I don't know what made me feel like that. I couldn't see or hear for a moment. I went blundering along the path and barged into a tree. At the same moment I heard my name called:

"Fairfax!"

It was the man I had been talking to, and he called a second time.

"Fairfax!"

I turned round. I had really only gone a pace or two. He was standing in the doorway holding up the lantern in front of him. As I turned, some one made a sound, a queer inarticulate sound of pain or distress. It seemed to come from the darkness behind him.

"What is it?" I asked.

"You're in too much of a hurry. Come back and talk things out."

"No use," I said. "I've made up my mind."

He turned half round and set the lamp on the table so that the dark side was between the light and the door. I saw all the left-hand side of the bare room in a yellow glow. He left the hut and came forward.

"Some one else wants to talk to you," he said. "You can come along to the car when you've finished." And with that he went past me and disappeared round the bend.

After a moment's hesitation I went back to the hut. I was very curious to see the other person—the some one else who had sighed in the darkness, and who wanted to speak to me. I went up to the door and looked in. Half the room was light, and half was dark. In the dark half some one was standing —a woman, in what looked like a black cloak and veil. The minute I moved she snatched up the lantern and turned the light on to my face. I don't know anything that makes you feel such a perfect fool as being stared at like that by some one you can't see. She took her time over it too, and just as I was beginning to feel like smashing something, she put the light down on the edge of the table and came across with her hand out.

"How do you do, Car?" she said.

I just stood there like a stock, for I was clean knocked out of time. She had on some sort of close cap with a black veil that covered her face and went round her neck like a scarf, but the minute she opened her mouth I knew her. It was Anna Lang.

Well, I never liked Anna, and there were reasons why both of us should find it awkward to meet. I hoped she didn't know as much about the reasons as I did—I couldn't believe she'd have come here to meet me if she did. I hoped with all my heart she didn't know that Uncle John had tried to bucket me into marrying her. I wished myself a thousand miles away, and yet, extraordinary as it may seem, one bit of me was pleased to see her. For one thing, when you've lived right away from your own people and your own pals for three years, it feels good to meet one of them again—it seems to bridge the gap a bit. And for another thing, I thought perhaps she might talk about Isobel; because, of course, they're near neighbors, and it isn't as if Isobel and I had even been engaged or anything like that, so I thought she might just happen to mention her. I didn't think all these things one after another as I've written them, but they were all there in my mind at once.

I stood there, and Anna's hand dropped down.

"Don't you know me, Car?"

Her voice is one of the things that annoys me about Anna. It's what you'd call a beautiful voice if it belonged to an actress spouting high falutin' blank verse stuff in a stage garden under a stage moon; in the family circle it's a bit too much of a good thing, and has always made me want to throw something at her.

I said, "Of course I know you. How do you do?" And I'm afraid I didn't say it very nicely. I don't know why some people always rub you up, but there it is.

When I said that, she laughed. She has the sort of laugh that is called "mellow" and "liquid" in novels. Personally I hate it. When she had laughed, she said,

"I don't do very well, and I'm afraid you don't either. Don't you think we might have something to say to each other?"

I didn't honestly feel that I had anything to say to her. I said so—politely of course. I put it that I hadn't exactly been making history, and that I wasn't going to bore any one with my horribly dull career.

She laughed again.

"You needn't be polite. It doesn't really suit you. I've come here because I want to talk to you. Will you give me ten minutes of your time?"

I couldn't say no to that.

"Well, let's sit down," she said. "One can conduct an interview standing, but one can't talk. I want to *talk*."

She stepped over the threshold and sat down on the step that ran the width of the door. I sat down too, in the opposite corner. I watched her unwind the black veil and throw it back. She did this very deliberately. Then she reached up behind her and turned the lantern so that the light shone straight between us and I could see her face and she could see mine. That's the sort of thing that riles me in Anna—she's stagey all the time. I suppose she's made that way. She used to get into a boiling rage when I told her of it—oh, about a hundred years ago when we were children and didn't mind what we said to each other.

She threw back the veil, and turned the light and looked at me, tilting her chin up a little and half closing her eyes. An artist once told her that she looked like the Blessed Damozel when she did that, and it's been her stock pose ever since. If you saw her painted like that, you'd say "How beautiful!" —and it would be quite true. But it's a trick all the same, and a trick ends in putting your back up.

I said, "You're looking very well, Anna," and she opened her eyes a little wider and looked mournfully at me. She's got those big, dark eyes that look as if they are just going to cry.

"Do I?" she said. "You don't—poor Car!"

I would have liked to say straight out, "For the Lord's sake, don't 'poor Car' me!" But I expect I looked it, for she said,

"Don't be angry. Can't you be friends and talk to me for ten minutes? Ten minutes isn't much out of three years. It's three years since we talked, isn't it?"

"Getting on."

"What sort of years have they been?"

"Oh, so so."

She put out her hand as if she were going to touch me. "Perhaps I know more about them than you think."

"There's nothing much to know."

"Shall I tell you what I know? It's not very pleasant telling—is it? So I think I'll leave it alone. It's been downhill all the way, and now you've got to the place where there isn't another step at all."

It sounds bald and brutal written down, but she said it in a sweet sad way, and at the end her voice broke into the sort of sigh which had come from the dark corner of the car.

"What did you want to talk to me about?" I said.

"You and me. Do you hate me, Car?"

"I wish you wouldn't talk nonsense!"

She laughed again, sadly. An ass who wrote poetry told her that her laugh had all the tears and all the music of the world in it. Of course, after that, she made a point of laughing sadly. She's had a lot of practice, and she does it awfully well.

"Look here, Anna," I said—and I admit that I was hot—"Look here, did you cart me all the way down from London into the middle of this wood to ask me whether I hated you?"

"Perhaps I did."

What can you do with a woman like that? I moved as if I was going to get up.

"Car—don't! I—I do want to talk to you. I—I've risked a lot to come and talk to you like this."

I never heard such rubbish in my life. You'd think she might know it wasn't any good talking like that to me. Anna and I are the same age, and we've known each other for the whole twenty-seven years. That's what annoys me—she ought to know better. I said so.

"What's the good of talking like that? What have you brought me down here for?"

"Bobby's been telling you."

Bobby. . . . When she said that, I knew where I'd seen the fat man before. Markham—that was his name—Bobby Markham. The Bobby did it, and his bulk. About a fortnight ago I tried for the job of secretary to a man called Arbuthnot Markham who is a partner in a big firm of timber importers. As they do most of their business with South America, and as I happen to have a smattering of Spanish, I thought I might have a chance. I hadn't. And after I'd seen Arbuthnot Markham I wasn't so sorry—I didn't like him. But beggars can't be choosers.

The fat man was in the outer office when I came through.

He didn't speak to me, though we'd had a nodding acquaintance some years before. He recognized me all right though—I could see that. It rather rubs it in when the people you didn't think good enough for you, start thinking you're not good enough for them. Not that I cared what Bobby Markham did. I didn't like him any better than I liked his brother. I suppose they were brothers; there was a good deal of likeness, only Arbuthnot was hard where Bobby was soft, and thick-set where Bobby was just fat. I put down Arbuthnot as a bully, and Bobby as a silly ass. Their voices were alike though.

"Oh," I said, "Bobby's been telling me?" That was Anna all over—she gave his name away as easily as saying good-morning. "And where do you come in? He talked about a client."

She tipped up her chin again.

"Oh, I was the client."

"Look here, Anna," I said, "what's all this nonsense? It doesn't take me in a bit, you know, this spoof offer of five hundred pounds and Mr. Bobby Markham's talk about a client who has forged a check and wants me to forge another so as to get him out of a hole."

I thought she turned paler.

"Not *him*," she said, "*her*."

"Meaning you?"

She *had* turned paler. For the first time, I thought she had stopped acting.

"Yes," she said, "yes. That's why I asked you whether you hated me, Car. If you do, yo'' 'e got your revenge to your hand."

I wanted to be quite sure what she meant, so I said,
"Yes?"

"Yes—*yes*," she said. "Do you hate me, Car? Because if you do, you've only to go to Uncle John and tell him just what Bobby and I have said to you to-night."

Of course she knew that I wouldn't do any such thing. She was playing up, but under all the theatrical stuff there was something that made me feel a bit sorry for her. You can tell when any one is frightened. I thought she was frightened, and I wondered what on earth she'd been up to.

I leaned back against the jamb of the door and tried to keep my temper.

"What have you been up to?" I said.

"Bobby told you."

"Good Lord, Anna, do you really want me to believe you've been forging checks?"

She nodded.

"One check—Car, it sounds worse than it is. Won't you let me tell you about it? I—I—it's been dreadful having no one to talk to."

"Mr. Markham?" I suggested.

"Bobby doesn't count."

I thought that was nice for Bobby, who was probably mixing himself up in a shady business because he was fool enough to be fond of her.

"I want to tell you about it. You'll listen—won't you? You must, because it wouldn't be fair if you didn't. I didn't mean to do anything wrong. I thought Uncle John was dying, and I knew he'd left me everything, because he told me so himself only the week before, so I didn't think there was any harm in my writing that check—he'd have given me the money twice over if I'd asked him for it."

"Why didn't you?"

"Because he was unconscious, and I couldn't wait. I had to have the money. And now I don't know what to do."

I gave her the best advice I could. She really was frightened.

"There's only one thing you can do—make a clean breast of it."

"To Uncle John?"

"Yes."

She sat there and looked at me for about half a minute. There wasn't any color in her face. Then she said,

"He'd never forgive me." She said that slowly; and then, like a flash, "You think that would play your game."

If she had been a man I should have struck her. Not that

it's any use anyhow—you can't strike the beastly mind that thinks that sort of thing.

She gave a gasp, leaned forward, and caught me by the arm.

"No—no—I didn't mean that! Car—I didn't mean it! Other people are like that, but not you. You'd help me out if you could. You're trying to help me out, even if you do hate me."

I wasn't going to answer that.

"I'm desperate—I don't know what I'm saying. If he knows, he'll cut me out of his will—and I don't know how to be poor—I've counted on the money always. If you were any one else, you wouldn't help me—but you're Car—you'll help me, won't you?"

"You can help yourself—I can't."

"No—no—*no*! He wouldn't leave me a penny, and if he doesn't leave it to me, it will all go to charities, for he told me so. You won't get it anyhow, Car—*no*, I didn't mean that—Car, I didn't—I don't know what I'm saying."

She turned from me, caught at the doorpost with both hands, hid her face against her arm, and burst into wild weeping. It was horrible to hear her. She wasn't pretending, she was really crying. Later on, when I touched her arm, I could feel her sleeve soaking wet with her tears. A woman crying like that makes a man feel a most awful fool, unless he can take her in his arms and comfort her—and that was just about the last thing in the world I wanted to do with Anna.

I sat down and waited, and I didn't say anything, because there didn't seem to be anything to say. After a bit she quieted down, and at last she let her arms drop and moved round so that she was facing me again. She put her hands in her lap and leaned her head back against the doorpost. Her face was wet, and her eyes were shut.

"I didn't mean it," she said.

"That's all right."

"I know you're not like that."

While she was crying I'd been thinking a bit.

"Look here, Anna," I said, "I don't really know what you've been driving at with this fake advertisement business, and getting me down here, but I do know one thing—if you've really been up to anything with Uncle John's check-book, you've given Bobby Markham a pretty dangerous hold over you. I don't know an awful lot about him, but what I do know wouldn't make me feel I should be safe in putting my reputation and—" I hesitated for a moment, and then I let her have it straight—"my liberty into his hands."

She looked at me between her wet black lashes and said, "Wouldn't it?"

"No, it wouldn't—not by a long chalk."

She gave a nod, quite casual and careless.

"Oh, Bobby's all right. He eats out of my hand." Then she leaned forward and put her left hand on my knee. "What about *you*, Car?"

"Me?" I couldn't make out what she meant.

"Yes, you—you—*you*. I've put myself in Bobby's power. Haven't I put myself in yours? Bobby knows about the check. What about you? Don't you know about it? If Bobby's got a hold over me, haven't you got one too?" She stared at me in the strangest way. "What about it, Car?"

"I don't know what you mean." I said that, but of course it wasn't really true. It had only just stopped being true though. You know how it is—what you're thinking runs ahead of what you're saying. The minute the words were out of my mouth I wished I hadn't said them, because she laughed in my face.

"How plainly have I got to put it? You know enough to damn me if you choose to go to Uncle John with your knowledge. No, that's too crude—you wouldn't do that—would you?"

"Am I to say 'thank you' for that?" I was very angry.

"No, you wouldn't do that—you wouldn't go to Uncle John. But if you met him, and he asked you, what would you do then? Would you give me away?" Her voice broke sharply in the middle of the last word.

"You mean if he asked me about the check? I haven't seen him or heard from him for three years. Why should he ask me?"

"I don't know." She sounded tired and bewildered. "I—don't know. I—was—just—supposing. Would you give me away?"

"What's the good of supposing?"

"Car—*would* you? I told you myself. It isn't as if you had found it out. I *told* you. You couldn't give away what I'd told you myself. Could you?"

I put my hand on her arm. That was when I felt that the sleeve was wet.

"What makes you think I'll ever have the chance?"

"Old men have fancies," she said. Her arm shook. She leaned nearer. "Suppose he sent for you. Suppose he asked you questions. Suppose you saw your chance of outing me and coming back to your old place." She wrenched her arm out of my hold and threw herself back against the half open door. "Oh, why did I tell you anything? Why was I such an utter, utter fool as to tell you?"

She had been trying me pretty high all along, and my temper got the better of me.

"What sort of damned cad do you take me for?" I got to my feet. "That's about enough," I said. "I'm going."

She jumped up and came to me with the tears running down her face.

"Car—will you promise not to tell? Will you swear you won't tell him what I told you? I'll believe you if you promise."

I was too angry to say anything, and I suppose she thought I was hesitating, for she began to catch her breath and sob.

"I only told you because I trusted you so. You *can't* use what I told you because I trusted you."

I got hold of myself again, but I expect my voice was pretty rough.

"I didn't ask you to tell me anything. I wouldn't have come within a hundred miles of this place if I'd had any idea of what you were going to tell me. But since you've known me all your life, I should think you'd have enough sense to know it won't go any farther. You'd much better make a clean breast of it yourself. But if you won't do that, keep clear of a fool's trick like forgery in the future. Uncle John's no fool himself, and you're bound to be found out."

"But not through you? Word of honor?"

"I told you so. Good-night."

She let me go a dozen yards, and then called after me.

"Where are you going?"

"To the car."

"It's not there."

"Where is it?"

She hesitated.

"I didn't want them hanging about. I didn't want—Bobby."

"How am I to get back? Where are we?"

"You don't know?"

I'd begun to think I did.

"Linwood Edge?"

"Of course. I thought you knew. I thought you'd see me home. I wanted to get rid of Bobby, so I told him to take the car to the corner by the bridge just out of the village."

I didn't in the least want to walk back through the wood with her but there didn't seem to be any way out of it. I knew where we were now—on the edge of my uncle's land with about a quarter of an hour's walk between us and the house, and another few minutes on to where Anna had sent the car to wait.

She picked up the lantern and fastened the crazy door. We went on down the narrow path again. The yellow light was round our feet, and everywhere all about us the woods were dark and very still. She didn't speak, nor did I. It was a long time since I had walked in Linwood. I had walked there with Isobel. Isobel's pool was there. I wondered where Isobel was. And then, breaking a ten minutes' silence, Anna made me jump by speaking her name.

"Isobel Tarrant's down here. I suppose you know that?"

I didn't see why I should tell Anna what I knew, so I just said,

"Is she?"

"Yes. I suppose we shall all be dancing at her wedding soon."

My heart stood quite still for a minute. It was a most horrible feeling. After a bit I said,

"Is she going to be married?"

I had to say it; but I had to say it so that Anna wouldn't notice anything. I think I managed it all right.

"It's not given out yet, so don't congratulate her."

"Who is it?"

"Giles Heron. He's since your time. He bought Brockington. He's a very good match for a girl like Isobel who hasn't a penny and never will have. Miss Willy has put everything into an annuity, you know."

I didn't say anything. I was glad it was so dark.

We came out on to the edge of the wood, and I could see the paddock stretching black between us and the drive. The elms that edged it were blacker still. The sky had a little faint light in it. The yellow lantern-light seemed to belong to a different place. Anna must have thought that too. She slid back the glass and blew out the candle.

We went on till we came to the road. Then I said good-night and began to walk down towards the gate, but she came running after me.

"Car—wait a minute."

"What is it?"

"It's—you. Why are you—so thin?"

"I'm not in the least thin."

"You are—*frightfully*. When I saw you——" Her voice choked. "What have you been doing to yourself?"

"Nothing."

"Car—"

"Good-night, Anna," I said. And this time I got away.

I found the car, not where she had said, but practically in the village street. It couldn't have been far short of midnight. The driver had the bonnet open and was tinkering away by the light of an electric torch. I asked him what was wrong, and he said he didn't know. There was no sign of Bobby Markham.

I thanked my stars it was so late and so dark. I certainly didn't want any one to come along and recognize me. I could just imagine how the village gossips would enjoy themselves.

The driver went on tinkering, and I walked up and down. There wasn't a light to be seen anywhere. Presently he called out and asked me to hold the torch. As I took it, I heard a car come round the corner where the street bends in the middle, and I saw the headlights. It was going slow—a small Morris—and just as it came abreast of us, the driver reached up for the torch, and in taking it turned the light right into my eyes and nearly blinded me.

The next thing I saw was the tail-light of the Morris going over the bridge. Then I lost it; but by the sound I thought it had turned in at my uncle's gate, and I wondered who was going there so late.

About five minutes later the driver got the engine going, and we drove back to town. I spoke to him when we had gone a little way, but he didn't answer me. Then I said something about the car, and he didn't answer that either, so after that I left it alone.

X

ANNA LANG STOOD JUST INSIDE THE BIG HALL DOOR OF Linwood House. She stood leaning on the door with her left hand, whilst with her right she held the catch that would slip the lock at a touch. She was listening intently. Behind her the house was dark except for the small lamp which burned beside the telephone. She had taken off her cap and veil and smoothed her shining black hair. It defined her head in close waves as formal and as natural as the marble ripple in the hair of some sculptured nymph.

She leaned against the door and listened intently. The moment she heard the car stop she pulled the catch and let the door swing in.

A man came up the steps with as much haste as a stoutish medical practitioner permits himself.

"I'm so glad you've come," said Anna.

Dr. Monk came into the hall.

"How is he?"

"I think he's asleep. I'm so glad you've come. I was so frightened."

"Well, well, I'll just go up and see him."

She went before him to the stairs and switched on the light on an upper landing.

"He didn't remember anything about it when I got him back to bed."

"Well, well, I'll just go up and see him."

She went up with him, and stood on the threshold of the large room where John Carthew lay sleeping quietly in a huge old-fashioned four-post bed. A nightlight burned on the double marble washstand. The room was shadowed, drowsy, and rather close behind the heavy crimson curtains which shut out the night air.

Dr. Monk went over to the bed. Anna held her breath. He mustn't wake.

Presently Dr. Monk came back, motioned her out of the room, and shut the door.

"He seems all right," he said. "Tell me what happened."

Anna spoke what she had rehearsed, with her large dark eyes looking at him mournfully out of a colorless face. Suppose he didn't believe her.

"He went to bed at ten. I read till after eleven. Then I went up to my room, and the servants shut up. I felt restless and hot, and after a bit I went downstairs and took a turn on the terrace. I suppose I was out half an hour. When I came in, I found my uncle's door ajar, so I looked in to see if he was all right. He was lying in a faint just inside the door. I got some cold water, and he came round at once and let me help him to bed. He didn't remember anything about it, and I thought I'd better call you up.''

"You're sure he was unconscious?''

"Oh yes.''

"He seems quite all right''—in a puzzled tone.

They moved together to the head of the stairs. As they began to descend them, Anna said,

"You must be feeling that I've brought you out for nothing. I'm so sorry.''

"Not at all,'' said Dr. Monk a little gruffly.

"If I ever have to come through the village at night, I always think how dead it is—as if it might have been dead a thousand years. I don't suppose you saw a soul.''

Dr. Monk gave a malicious snort and rubbed his hands together.

"Then you suppose wrong, for I saw Car Fairfax.'' He took a step down as he spoke, but Anna stood perfectly still above him, her hand on the banisters.

"*Car? Car?*'' she said in a low voice.

"Car Fairfax,'' said Dr. Monk, looking up at her with his small gray eyes. He had begun to feel distinctly less cross. He admired Anna a good deal, and was pleased at the effect of his speech.

"*Car?*'' said Anna. "Car Fairfax—*here*?''

"Just outside Turner's, holding a torch for a chauffeur who was doing something to a car. The man took the torch from him as I passed, and the light went right on Car's face. It was Car all right.''

"Oh, don't!'' said Anna. She had begun to tremble very much, and the words were hardly audible.

"Why? What's the matter?''

She shook her head.

They came down the rest of the flight into the hall.

"Dr. Monk——"

"What is it?"

"Do you think Car came here?"

"What makes you think that?"

"I don't know if I ought—oh, I must tell some one."

"What is it?"

"I told you I went out. I came in because the library window was open."

"You mean you left it open."

"No—I didn't go out that way. I went out through the garden door. It has a spring lock, and I had the key. It was shut all right, because I tried it, but the library window was ajar."

"Do you think Mr. Carthew——"

"I don't know what to think. Suppose he came down and let some one in, or suppose he heard some one in the library and got up. His room is just above. I don't know what to think."

"The window was open. Was anything disturbed?"

She hesitated. Then without speaking she crossed the hall and opened a door. Dr. Monk followed. She touched a switch, and the library sprang into view—a heavy, handsome room with maroon curtains and old, comfortable leather chairs.

"The curtains were drawn, but the door was open," said Anna slowly.

The room was high. There were two windows—long French windows, opening to the ground, as Dr. Monk well knew. Between the windows stood a large mahogany bureau with a cupboard above and three drawers below. The top drawer was not quite shut.

Dr. Monk walked across and looked at it.

"That drawer——"

"I know."

"Did you look to see if anything's missing?"

"I didn't like to. I—I was frightened."

"Well, you'd better see now." He pulled out the drawer.

"Doesn't keep valuables here, I suppose—does he? Hullo! Some one's been rummaging!"

The papers in the drawer had been turned over. A check book lay open across them.

"Hullo!" said Dr. Monk again. "Hullo, hul*lo*! Some one's been up to something—yes, by Jove, they have!"

Anna tried to push the drawer in, but her hand shook. She leaned against the desk and said in a choking voice,

"Oh—don't!"

Dr. Monk glanced at her sharply.

"Would you know if anything had been taken?"

He pulled down the flap of the bureau and exposed more confusion. There was a row of pigeonholes above the desk. Everything had been bundled out of them—papers, a time-table, pencils, an old pen, a bunch of seals, stamps, and some neatly docketed bills; whilst, across the tangle, stretched a light chain ending in a bunch of keys.

Anna exclaimed and caught it up. The keys fell jangling against the wood.

Dr. Monk looked at her. Those big eyes of hers were brimming over with fear. Odd. He would never have suspected her of being easily frightened. She was as white as a sheet of paper. Those very beautiful lips of hers had lost all their red.

Dr. Monk admired Miss Lang more than a little. He was fifty, and a very comfortable bachelor. He didn't want to marry any one, but Anna made him feel agreeably young. Her pallor and her distress moved him dangerously; he didn't feel at all sure that he might not commit himself in some way if she went on looking at him like that. Dangerous—very dangerous. But how agreeable. Lovely woman. Midnight. Danger. The position of consoling friend——

"My dear Miss Anna——" said Dr. Monk. He said it warmly and with a slight tremor in his voice.

Anna's eyes came to his face. Then suddenly her lashes fell; a shiver went over her. She gathered up the keys and, turning, shut the bureau top with a jerky movement. There was an awkward silence. She broke it at last, speaking in a low voice and not looking at him.

"You won't—tell any one—will you?"

"My dear Miss Anna——" said Dr. Monk again.

"I shall have to tell my uncle," she said. "I wish I needn't, but I must."

He felt more and more puzzled.

"Is anything missing here?" There must be some reason for this extraordinary agitation of hers.

"I don't know." Then, with an abrupt change of voice, "Are you sure that it was Car whom you saw?"

"Oh, quite sure."

Was she changing the subject? Or did she mean—what did she mean? Some of her color had come back.

"I'm keeping you, and it's most dreadfully late. Good-night."

This was dismissal. He accepted it with a sense of danger averted. He might have made a fool of himself in another minute. It was, somehow, disappointing not to have had the chance. He felt a little dashed as he said good-night and stepped out into the dark. But before he reached the car Anna called him back.

"Dr. Monk!"

He could see her only as a soft black shadow against the dimly lighted hall. She stood in the half open door and spoke quick and low.

"Did he look ill?"

"Who?"

"Car."

"Bless me—no! Why should he? I only saw him for a moment. I thought he looked a bit thin."

"You didn't think he was ill?"

"Has he been ill?"

"I don't know." She opened the door wider and slipped across the step. "Dr. Monk——"

"What is it?"

"You won't—you won't tell any one you saw him?"

Now why should she ask him that?

Her hand touched his arm just for a moment.

"Please."

"But why?"

"But I can't tell you. You won't tell any one—will you?"

Dr. Monk said he wouldn't, and then went off wondering why she had asked him that, and what in the world Car Fairfax was doing in Linwood at that hour of night, or at any hour, if he wasn't seeing his uncle. Then quite suddenly the keys, Mr. Carthew's swoon, the ransacked bureau, and Anna's frightened eyes rushed together in his protesting mind and supplied an answer which upset him a good deal.

XI

MRS. BELL PANTED UP THE STAIR WITH A PLATE OF HOT meat pudding in one hand and a letter in the other. Both hands being occupied, she knocked on Mr. Fairfax's door with the edge of the plate and then, taking the letter between her teeth, wrestled with the rather stiff handle for a moment and burst in.

Mr. Fairfax was standing at the window with his back to the room. As soon as she had retrieved the letter she burst into speech, at the same time setting down the plate with a bang calculated to attract the most absent-minded person's attention.

"And if you please, sir"—it was Mrs. Bell's way to start sentences in the middle—"and if you *please*, sir, there isn't nothing nastier nor cold suet—or if there is, I haven't come across it, not yet I haven't."

The meat pudding had a mound of potato on one side of it

and a little hill of green cabbage on the other. There was plenty of gravy. Even cabbage smells good to a very hungry man.

Car turned round in a hurry.

"Mrs. Bell, you shouldn't—I can't," he stammered.

Mrs. Bell slapped the letter down beside the plate. Her large round face was hot and red with cooking. Her large red hands were still steaming from the hot water in which she had just plunged them. Her apron was not very clean, and she had a smudge on her cheek. She spoke in a tone of angry authority that carried Car back to his nursery days:

"Now, Mr. Fairfax, you look here! What ha' you had to eat these last two mortal days? Bites, and crusts, and chippings of cheese, and such-like. You set right down and eat a proper meal whilst it's hot! And if you wants to argue you can do it afterwards—for suet's a thing that won't be kept waiting, not if you was a duke."

"Mrs. Bell——"

"Take and eat it up!" said Mrs. Bell in a warning voice. She backed through the doorway and banged the door.

When Car had finished the last shred of cabbage, he opened the letter. It had a London postmark and had been cleared that morning. He read it with steadily increasing surprise:

Dear Sir,

I must apologize for not having kept the appointment made with you yesterday over the telephone. I hope you did not wait very long. I was delayed by a slight accident to my car, and did not reach Churt Row until nearly eleven. As you were not there, I presumed that you had given me up and gone home. If you will be at the same place at the same time this evening, I will endeavor to be more punctual.

Yours truly
Z.10 SMITH

The writing was clear, upright, and a little formal. Car

stared at it. There was no word that he could possibly have misread. There was not the slightest ambiguity about the phrasing. Mr. Smith was apologizing for not having kept his appointment last night. But somebody had kept it—the fat man had kept it. The fat man was Bobby Markham. Or was he? For the moment he didn't feel sure about anything.

Then he took hold of himself. He was quite sure that he had talked with Anna Lang in Linwood last night, and Anna had spoken quite openly of Bobby. Yes, the fat man was Bobby Markham. And it was Bobby Markham who had gone through the tobacconist's shop and into the inner room whilst Car was waiting to make his inquiries about the International Employment Exchange. Where, then, did Mr. Z.10 Smith come in? So far he existed, very elusively, as a profferer of five hundred pounds; as Box Z.10 ; as a voice on the telephone; and now, as an apologist for having failed to keep an appointment.

Bobby Markham had kept the appointment. But how did Bobby Markham know that there was an appointment to keep? And how did Bobby and Anna know that Box Z.10 was offering him five hundred pounds? Of course any one might read an advertisement. But how did they know that this particular advertisement had been thrust upon Car Fairfax? It was all very complicated, and if there had been a little more margin between him and sheer starvation, he would have put Mr. Smith's letter into the waste-paper-basket and thought no more about it. He wouldn't starve to-day, thanks to Mrs. Bell's meat pudding. He had been giddy with hunger all the morning. To-morrow he would be hungry again. Five hundred pounds was five hundred pounds. He wouldn't forge a check for it, but he would do a good deal; and if the job was a risky one, so much the better.

He pushed the whole thing away, carried his plate down to save Mrs. Bell the stairs, and went out.

He tramped five miles to answer an advertisement in Hampstead, found the post filled, and tramped back again. The sole of his boot still held.

He opened the street door upon Mrs. Bell and a girl.

"And here he is!" said Mrs. Bell. "In the nick of time, as you might say."

What with the open door, and three people, the narrow passage seemed quite full. Mrs. Bell leaned on the door and breathed heavily. Her apron was a little dirtier than it had been three hours before, she had another smudge on her cheek, and her gray hair displayed more wispy ends and hairpins than one would have thought possible.

"The young lady come and asked for you not five minutes ago, and just going, only as you may say, before I could put my hand on the handle to let her out, in you come."

Car looked past Mrs. Bell to the girl. The first thing he noticed about her was the interest with which she was regarding him. Her pretty, bright eyes were full of it. The parted lips, the tilt of her chin, the little hands in their gray suede gloves, all said, "Here's Mr. Fairfax!" She was in gray from head to foot; not gloomy gray, but the gray of her own eyes, and that was a very pretty color indeed. Her little hat framed her face so close that her hair might have been any color, or she might not have had any hair at all. It came down over her ears and then sprang out in two quaint wings. They gave her a Puckish look, and the way she tilted her head and looked up at him deepened the impression of something light, airy, elfin. She spoke in a sweet, high voice that had learnt its pitch on the other side of the Atlantic.

"Are you Mr. Fairfax?"

"Yes, I am."

Instantly his hand was being shaken. The gray eyes were beaming with a delightful friendliness.

"Then I'm very pleased to meet you." She went on shaking hands. "Well now, Mr. Fairfax, if this isn't delightful! And just when I had given you up. Well, you'll never know how disappointed I was, and I couldn't begin to tell you. No, it didn't seem *right*. And just as I was telling Mrs. Bell what I felt about it, the door opened, and I knew it was going to be you."

She stopped shaking hands and stepped back. She had the quick, sure grace of a kitten. Yes, that was what she was like—a gray kitten, with wide-set, innocent eyes and an alert but friendly poise.

Car smiled at her because he couldn't help it; but he hadn't the ghost of a notion what to say, so he didn't say anything. She tilted her head and looked at him with her eyes very wide indeed.

"You don't say you don't know who I am!"

"*There* now!" said Mrs. Bell.

"I—I'm afraid——" said Car.

"I'm Corinna Lee——" She stopped, gazed blankly at him, and clapped her hands together. "Gracious! Don't say you've never heard of me!"

"I—I'm afraid——"

"You haven't! You must be thinking I'm crazy then. Peter didn't tell you I was coming?"

"Peter——"

"Peter Lymington. You're not going to tell me you've never heard of *him*!"

She liked the way Car smiled.

"Yes, I've heard of Peter."

"And Peter'll hear from me," said Miss Lee firmly. "Letting me come here and act as if I was crazy, instead of writing to tell you to get ready to ring the joy-bells!"

"How am I to ring them?" said Car.

"By coming out to tea with me at my hotel. I'd been fixing it with Mrs. Bell before you came, but now you've come, we'll just go along together, and first I'll explain about me, and then I'll tell you all about Peter—and if he doesn't write, he's sent you a good few messages."

Mrs. Bell let go of the door and stepped ponderously back. Fay was coming down the stairs. She was dressed in black, and she carried a scarlet bag. Her hat resembled Pierrot's cap, her face was powdered as white as his, her lips painted as startling a crimson. She swung her scarlet bag and came down slowly, looking neither to right nor left.

When she reached the bottom step, she stopped and spoke to Car.

"Going out—or coming in?"

He said, "I've been out."

She kept her shoulder turned to Corinna Lee.

"Come and have tea with me," she said.

He thought she must have heard Corinna's invitation.

He said, "Thank you—I'm afraid I can't." And then, "This is a friend of Peter's—Miss Lee. Miss Lee——" He hesitated for a moment. Fay's shoulder was a barrier. "Miss Fay Everitt."

And then he had a doubt. Fay called herself Miss Everitt. She had never called herself Mrs. Lymington. But all the same——

If she acknowledged his introduction at all, it was with the very slightest movement of her head. She neither turned towards Corinna Lee nor looked at her. She looked at Car, and standing on the bottom step, opened her scarlet bag and extracted from it mirror and lipstick.

"Come and have tea with me, Car."

"I'm afraid I'm engaged."

She transferred her attention to the mirror, ran the lipstick over the painted curves of her mouth, and then very deliberately looked him up and down. Without a spoken word Car understood just how shabby he looked, and how impossible as an escort except by the indulgence of old friendship. Mirror and lipstick went back into the bag. Fay passed carelessly out. The tapping of her heels died away.

"*Well*!" said Miss Corinna Lee.

Car did not know what to say. Fay wanted shaking. If this pretty creature was a friend of Peter's, things were going to be awkward. If they were great friends, she probably knew about Peter's marriage. Perhaps he ought to have introduced Fay as Mrs. Lymington. He had never been able to see why there should be any secrecy. Well, it wasn't his business.

By the time he reached this conclusion he was walking down the street with Miss Lee, and she was telling him how polite English railway porters were (was there a spice of malice here?) and how surprised she was to see London bathed in sunshine and with a blue sky overhead.

"I thought there would be a fog. Now you're not going to tell me that London fogs are a myth?"

"We have them."

"Now that's a great relief! Will there be one tomorrow?"

"I don't know. I hope not."

"You *hope* not. But I *want* to see a fog!"

Car laughed at her.

"Do you get everything you want?"

She looked as if she did. There was something of the unspoilt darling child about her. She looked as if she had sunshine and love always. Perhaps she wanted a fog for a change.

"Most of the time," she said, and cocked her chin at him. "I've wanted to meet you."

"That's very nice of you."

She went on as if he had not spoken.

"Because of Peter—and because of your name."

"Fairfax?"

She shook her head.

"I'd have liked it to be the Fairfax part of your name, because that's romantic and historical, but I can't tell a lie any more than Washington could. It would be a pity if I hurt myself trying to—wouldn't it?"

"*Rather!*"

She looked at him with just a shade of anxiety in the round gray eyes.

"I guess I sound real crazy. But I'm not—I'm trying to break it to you that I'm a cousin."

"It would have to be broken very gently."

"I'm being as gentle as I can. You won't fall right down in a faint, will you?"

"I'll do my best."

She stopped at a street corner and looked up at him.

"Well then, your name's Carthew, and it was your mother's name—wasn't it?"

Car nodded.

"And she came from a place called Linwood?"

"She did."

"And so did my grandmother," said Corinna. Her eyes, her face, her voice all held a sort of quivering blend of earnestness and mischief.

"How topping!" said Car.

"I'm glad Peter didn't tell you. I told him he wasn't to."

"Perhaps that's why he didn't write," said Car.

They shook hands earnestly. Her hand was very small and soft. For the moment mischief was subdued. It was evidently an occasion—and an occasion ought to be celebrated. With a horrid sick feeling Car remembered that he couldn't ask her to celebrate it. Fay's look came back. His hand felt cold as it let go of Corinna's gray glove.

"What's the matter?" said Corinna.

"Nothing." Why on earth had he let her carry him off like this?

"Didn't I break it gently enough?"

"You broke it beautifully."

"Then come along."

"I——"

"What is it? Don't you like me for a cousin?" The gray eyes were still mischievous, but the mischief was very faintly clouded over—mist over sparkling water.

Car felt himself getting hot.

"It isn't that. I—I'm not dressed for a tea-party."

"Carthew Fairfax—if you don't come and have tea with me, I shall burst out crying, right here. Did you think I was asking a suit of clothes to tea? Because if you did, you've got to think again. Now, have I got to cry?"

Car's embarrassment left him. Gray kittens have no conventions. They do not look at the seams of your coat or the bulges in your boots.

Corinna produced a handkerchief four inches square and wrinkled her nose in a preparatory sniff.

"Thank you very much for inviting me," said Car.

XII

HALF AN HOUR LATER THEY WERE TALKING AS IF THEY
had known each other always. Miss Lee was staying at the
Luxe, and they had a *tête-à-tête* tea in her own sitting-room,
with her own cushions making bright, delightful spots of
color, and a large photograph of Poppa in the middle of the
mantelpiece, and a small snapshot of Peter on either side of it.

He had learned that Poppa was the head of the Lee-
Mackintosh Corporation, and that he thought a heap of
Peter. He thought Peter was a real fine boy, and he didn't
mind his being English—at least, not much. Car gathered that
continuous pressure was being brought to bear upon Poppa to
think even more highly of Peter. He also gathered that Poppa
had perfectly effete ideas about daughters traveling alone, and
that Corinna was therefore saddled with a chaperone in the
shape of Cousin Abby Palliser. She seemed quite capable of
managing her however. Cousin Abby, having a passion for
historical monuments, could always be sent to see St. Paul's,
or Westminster Abbey, or the Houses of Parliament if Corinna
wanted to get rid of her. This afternoon she was doing
Westminster Abbey, and as she was an extremely conscientious
sightseer, it would certainly take her several hours.

"And now," said Corinna—"*now* I'm going to ask you
questions."

"All right."

"You don't mind?"

"Not a bit."

She was sitting behind the tea-table with her elbow on her knee and her little round chin in her hand.

"Sure?" she said.

Car wondered. He laughed and said,

"What are you going to ask?"

"Wait and see." She waited herself for a moment, and then said, "Peter's told me a lot, and I've guessed some of the things he didn't tell me. If I've guessed wrong, you can put me wise. You know, Peter thinks the world of you, but he's considerably worried, because he doesn't think you're getting a fair show. Now if my grandmother was a Carthew, I suppose that lets me in so I can talk about the Carthews without offending you. And if that's so, well, the first thing I want to ask is why your Uncle John Carthew didn't rally round when things went wrong."

"He helped my mother," said Car.

"But not you."

"No—not me."

"Why?"

"Well, I don't know why he should."

"Didn't he offer to help you at all?"

"Yes—on conditions."

"And you couldn't take them?"

"No."

She didn't ask what they were—that was a relief; she just sat and looked at him with perfectly round innocent eyes under a fluff of dark hair. The little gray hat lay on the floor beside her chair. Her hair was darker than he had expected. Its brown was the soft velvet brown of a bulrush. It increased her resemblance to a kitten, for it had the light, soft look of fur. It was very thick, and yet very light.

After a bit she said, "The job Peter got was offered to you first."

Car flushed up to the roots of his hair and objurgated Peter in his heart.

"Oh well, it was for either of us. It—it wouldn't have suited me to leave England then."

She nodded.

"You let Peter have it. How many jobs have you had since Peter went out?"

"I couldn't say."

"Have you got a job now?"

"Not just at the moment."

A look came over her face like a shadow passing quickly.

"You think I'm very inquisitive. *I'm not.* I've got to ask you something more, and I'm scared you'll be angry with me."

She didn't look in the least scared; she looked as friendly as the friendliest importunate creature that does not know what it is to get no for an answer.

"I've got to ask you a very impertinent thing. If you've had a lot of jobs, what's the reason you haven't kept any of them?"

Just for a moment Car was angry.

"My own incompetence, I suppose," he said.

"*Well*!" said Corinna. Her sparkling look accused him of mock humility. She sat up, dimpling. "Do you want me to believe that?"

"I'm afraid it's true."

She went suddenly as grave as a judge.

"Carthew Fairfax—you've got to tell me the truth. Was it your opinion that you were being incompetent *before* you got fired from those jobs?"

After a moment he met her look squarely.

"No, I thought I was doing pretty well."

"There hadn't been any complaints?"

"No."

"They just fired you all of a sudden?"

"Yes."

"Every time?"

He thought for a moment. Beecher—he'd been getting along like a house on fire with old Beecher—and then, "I'm sorry, Mr. Fairfax, but we're cutting down the staff." Prothero—yes, that was sudden enough. Craddock—you couldn't count Craddock, who was just pure beast. But Gray—Gray had been full of a decent embarrassment.

"Why did you ask me that?"

"I'm going to ask you something else," said Corinna. "I'm going to ask you whether you've got an enemy. No, I'm not—I'm going to ask you who your enemy is. I don't need to ask whether you've got one." A little hot color stood in her cheeks. Her eyes met his squarely.

Car leaned back smiling.

"I'm afraid I'm my own enemy, Miss Lee."

She clapped her hands together sharply.

"You *don't* like me for a cousin!"

"Why——"

"Didn't I call you Carthew right away? If it isn't the worst slap in the face I've ever had, to be called Miss Lee as if I was my own chaperone and at least as old as Cousin Abby!"

Car laughed, as one laughs at a child.

"My mistake! Let's begin all over again. I'm Car, and you're Corinna."

"And we're talking business," said Miss Lee reprovingly.

"Are we?"

"I am." She put her head a little on one side, let her lashes fall just a shade, and asked,

"Who was that girl on the stairs?"

"Fay Everitt?"

"Fay Something—I didn't get her whole name. Who is she?"

Car experienced an extreme embarrassment. What was Peter playing at? Had he told this child he was married? He seemed to have told her a good many intimate things, but he didn't seem to have told her that; and it wasn't like Peter—it wasn't in the least like Peter. If Peter hadn't said he was married to Fay, it was going to be uncommonly awkward for any one else to say it. He wondered if it was Fay who was insisting on this rotten secrecy. He looked very nearly as embarrassed as he felt when he said,

"Didn't Peter mention her?"

"No. Is she a friend of Peter's?"

"Yes—she was."

"You mean they've quarreled?"

"Oh no."

"Is she a friend of yours?"

Car wondered. He wasn't sure, but he supposed that Fay would have claimed him as a friend.

He compromised with, "I've known her for some time," and to his horror felt the color rise in his face.

" 'M—m—m——" said Corinna. "She didn't act in a very genial way—did she?"

"Not very."

"Why?"

"I don't know," said Car.

She waved Fay Everitt away.

"Do you know what I'm doing to-morrow?"

"Something pleasant, I hope."

"I hope so too. I'm going to Linwood to see my grandmother's nephew, John Carthew. Will it be pleasant?"

"If he likes you. He's charming to people he likes."

"And he doesn't like you?"

"He likes people as long as they do everything he wants them to. If they want to do something else, there's trouble."

"And you wanted to do something else?"

"I like my own way too," said Car.

XIII

Car Fairfax's Diary:

September 18*th*, WEDNESDAY—I'M *BLOWED* IF I CAN UNDER-stand what's happening. I'm going to keep on writing everything down. I don't like the feel of things. Yesterday morning I got a letter from Z.10 Smith—he signed it like that—and it was an apology for not having kept the appointment he had made with me over the telephone. He said he'd been delayed by an accident to his car and didn't get to Churt Row till nearly eleven, and he finished up by asking me to be at the same place at the same time that evening. I can't copy the letter or attach it, because it has disappeared. My letters seem to be getting a habit of disappearing. That's one of the things I don't like. I'm prepared to swear I left it inside my blotter when I went out, and when I came back it was gone. I didn't get back till pretty late—that is, I didn't get up to my room till pretty late—because I met an American cousin on the doorstep, and went off and had tea with her at the Luxe. That looks funny written down; but after the first ten minutes or so it didn't feel funny. She's a ripping kid, as friendly as they're made. Her name's Corinna Lee. She's going down to Linwood to-day. I wonder if she'll see Isobel. I didn't say anything about Isobel, because I was afraid of giving myself away. Corinna is as sharp as a needle.

Well, at half-past nine I started to walk down to Putney. I found Churt Row without asking this time. I hadn't heard the clock strike, so I didn't know whether I was early or not—I thought I must be. There wasn't any car in sight. I walked as far as Olding Crescent and stood at the corner looking down the road. I hadn't been there more than half a minute before some one came out of the shadow of the long brick wall which I had noticed the other day. He didn't come very far across the road. He stood there and said, "Mr. Fairfax?" and as soon as I moved to meet him he went back into the shadow again. I followed him into what was practically pitch dark, because the branches of big trees growing inside the garden came down over the wall nearly the whole way along it. The wall must have run three or four hundred yards, and the nearest lamp-post was a good way off on the other side of the road. I stood still when I got in under the trees. I thought it was up to him to begin.

He said "Mr. Fairfax?" again, and I said, "Mr. Smith?"

"Z.," he said; and when I didn't say anything, he went on in a dry, impatient whisper: "What's the number? If you're Fairfax, you know the number."

So then I said, "Z.10."

That seemed to satisfy him.

"I was vexed to miss you last night. I suppose you gave me up?"

I didn't answer that. He either knew what had happened last night, or he didn't. If he didn't, I wasn't going to tell him. I waited a bit, and he made an impatient sound, and went on:

"Well, Mr. Fairfax, you're here now, so I take it you're interested in the possibility of earning five hundred pounds?"

I thought I might agree to that, so I did, and I wondered what he was going to ask me to do. I hoped it wasn't going to be forgery. I felt somehow as if I should like a change.

"Five hundred pounds is a large sum of money," he began.

"There are larger sums."

"They're not so easily come by."

"Is this one easily come by?"

"Very much to the point, Mr. Fairfax—very much to the point." He took me by the arm and began to walk me down the road away from the corner. "The matter, as you most certainly will have guessed, is of a very confidential nature. Now I put it to you—does one hand over a large sum of money and a confidential mission without making sure that one's choice is a wise one—wise and—er—*safe*?"

He had very hard and bony fingers, and a singularly inexpressive voice. He seemed scarcely to touch my arm, and yet his touch cramped me. He was a little man with a fidgety manner and a way of putting up his hand—to adjust his glasses, I thought. There was a flavor of formality about his way of speech. I felt quite sure that I had never talked with him before, except perhaps on the telephone yesterday morning. He went on speaking, and when we came to the end of the long brick wall, he turned and walked me back again.

"The matter being of such a very confidential nature, you will not think it unreasonable if there is some little delay about entrusting it to you. To be quite frank, my principal would like an opportunity of testing your capabilities."

"In what way?" I asked.

He did not answer me directly.

"My principal proposes that you should be paid a retaining fee until such time as it may appear advisable to call upon you for the service which will earn the offered five hundred pounds."

I repeated the words "a retaining fee" with a question in my voice.

"A sum of ten pounds down, and a salary of three pounds a week."

I stood stock still in amazement and heard the crackle of a bank note not six inches from my right elbow. Ten pounds. . . . It sounded like the sort of dream you have when you've gone short of water and you think you hear a running stream. That happened to me once in Africa. It was a dream, and I woke up and there wasn't any water. The crackle of that note sounded awfully real.

Old Z.10 had let go of my arm and was doing something with a pocket-book. All of a sudden there was a click and a little round blob of light no bigger than a shilling popped out of the dark and slid across the tarnished silver edge of a leather note-case and the black and white of a half unfolded note. It came to rest on the big "Five" in one corner. If a note sounded good, it looked even better. I had sixpence in my pocket—*sixpence*. And if I pawned anything more, I shouldn't have a change of clothes. Five pounds—ten pounds—ten pounds down. . . . I heard the running stream, and I wondered when I was going to wake up.

"Well, Mr. Fairfax?"

I made myself look away from the patch of light.

"What have I got to do for this?"

"For this? Nothing. It is merely a retaining fee."

"To what extent does it commit me?"

"It does not commit you at all—it merely enables my principal to make the observations which he considers necessary and advisable. Let me explain. He wishes to see you without being seen. To this end he wishes you to go to certain public places, which will afford him an opportunity of observing you. To do this you will have to replenish your wardrobe. Ten pounds will not, perhaps, go very far, but it should enable you to pass muster. You possess dress clothes?"

I didn't think it necessary to tell him that they were in pawn, so I said,

"Yes."

"Well, Mr. Fairfax," he said again, "do you accept?"

There was something I meant to ask, but I didn't know how to put it. I hesitated, and then got it out.

"Is your principal a woman?" Because if it was Anna, I thought I was going to prefer the workhouse after all.

He sounded most awfully surprised as he said,

"A woman? Certainly not. May I ask what suggested this idea to you?"

Naturally I wasn't going to tell him that.

He slid the spotlight back on to the case, picked up two fivers, and held them out.

"You accept then?"

I took the notes and put them in the pocket with the sixpence.

"What am I to do?" I asked.

His hand with the torch in it had fallen to his side. The little circle of light swung to and fro on the worn edge of the road. It had been tarred, and the tar had broken away into holes that looked like the pictures of dead craters in the moon.

"Why," he said, "nothing very arduous. This is Tuesday. To-morrow you will dine at Leonardo's."

"Alone?" I said.

"No—no——" He seemed to be considering the question. "No—I don't think so. You had better invite a lady to accompany you."

I laughed. I don't know why, but the thing tickled me.

"I'm afraid I don't know any lady whom I could ask."

The little round shilling's worth of light went swinging to and fro over the dead craters of the moon and a dry leaf or two and the dust of the road.

"Surely—*surely*," he said. "Come, Mr. Fairfax—you do yourself an injustice. There is surely some one."

"There is Mrs. Bell," I suggested, and as soon as I'd said it I could tell that he knew Mrs. Bell was my landlady.

He moved sharply and was going to speak, and didn't speak. I wondered how much he really did know about my circumstances. I began to think that he knew a good deal.

"And who is Mrs. Bell?"

"A British matron and my landlady."

"Ah," he said—"yes. But I have no time to waste on landladies. Come, Mr. Fairfax—you will not ask me to believe that your landlady is the only woman you know. I am informed that you have at any rate an acquaintance with one of your fellow lodgers. Would she not perhaps be a more suitable companion?"

I don't know why I hadn't thought of Fay, but I hadn't. She would certainly be—suitable.

"I could ask her," I said. "But it's short notice—she might be engaged."

"Well, well," he said again, "if she is, something must be done about it. If you arrive alone, a partner will be provided—but the other would be better."

He turned out the light on the pocket-book and took out five one-pound Treasury notes.

"For expenses," he said, and handed them over.

He then shut the pocket-book and put it away.

"Your engagement begins to-night. Your salary will be paid you to-day week. Your instructions will reach you from time to time either by letter, telegram, telephone, or word of mouth. Written communications will be signed 'Z.10.' Messages will be preceded by 'Z.10' as a pass-word. That is all. Good-night."

He switched off the light, turned sharp round, and walked

away down Olding Crescent. I could not see him, but I could hear his footsteps getting fainter and fainter. When I couldn't hear them any longer I went home.

XIV

September 19*th*—I WOKE UP NEXT MORNING WITH THE feeling that something had happened, or was going to happen. I wasn't really awake, and I wasn't really asleep. The sun was making a bright golden line all round the edge of my blind, and the room was full of that happened feeling.

Then I remembered that what had happened was fifteen pounds—two five-pound notes and five Bradburys. And what was going to happen was new boots, a suit of clothes—and dinner at Leonardo's. It all felt pretty good, and at the moment I wasn't bothering about what my principal, or Z.10's principal, might be going to ask me to do. I was going to get some new boots even if the skies fell.

I got up and made a list.

A reach-me-down suit—five guineas.

To get my dress clothes out of pawn—thirty bob (I ought to have got more on them, for they were brand new just before the crash, and I've hardly had them on since).

Two soft shirts—say, eight and six apiece.

Boots—fifty shillings.

That brought me up to ten pounds two. My hat's pretty bad, but it will have to carry on for a bit.

I went out and shopped, and came home with my parcels. Then I went and asked Fay if she'd dine with me. I was rather fed up about having to ask her, because she was most awfully rude to Corinna Lee when I introduced them. Corinna is a friend of Peter's, and I said so, and Fay gave an exhibition performance of bad manners that would be pretty hard to beat.

Well, I asked her to dine at Leonardo's. She jumped at it, and wanted to know if I'd come in for a fortune. I said Henry Ford had just sent me a check for half a million, so she'd better wear her best dress.

We dined at eight. Leonardo's wasn't going three years ago, so I'd never been there. The place was crowded, and the dinner was top-hole. The whole thing felt awfully queer. I kept on finding my thoughts wandering, so that I didn't hear what Fay was saying. One of the people, at one of the tables, was my employer, making his ''observations.'' I wondered if I would pass muster, and exactly what would happen if I didn't. Anyhow I'd spent that ten pounds, and he couldn't very well take my boots away. It was a very queer evening. I didn't know a soul in the room. But one of these people knew me, and I naturally wanted to know which of them it was.

All at once I saw that Fay was watching me. She was smoking. The smoke hung round her, and she was looking through it at me. I apologized for being a bad host, but she didn't answer; she just went on looking through the smoke. Her mouth was all plastered with paint, but the rest of her face was pale. She looked like something artificial in a glass case—beautifully finished and all that, but you wonder what on earth any one would do with it if they had it.

Just as I was beginning to feel annoyed, she said,

''Why did you ask me to dine with you?''

I said the obvious thing.

''Why didn't you ask Peter's friend?'' she went on— ''Clarissa what's-her-name.''

''Corinna Lee.''

''Who is she?''

''An American cousin of mine.''

''And a friend of Peter's?''

''Yes.''

"What did you tell her about me?"

"I didn't tell her anything."

She put her elbows on the table and leaned towards me.

"Did you think I was rude to her?"

"What do you think yourself?"

"I can be ruder than that," she said, and laughed.

I didn't like the look in her eye. When I didn't answer, she began to talk about Rena La Touche the dancer, who had just come in with a boy who looked as if he oughtn't to have left school, a young ass with pale hair and eyes like a love-sick rabbit. Fay told me his income, and her salary, and how many lovers she'd had in a year, and just what she'd paid for the feather frock she was wearing. She was all feathers and pearls, and bare back, and enormous eyes like pools of ink.

And then all of a sudden she asked,

"Did you tell her I was Peter's wife?"

"Rena?" I said.

"Don't be so outrageously stupid! That Clarissa girl."

"Corinna Lee?"

"It's all the same thing. Did you tell her?"

"No."

"Then you're not to. Do you hear?"

I told her what I thought about this idiot game of secrecy, but she only began to talk about Rena La Touche again.

After dinner we danced. Fay dances beautifully, and the floor was topping. She taught me the new steps. She can be very attractive when she likes. I can understand why Peter... It's perfectly asinine of them not to give their marriage out.

When we were walking home, I thought she must be thinking me a brute, because the last time we really talked she told me she was absolutely up against it and she asked me to help her. Helping her was going to mean five hundred pounds, and as I hadn't five hundred pence, it didn't seem much good talking about it. It was one of the things that made me dally with Z.10 and his offer, so I hadn't really forgotten Fay—or if I had, it was only for a few hours. It seems stupid to have forgotten a person when you're actually dining and dancing with her. The fact is, the dining and the dancing rather went to my head—it was like going back to a bit out of the old life—and though I was talking to Fay and dancing with her, I wasn't thinking about her at all; the nearest I got to her was Peter. When we were walking home I sort of woke up.

It was Fay who wanted to walk. Personally, I was feeling as if I could have walked to Brighton but I should have thought a taxi would have been more in her line. I was feeling a bit reckless, and I thought the exes would stand a taxi all right. She said no, she wanted to walk, so we started off, and for about a mile neither of us said a word.

It was a topping night, warm and windy, with the wind sounding like wings. Fay kept close to me, and all at once I heard her sigh, so I asked her if she was tired, and she said "No" and sighed again. And then I began to feel a brute. I was just going to say something when she pressed up against me and said,

"Have you really come into some money?"

I said "No—I've got a job—and part of the job is going and dining at Leonardo's."

"With me?" she sounded rather frightened.

"With any one."

"How odd! I was hoping—Car, is it a good job?"

"I don't know yet." Then I went on, "Fay, did you mean all those things you said the other day?"

She slipped her arm through mine.

"Oh, I don't know. What did I say? I'm damned miserable. Did I say that?"

I felt her shiver up against me.

"You said——"

"What's the good of talking about what I said?"

"You said you must have five hundred pounds."

"Can you give it me?"

"No—I can't."

"Then what's the good of talking about it?"

"The man you mentioned—Fosicker—what is he like?" I don't know what made me think of that, it just came into my head.

"I never mentioned any one."

"You did."

"I don't know any one called Fosicker."

"You said you got money from him."

"Are you trying to insult me?"

"You said he paid you."

She let go of my arm and pushed herself away from me so violently that I stumbled on the curb and nearly lost my balance.

"Hold on!" I said—I was furious. "You told me he paid you for distributing dope."

She turned round on me in a sort of whirling fury.

"How dare you?" Then she seemed to catch hold of herself and calm down. It would have been more natural if she had gone on being angry. But she didn't; she laughed and slipped over to me and took my arm again. "You've been dreaming, Car darling," she said.

I wondered what on earth her game was. I could see she was frightened. Had she frightened herself—or had Fosicker frightened her? And who was Fosicker?

XV

September 20*th*—I GOT A REGISTERED LETTER NEXT MORN-ing. There were five more one-pound notes and two lines of type on a sheet of plain foolscap. They were:

Repeat last night. Post this back to me at old address.
Z.10.

I did what I was told—posted his own letter back to Box
Z.10, International Employment Exchange, and the rest.

This is one of the things I don't like—his first letter
disappearing, and his second to be posted back to him. The
more I go over the whole thing, the less I can make of it and
the less I like it.

1. I have a printed advertisement thrust on me in the
    street. "Do you want to earn £500? If so, apply to
    Box Z.10, 187 Falcon Street."
2. I write to Z.10 and I go to Falcon Street to make
    inquiries, and I hear Bobby Markham talking to a
    little Jew tobacconist about Benno having planted
    some one with something. No reasonable doubt that
    they were speaking about me and the advertisement.
    I vamoose without being seen—or at any rate I hope
    so.
3. Letter from Z.10 (signed Smith) asking me to ring up
    a number afterwards identified as paper shop.
4. Telephone conversation with Z.10 Smith. Tells me to
    be at corner of Churt Row and Olding Crescent
    (Putney) ten o'clock same evening.
5. I keep appointment. Am taken by car a long way
    (Linwood). Anna in car—not recognized till later.
    Driver perhaps Benno—not sure.
6. Interview in hut on Linwood Edge with Bobby Markham,
    and then Anna. Anna offers £500 if I will forge my
    uncle's name and go to prison for it. She has a
    nerve!
7. Anna and I walk through Linwood; she to the house, I
    to village street, where driver and car are waiting—
    engine trouble. Some one passes in car and goes up
    to the house—probably Dr. Monk. Sounded like his
    old Puffing Billy, but I should think it must be dead
    by now. Wonder if my uncle is ill.
8. Letter next morning from Z.10 Smith, apologizing for

> having failed to meet me—accident to his car. Asks me to meet some place that evening.
>
> 9. Meet Z.10 Smith in the dark. Offers me retaining fee of £10 down, £3 a week, a fiver for expenses, pending decision of unnamed "principal" as to my fitness for post (Second Murderer?). Duties, *pro tem.*, to dine and dance at Leonardo's. Curiouser and curiouser!

I can't make anything of it. It's just possible that Markham and Anna butted in on a plan that hadn't really got anything to do with them. I mean Z.10 may be genuinely wanting some one to do a confidential job for him, and either Markham or Anna may have got to know about it. One of them might have been buying papers while Z.10 and I were talking on the telephone—no, that won't do, because Morgan was talking to the tobacconist about Benno having pushed off the advertisement on to me before I talked to Z.10 at all. Well, that doesn't matter, because of course there are dozens of other ways he might have got to know about the affair— he, or Anna. And I suppose Anna could have jabbed a hatpin into his tyre and made him late for his appointment with me. I wonder whether Anna is really in a hole, or whether she's just trying to get me into one.

And that's another thing that's odd. Anna says she's in a hole, and will I please commit a forgery and do seven years, or whatever it is they give you for forgery, to help her out of it, and she'll say "Thank you kindly," and press five hundred pounds into my hand. And Fay says *she's* in a hole and can't possibly get out of it unless I give her five hundred pounds—at least that's what she said to start with, and now she says she never said anything of the sort, and that I must have been dreaming.

Now is there any connection between these two things? Or is it just a coincidence that Fay should be in a hole, and Anna should be in a hole, and that they should both, as you might say, harp on the sum of five hundred pounds? Can't make head or tail of it. I can only go on writing things down as they happen.

Quite a lot happened last night. We got the same table at Leonardo's. Fay seemed awfully bucked about coming, and about half way through dinner it came over me that I didn't really care a damn about Z.10, or Anna, or anything else. My spirits went up with a run and I felt like taking on any old thing that was going to turn up.

Rena La Touche was there again, in what looked like a gold snake-skin. Fay told me she was wearing the largest emerald in the world. It was about an inch square, and she said it was flawless. I wondered whether nine hundred and ninety-nine people out of a thousand would have known the difference if it had been suddenly changed for a bit of colored glass. As long as they went on believing it as the biggest emerald in the world they'd have got just the same amount of thrill out of it.

She passed quite close to our table, with the love-sick rabbit about half a pace behind. Just as she was level with us she dropped her bag, a little gold affair with a handle made of twisted snakes. The rabbit picked it up as I was going to make a dive for it myself. She gave me a sort of perfunctory "come hither" look as she put out her hand to take it. She didn't look at the rabbit at all, and I thought what a jolly time the poor devil must have, fetching and carrying and paying the bills, and buying her emeralds, or seeing other people buy them for her. She took the bag out of his hand, still looking at me, and began to move away.

Our table was against the wall, set into a recess. Just as Rena moved, she looked for an instant at Fay, and it seemed to me that the look asked a question, and it seemed to me that Fay's eyes said "No." Rena went on down the room with every one looking at her. Every one was looking at her all the time—they always do. But only Fay and I could have seen her ask that question. I don't count the rabbit—subhuman and a poor specimen at that.

Fay began to talk rather fast. She pointed out Delphine,

the woman whose shop she works in, on the other side of the room.

"Isn't she smart?" she asked.

I thought she was perfectly hideous. Light-red hair scraped right off her forehead and curling up in wisps at the back of her neck; a sort of hatchet face made up a nasty yellowish white; and bright orange-colored lips put it rather thin and curly. I said what I thought, and I didn't hear what Fay said, because just then I saw Isobel.

She was coming down the room. She looked pale and a little sad. She used not to look like that; she used to be all sparkle and life and happiness. She wore a dress of some soft blue stuff that was just a little darker than her eyes, and she had a string of pearls round her neck. She looked very beautiful. When I realized that I must be staring, I got my eyes away from her face and saw that she was with a party. There was a dark man with her, a strong stocky sort of fellow, not very tall.

I remembered what Anna had told me, and I wondered if it was Giles Heron, and whether it was true that Isobel was going to marry him. I shouldn't believe anything just because Anna said it—she's always been one of our leading amateur liars.

After Heron—if it was Heron—came Miss Willy Tarrant, full of *joie de vivre* and talking all the time. She hasn't changed a bit. She was dressed in something that glittered and clanked like chain mail. Behind her came Bobby Markham. They went right up to the top of the room.

I felt Fay touch my arm. I think she'd been saying something that I hadn't heard.

"Car—wake up! You're pretty far gone if she sends you into a trance the moment she appears on the scene."

I stared at her. She doesn't know anything about Isobel, so I didn't know what she was driving at. She looked as if she was angry too. I suppose she thought I was neglecting her.

"What are you talking about?" I said.

She primmed up her lips—I should like to tell her it's not

at all becoming; it always makes me want to slap her—and then she tossed her head.

"Your Clarissa—the very new cousin that no one's ever heard of before—are you going to pretend you haven't seen her?"

I hadn't until that minute, but when Fay said "Clarissa" like that, I saw that Corinna Lee had joined Miss Willy's party. There was a thin elderly woman with her, whom I took to be Cousin Abby, and two men, one middle-aged and the other young. Corinna had come out of gray, and was as gay as a humming-bird. I wondered if Anna and my uncle were going to turn up next, and then I saw that the table was full. I turned back to Fay.

"Why do you call her Clarissa?" I said.

"Isn't it Clarissa?"

"No—Corinna—Corinna Lee."

"What does it matter?"

The rest of dinner was rather a strain. Isobel had her back to me, but it was very difficult not to watch her. I didn't want Fay to notice that, but I'm afraid she did. I hoped she'd go on thinking I was looking at Corinna. I don't know what we talked about, but I must have kept my end up pretty well, because Fay seemed quite pleased.

XVI

AFTER DINNER WE DANCED. THE TABLES ARE ALL ROUND the edge of the room, and there is an open space in the middle. The first time we passed Miss Willy's table they were talking, Miss Willy loud enough for two, and no one

looked at us except Bobby Markham, and he looked and
looked away like you do when you've seen some one you
don't want to see. I went on doing the step Fay was teaching
me, and wondering about Bobby. I wondered if he was my
employer. It went a good deal against the grain to think he
might be.

We went on dancing. Isobel never looked round. The
man that I thought might be Giles Heron was on one side of
her, and the elderly man who had come with Cousin Abby
on the other. Heron was bending towards her and talking
most of the time. He looked a good chap, solid and capable.
About the third time we came round, Corinna saw me and
waved her hand. She was between Bobby Markham and the
young man she had come in with, a red-haired lad with a
cheeky grin. They seemed to be getting on like a house on
fire.

Just after we'd passed, the music stopped, and so did Fay.
We were by Delphine's table. Fay turned round to speak to
her, and the minute she saw that, Corinna jumped up and
came across to me with her hand out.

"If this isn't just lovely!" she said; and then, "Are you
going to dance with me?"

"You've got your party and I've got mine," I said. I
should have liked to dance with her very much.

"Come and join us," said Corinna. She made a dart at
Fay, who was just turning back. "It's Miss Everitt, isn't it?
How do you do? I was just saying, won't you both come
and join our party?"

I was hoping Fay wouldn't snub the child too hard, when,
to my surprise, she said in a hesitating way,

"That's very kind of you."

"It will be very kind of you," said Corinna prettily. "It's
my party, and I think Car knows Miss Tarrant and her
niece—You do, Car, don't you?"

I said "Yes." I wondered if Isobel knew that Corinna was
bringing me into her party. I wondered if I ought to refuse.

"And the others are my cousin Abby Palliser, and Mr.
Heron, and Mr. Markham, and Jim O'Hara—a sort of

cousin of mine too—and Mr. John Brown, who is a friend of Poppa's.''

She introduced us all and pressed coffee and chocolates on us, and I found myself sitting opposite Isobel, and presently dancing with her. It seemed quite natural, just as in a dream the strangest things seem natural. From the moment I had seen her I seemed to myself to have crossed the line between the everyday world and the secret place where one keeps one's dreams. I felt as if anything might happen—as if I could say anything to her just as one does in a dream. As a matter of fact, I don't think I spoke at all for some time.

Isobel talked about Corinna. She said she had made a complete conquest of Uncle John and was going down to stay at Linwood next week.

''She actually got him to say he would come to her party to-night. What do you think of that?''

''Is he coming? I don't want to meet him, Isobel.''

''I wish you could meet him. But he's not coming—Anna got Dr. Monk to forbid it. I believe it would have done him good; but she's anxious about him. She gave up coming herself, which was good of her. I think she's really devoted to him. Car, *don't*!''

I hadn't said anything. I didn't believe Anna was devoted to Uncle John, but I didn't say so.

Isobel went on looking at me reproachfully.

''Car—'' she began.

''Don't waste time,'' I said. ''I don't want to talk about Anna and Uncle John, and I *won't* talk about Anna and Uncle John.''

The dimple at the corner of her mouth came out in just the old way.

''I don't really want to talk about them either—I want to talk about you.''

''I don't.''

''Well, what do you want to talk about?''

There was only one thing that I really wanted to talk

about, and I knew I mustn't. I oughtn't to have asked her to dance. I ought to keep away from her.

She smiled her lovely smile and said,

"We'll talk about you to start with. What are you doing? Have you got a job?"

"Not properly—I'm on appro'."

"Car—what do you mean?"

"I'm being tried out. At this very moment the secret eye of my employer is probably boring into my back. I don't know what I'm supposed to do, or when I'm to do it—I'm on appro'."

"How desperately mysterious! Tell me all about it from beginning to end."

"I can't my dear." I oughtn't to call her that, but it slipped out.

She didn't say anything for about a minute. I saw her color rise, and I wondered if I had vexed her, but when she looked up her eyes were very kind. It would be easier if she weren't so heavenly kind to me.

"Car dear, you look better," she said.

"I'm in the pink."

We passed Corinna with Bobby Markham.

Corinna said, "Dance the next one with me," and looked back smiling.

"That's a nice child," said Isobel.

"Who—Bobby Markham? He's a bit fat for my taste."

She laughed.

"Don't be silly!"

I was wondering again if the secret eye of my employer was in Bobby Markham's head. I did hope not.

"Where did you come across him?" I asked.

"He's Aunt Willy's latest—he practically lives with us. I think he's dined with us every night for a fortnight. He's been staying at the George."

"Every night?" I said.

"Yes. Awful—isn't it?"

I began to sit up and take notice.

"He didn't dine with you on the sixteenth?"

"The sixteenth? Yes, he did."

"Not Monday, the sixteenth?"

"Why? How mysterious!"

I was making a calculation. If Markham had spent the evening with the Tarrants, could he have been in the hut at Linwood Edge by eleven? I should think it would have been just about eleven when I got there. My watch went west long ago, but I'm pretty good at reckoning time, and it couldn't have been much more than eleven—perhaps it wasn't as much. I wondered when he had said good-night. I thought I would make sure.

"Did he just bolt his food and dash off?" I asked.

"No, of course he didn't. You don't get as fat as that on bolting. He stayed till eleven—he always does, and then he makes a joke about his beauty sleep, and Aunt Willy's beauty sleep. It's a frightfully complicated joke, and he finishes up by saying, 'I don't need any. I'm so beautiful already, you see.' And then he presses our hands in a long, long, lingering clasp, and by that time it's nearly twenty past."

I sat up a good bit more. This looked like an absolutely cast-iron alibi for Bobby—and if it wasn't Bobby I met in the hut, who was it?

"Isobel—are you sure?" I said.

"Quite."

"Quite sure he was with you all the evening of the sixteenth—Monday the sixteenth?"

"Yes, I'm sure. Why, Car?"

"Because I thought I saw him somewhere else on Monday night," I said.

We went round the room in silence. Bobby Markham had broken into our dream, but it began to flow back upon me. I didn't want to talk; I just wanted to go deeper and deeper into the dream with Isobel and never come back any more. She gives me a kind of quiet, happy feeling which I have never had with any one else. Every now and then something like a knife jabs into me, and I know that I oughtn't to be there, and that it can't go on, and that she ought to marry somebody else. That hurts like hell. And then all of a sudden it stops hurting, and I only feel that I'm with her and that nothing else matters. She makes all the beautiful things in the world seem natural.

After a bit we passed Giles Heron, and I had another look at him. He was standing by himself, looking on. I thought again that he looked a first-class sort of chap. I said so to Isobel, and she said,

"Yes—he is."

All at once it was quite easy to ask her what I wanted to know, and I said,

"Are you going to marry him, Isobel?"

She said, "Who told you that, Car?"

I thought I'd braced myself, but when she said that, it caught me like a knife jabbing into an old wound.

I said, "Is it true?" and for an empty, endless minute she didn't say anything at all. We were dancing all the time.

Then she looked up at me right into my eyes, and she said,

"Would you mind if it were true?"

I hadn't had any hope for years, but somehow that hurt unbelievably. But I managed not to look away, and I managed to say,

"I want you to be happy."

There was a sort of shining look in her eyes and a bright rosy color in her cheeks. She looked like she used to look before everything went wrong. I thought it was for Heron, and I didn't know how to bear it. Then she said,

"I couldn't be happy if you were sad. Don't you know that yet, Car?"

I don't think I said anything. I tried to say her name, but I don't think I got it out.

She said, "When you're happy, I'm happy, and when you're sad, I'm sad."

And there, just there, the music stopped, and the dream broke.

XVII

I DANCED WITH CORINNA NEXT. FAY SEEMED TO BE OFF my hands all right. She had clicked with the Irish cousin.

Corinna was most awfully pleased with England, and her English relations, and Linwood, and Uncle John. She said he was a perfect lamb; and I thought he must have changed an awful lot, or else Corinna had really made a complete conquest. She raved about every one and everything except Anna. I noticed she didn't say much about Anna; she just slid away from her. I brought her back firmly.

"What about Anna?" I said. "Is she a perfect lamb too?"

Corinna gazed at me earnestly.

"I don't think you've got at all the right idea about your Uncle John."

"Don't you?"

"No, I do not."

"But we weren't talking about my Uncle John—we were talking about his wife's niece, Anna Lang, and I was asking you whether she was a perfect lamb."

She made a wicked face.

"She's very handsome."

"Handsome is as handsome does."

All at once she looked very serious.

"What does she do, Cousin Car?"

"I don't know," I said.

She looked across at Isobel, who was dancing with Heron.

"I love Isobel. Don't you?"

I believe I blushed.

Corinna laughed.

"I think your Isobel's perfectly sweet." She cocked her chin at me impudently, waited a minute, and said, "Why don't you say, 'She's not my Isobel'? You don't know your part a bit. That was your cue, and you didn't take it."

I laughed a little too.

"I'm not on in this play, really."

"Isobel thinks you are," she said.

I changed the subject.

"We're not going to talk about Isobel—we're going to talk about Bobby Markham."

"Why?"

"Because I want to. Where did you meet him?"

"Cousin John had the Tarrants to lunch, and they brought him with them, so I said would they all come to my party to-night, and they said they would—only Anna wouldn't let Cousin John come after all. Don't you think it was real mean of her? But if she's a *great* friend of yours, perhaps I oughtn't to say that. Is she a great friend of yours?"

"No, she isn't."

"She said you were a great friend of hers."

"I'm not."

"I thought a gentleman never contradicted what a lady said."

"Then I'm not a gentleman. I don't like lies and I always contradict them."

"Aren't you *fierce*!" said Corinna. "What shall I say to Peter when I write to him?"

"Are you writing to him?"

"Of course I am. I write to him by every mail. Wouldn't you like to know what I'm going to say about you?"

"Not if it's very bad. I'm a sensitive plant, and if you wrote harshly about me—I should just fade out."

" 'M——' " said Corinna. She looks awfully pretty when she says " 'M——' " I expect she knows it too.

Our dance was just coming to an end, when she exclaimed and pulled me out of the stream.

"I've got a note for you, and I'm forgetting all about it!"

I felt very much surprised, because I couldn't think who could have given her a note. She took it out of a little silver bag and gave it to me. I felt more puzzled than ever. There was a small square envelope with a typed address, "Carthew Fairfax, Esq.," and that was all.

"Who is it from?" I asked.

"I don't know."

"But who gave it you?"

"A waiter put it down on the table in front of me."

"A waiter?"

She nodded.

"Open it—that's the way to know who it's from."

The music had stopped, and there were a lot of people passing us. I stood back to get out of their way and tore open the envelope.

There was a plain sheet of paper inside, or rather, part of a sheet of paper, for the top of it had been torn off, leaving the docked sheet almost square. Across this square was typed:

Accept any invitation extended to you. You are to go about and make friends. Look up old acquaintances and make new ones. Funds by first post to-morrow.

Z.10

I stared at the paper. It was thick and expensive. The bit that had been torn away would have had an embossed address on it and a telephone number—I'd have given something to see them. I put the note away in my pocket, and found Corinna looking at me with eyes like saucers.

"Well?" she said.

"I'm not any the wiser."

"Really?"

"Really. Would you know the waiter who gave you the note?"

"No, I shouldn't—I never saw him."

"What do you mean?"

"It's perfectly intriguing," said Corinna. "I had just

finished my soup, when a hand came over my shoulder—
and of course I thought it was going to take my plate, but it
didn't—it just put down that note and went away. And I was
too perfectly surprised to do anything but stare at the
envelope—because I didn't even know you were in the
room. And when I turned round, you couldn't say there was
any particular waiter near our table at all.''

Of course it's the easiest thing in the world to tip a waiter
and tell him to let a girl have a note without seeing who
gives it to her. I just wondered who had tipped the waiter.
And as I was wondering, Corinna said "Oh!" and I looked
down the room, and at the far end, coming through the open
folding doors, I saw Anna Lang.

"Well, I'll tell any one she's handsome," said Corinna,
in the tone of one who concedes a single virtue.

Anna came in alone. The dancing floor was empty for the
moment, and she crossed it slowly and with the most
complete self-possession.

Corinna was quite right—she's handsome. and I'd never
seen her look handsomer. She was dressed in some sort of
rose-colored stuff which sparkled all over as if it were
powdered with diamonds. She holds herself magnificently,
and she walks like a Spanish woman or an Indian. Every
one in the room was looking at her.

She came up to Corinna and shook hands. I didn't know
whether she'd seen me or not.

"I've come after all," she said. "Uncle John was so
distressed at my missing your party. He begged me to take
the car and run up—and as he really was going straight to
bed after his dinner, I came."

When Corinna had been nice and polite, Anna looked at
me, and was surprised. I don't know how she thought I was
going to believe she'd only just seen me, because I am six
foot one to Corinna's five foot two, so it stands to reason
she couldn't very well have seen her and missed me.

She said, "Car! What a surprise!"

I said, "Is it?" and Corinna laughed.

"Is it?" said Anna. "What am I to say to that? It's a very

pleasant surprise to all your friends to find you've come out of your shell again." She turned to Corinna. "We're very old friends, you know, and though I've come so late, I hope he's not too much booked up to dance with me."

I was dancing the next with Fay, and I said so; but as I said it, she came up behind us and told me quite coolly that she was cutting my dance. After that there didn't seem to be any way out of dancing with Anna, so we danced. But when we had gone about half-way round the room, she said, in a low voice,

"I don't want to dance—I want to talk to you. Let's go and sit out somewhere. Up in the gallery's a good place if it's not too crowded."

First of all I hoped it would be crowded, and then I decided that it might be just as well to have a good straight talk with Anna. If she was my mysterious employer, I was through, and the sooner she knew it the better.

The gallery runs across one side of the room, and at either end of it there are palms in pots, and a couple of chairs which are pretty well screened from view. She made a beeline for the nearest pair of chairs, and it just went through my mind that she seemed to know all about the place. And then I saw something that gave me the most furious amount to think about. Anna was looking at me, and I hope my face didn't give anything away. I stood aside to let her sit down, and then I took the outer of the two chairs myself.

What I had seen was this. Lying on the floor in front of my chair was one of the little sparkling diamond things which were sewn all over Anna's dress. I put my foot on it, because I didn't think she'd seen it, and I didn't want her to see it. It meant that Anna had been up in this gallery already to-night. She hadn't just come—she'd been up in the gallery in one of these screened seats, watching us all. It looked very much to me as if I had found my employer all right, because if she wasn't watching me, why should she first say she couldn't come, and then pretend she'd only just arrived, when, as a matter of fact, she must have been here some time? I felt most awfully sick about the whole thing, and I was determined to have an explanation.

All this takes a long time to write, but it didn't take any time to think. I just saw it in my mind like you see a picture hanging on a wall. By the time Anna had finished settling herself and getting into a becoming attitude, I was ready.

"I was very glad to see you," I said.

"Were you? How nice of you!"

"Not very. I'm glad to see you because I want an explanation."

"Do you? How unpleasant!"

Anna does annoy me when she talks like that. I wish she'd realize that making her voice sweet and arching her eyebrows at me simply doesn't cut any ice at all. If we were only happily uncivilized, I should shake her when she does it. Unfortunately one can't go about shaking people in modern evening dress—I think it's rather a pity myself. I expect I glowed a bit, but I wasn't going to let her put me off. I said,

"Look here, Anna, I want to know straight out whether you're my employer?"

Her eyebrows went nearly up to the roots of her hair.

"My—dear—Car!"

"Yes or no—are you?"

"No." She began to laugh. "No, no, no, no."

"I don't see anything to laugh at."

She stopped laughing so suddenly that there was something startling about it. Her face turned tragic. She doesn't really look her best when she laughs, and I expect she remembered that and switched off into being the tragic muse.

"Why did you say that?" she asked.

"Because I wanted to know. The other day I had an appointment to meet some one with a view to earning five hundred pounds. You and Bobby Markham kept the appointment and took me down to Linwood. You offered me five hundred pounds to do something which I refused to do." I stopped because I wasn't sure how much to tell her—I've never had what you might call an urge to tell Anna anything about my private affairs. At the same time I'd got to find out whether I was being jockeyed into taking money from her.

She looked at me rather strangely, leaning a little forward in her low chair.

"Yes, Car," she said; and then, "You refused. I went home. That was all."

"Was it? That's what I want to know. You see, next morning I got a letter saying that my original correspondent had not kept his appointment. He made another."

"You went?" Her voice shook.

"Yes, I went."

She had turned pale—I swear she had.

"And——"

"Don't you know?"

"No. Car, can't you see that I don't? You *must* see." If it had been any one else, I should have said she was speaking the truth. "Tell me what happened."

"No—I don't think I will. If you're not mixed up in it, you're not. But what I want to know is—why did you butt in on that first appointment of mine? If you're not in the affair now, what brought you into it then? You say you're not in it now. Well then, it was a private affair between me and some one else—a very private affair. How did you come to know about it? Why did you keep that appointment? Where, in fact, do you come in?"

She leaned back in her chair as soon as I began to ask my questions. This brought her face into shadow. The little sparkles on her dress caught the light when she moved. Then she stopped moving and there was one of those silences that feel as if they might go on forever. I wasn't going to break it. I wondered if she was thinking up a lie, or trying to make up her mind to tell the truth. Anyhow, it was up to her.

After a long time she sighed as if she was tired. Then she said,

"Car, if I tell you the truth, will you believe me?"

"Yes—if you tell me the truth," I said.

"I don't suppose you will believe me, but this is what happened. I had come up to town, and I was looking for a place in the City where a friend of mine had told me you can get a marvelous reduction on Persian rugs—I wanted one for my bedroom. I couldn't find the number."

I wondered what all this rigmarole was about. It sounded to me as if she was giving herself time to invent something, or to put the finishing touches to what she *had* invented. She looked at me all the time—the dark, mournful gaze stunt.

"There were two men walking just in front of me, and one of them said your name—he really did, Car. So of course I was startled and interested, and I came up a little nearer and listened to what they were saying. You know how people will talk in a London street when they think no one knows them."

"What did they say?" I asked.

"One of them said, 'I've talked to him on the telephone and made an appointment to meet him to-night at ten o'clock at the corner of Churt Row and Olding Crescent.' The other man said, 'Will he come?' and the first man laughed and said, 'He'd go farther than Putney for five hundred pounds! So would I if I were in his shoes!'"

"Well?" I said.

"They went on talking," said Anna. "One of them was a little man in glasses, and the other was tall and thin. It was the little man who was going to meet you."

I wondered about this little man. For the first time, I thought Anna might really be speaking the truth. Z.10 had kept under the shadow of the wall in Olding Crescent; but even in the dark you can tell a little man from a tall one, and I put him down at five foot five or so. And he wore glasses, because he kept putting up his hand and fiddling with them whilst we were talking. It wasn't so dark but that I could see when we moved.

I said, "A little man with glasses?"

"He had gray hair and a pointed ferrety nose," said Anna. "He said, 'Mind you, I shall test him very carefully before I use him. To begin with, I have made an appointment with him for to-night. But I shall not keep it—I shall leave him to kick his heels, and then make another appointment. That will test his temper and his keenness.' ''

I was getting interested. Anna stopped, so I said,

''Go on.''

''There isn't any more,'' she said. ''The tall man looked round, saw how near I was, and said something that I didn't catch. They began to talk about other things, and a moment later they separated.''

I thought about that. It might have happened. A month ago I was walking down the Strand, and a man and a girl in front of me whom I had never seen before in my life were talking about Billy Rogers who was at my prep school. Things like that happen.

Anna went on looking at me as if she expected me to say something. After a bit I said,

''Why did you keep that appointment?''

She said ''Oh!'' as if I had made her angry.

''Well,'' I said, ''it seems to me it's a very natural thing for me to ask. What made you butt in on a business affair between me and some one you didn't know anything about?''

She lifted her hand and let it fall again on to her knee.

''I hadn't seen you for three years.''

That's the sort of thing that's most frightfully difficult to answer. It made me angry, and she said quickly,

''You don't believe that.''

I let that go.

''And what made you think of asking me to forge a check?''

''Hush!'' she said. ''Car—you promised—you promised!''

I thought she was frightened. She was acting of course. I don't think she can help acting—but under the acting she was frightened. I came to the conclusion that she really had been monkeying about with Uncle John's money, and I did just wonder whether she hadn't told me about it in confidence so as to shut my mouth. I didn't see how it could have come to my knowledge—but Anna would have known more about that than I did. Well, I thought that was about enough. I pushed back my chair, but she caught hold of my arm.

"You *promised*, Car! You'll keep your promise, if you won't help me in any other way."

"I won't forge," I said, "and I won't do seven years, if that's what you mean by helping you." My temper was getting up a bit.

She still had her hand on my arm. She clenched her fingers down on it, and she said in a sort of whisper,

"You would do it for Isobel."

I pulled my arm away and got up. She had lost her temper first after all.

"Leave Isobel out of it!" I said.

"You'd do it for her—you would—you *would*!"

She was one of her rages, all white and shaking. I emptied the watering-pot over her once when we were about eight. That's the only thing I've ever known stop her.

"Isobel would never be in a position to need that sort of help," I said.

Anna seemed to pull herself together when I said that. She went quiet and still for a minute, but she was frightfully white. I hoped to goodness she wasn't going to faint—it would be just like her to score off you that way and make you feel what a brute you'd been.

Just as I was thinking that, she said, "No?" She said it under her breath, holding on to the word and making a long question of it.

I'd had enough. Anna's one of the people who think no one has any nerves, or a temper, or feelings except herself. I turned round and went away. Honestly, I was afraid of what I might do if I stayed.

XVIII

I DANCED AGAIN WITH ISOBEL. I DIDN'T MEAN TO, BUT she came up and asked me in front of Fay. I only danced about one round, because she wanted to talk to me about my uncle. That's why she asked me to dance.

We went and sat down at a table, and I ordered her some lemonade—she wouldn't have anything else. She told me I ought to go and see my uncle, and when I said I couldn't, she said she thought I would feel different if I were to see him. She says he's changed a lot, and that several times lately he has spoken about me to her and to Miss Willy.

"You know, Car," she said, "one doesn't like to say things like that—but I have thought, and so has Aunt Willy, that he isn't——" she stopped. "Car, I feel as if it was horrid of me."

"Never mind about being horrid. What isn't he?"

The color flew into her cheeks.

"Not—not quite—a free agent."

"What do you mean, my dear?"

"Anna's devoted to him, of course," said Isobel, "and she's run the house and done everything for so many years—she couldn't have been more than sixteen when Mrs. Carthew died—so it's natural he should lean on her, but——"
She stopped and looked at me in distress.

I laughed.

"My dear child, if you're trying to be tactful about Anna, it's a bit late in the day as far as I'm concerned! I've no doubt at all that by this time Uncle John can't call his soul his own!''

"You're not quite fair to her. I mean—Car, I don't think I'm fair to her—at least I hope I'm not—oh dear, I'm getting so tied up! But I do hate saying this sort of thing.''

"I don't think you need mind what you say about Anna—it'll always fall a good bit short of the truth.''

"Don't, Car! And don't let's talk about her. I really only wanted you to see that Mr. Carthew needs you.''

"I don't see it.''

"He does, Car.''

"How do you know?''

"Because he told me.''

"He told you?''

"Yes, he did—really. It was the first time I'd seen him alone for a long time. I was coming up from the village, and I overtook him. He was walking so slowly, not a bit like he used to, and he said, 'Ah, you young people!' And when I told him how wonderful I thought he was, he said, 'That's all very well, but one wants some one to hand things over to. There's no one to take an interest, and no one who really cares.' We were walking along, you know, and talking as we went. I'm only telling you bits.''

"Well—I don't see where I come in.''

She blushed.

"Don't be angry, Car. I did say, 'If Car were here, he could help you.' ''

I laughed again.

"Jesuit!''

"I'm not. You should have seen how he jumped at it. He looked very gruff, like he always does when he's feeling anything, and he said, 'I'm nothing to him. We quarreled, you know. He wouldn't come near me now. He's got his pride like the rest of us.' '' She blushed again, and looked at me in an undermining sort of way.

When Isobel looks at me like that, I would give her the whole of my kingdom if I had one.

"What did you say?'' I asked as sternly as I could. I tried

to frown, but I don't know whether I managed it or not. Isobel is frightfully undermining when she blushes.

She looked guilty.

"I said I was sure you'd be ready to make up your side of the quarrel if he really wanted you to."

"Oh, Isobel!" I said.

"You would—wouldn't you, Car dear? Because he's old, and he's lonely, and he really, *really* wants you."

"He'll have to tell me so," I said.

"And I thought," said Isobel, "that if Aunt Willy were to ask you to come and stay——"

I said "No!" and pushed back my chair. Go and stay— see her every day—see Heron making love to her, and not break down and say things that I've no business to say to her. . . . I couldn't do it.

I don't know what she thought. Her color was all gone. Perhaps she thought I was angry with her—I don't know. I felt I must get away, because if I didn't, anything might happen. I didn't realize that the music of the next dance had begun until Isobel put her hand on my arm.

"I'm dancing this with Giles," she said, and I took her across the room to where Heron was waiting for her. We did not speak a single word.

I'm afraid Fay must have found me a dull partner.

As soon as I got hold of myself I went over what Isobel had said about my uncle. It seemed to me that it fitted in with Anna's story. It seemed to me that if Anna knew that Uncle John was wanting to get into touch with me, she might very easily get the wind up and be afraid of my finding out what she'd been up to—that is, if she'd really been messing about with his banking account. And if she was afraid of my finding her out, it would be just like her to try and muzzle me in advance.

The sort of half guess which I had made when she was talking to me looked a good deal more likely now. If I was right, it wouldn't be the first time Anna had played that trick. I remembered her stopping her nurse's mouth that way when she couldn't have been much more than seven. She had thrown a ball through one of the drawing-room windows, and she got nurse to promise she wouldn't tell Uncle John if she told her something. I don't know what Nanny thought she was going to tell her, but she promised, and she kept her promise; though I can remember her crying bitterly because I was punished, first for the window (it was my ball) and secondly for telling a lie and saying I hadn't been near the place. Those are the sort of things that have made me love Anna.

I had her name in my mind, when I looked across Fay's shoulder and saw her not a yard away. I don't know what Fay had been saying, but she must have said it more than once, because when I did hear her she sounded really peeved.

"Car, are you deaf? I want to stop—my brooch has come undone."

I had to stop, because the brooch fell and rolled almost under Anna's feet. She was sitting alone at a table; but I could see she hadn't been along long, for there were two glasses, and a chair pushed back. I retrieved the brooch and got up with it in my hand, and just as I was giving it to Fay, I saw Bobby Markham coming along with his brother. They came up to Anna, and Bobby said,

"May I introduce my brother Arbuthnot?"

Anna wasn't too effusive—and I don't wonder. Arbuthnot Markham isn't exactly a human ray of sunshine. Bobby's a fat-headed-looking sort of chump; but there's something about Arbuthnot that makes me want to go home. He'd look better if he was bald like Bobby—his hair's too black and shiny.

I heard him say, "I took the liberty of asking my brother to introduce me." Then he asked her for a dance, and Fay and I finished ours.

I went and talked to Miss Willy after that. I was afraid she'd want to dance—and it's just like dancing with a steam-engine. But she said she wanted to talk to me, and then I wondered whether it wouldn't have been better to risk being crushed. She's a most overpowering person, and I don't know how Isobel stands living with her. If it weren't for Isobel, she'd have come some awful smash long ago.

I've never met any one with so much exuberant enthusiasm going to waste.

She began at once to talk about my uncle, and about Anna. She hadn't any of Isobel's hesitation. She called Anna quite a number of things that made me feel better, and she was wildly indignant on my uncle's behalf.

And then she broke off to tell me all about a row she'd had with old Monk, and from that she got on to another row with the Vicar—I think the one with Monk had something to do with Anna, but not the one with the Vicar—and in the middle of the second row she suddenly switched back on to Uncle John and said I must come down and be reconciled to him. Now I happen to know that Miss Willy hasn't had a good word to say for me ever since the smash. I don't blame her, because it was on Isobel's account; but I wondered why she should be all over me now. Then it came down on me like a cartload of bricks. If Isobel was going to marry Heron, I didn't matter any more—Miss Willy could let her naturally kind instincts rip, have me to stay, reconcile me to Uncle John, and annoy Anna, all at one blow. I discovered that she had heard Anna allude to her as a blatant old maid. That clinched it—I was convinced that she regarded me as a convenient retort.

I seem to have written reams about last night, but I'm nearly through. I want to get it all down, and then go over it and see what I can make of it. There are just two more things to get down. I think one of them's important.

Fay said she'd go home in a taxi, and I went out to get one. When I was coming back, I saw Anna come down the steps with Arbuthnot Markham. There wasn't room for my taxi to draw up, so I nipped out and cut across behind the car Anna was getting into. There was rather a jam and a crowd on the pavement, and I didn't particularly want her to see me, so I stood and waited for her to get in and shut the door. She got in, and then she leaned out of the window, and she said to Arbuthnot Markham, ''He *mustn't* go to the Tarrants—he *mustn't*.''

He said something I didn't catch.

Anna's got a carrying voice. She said,

"You must stop him somehow."

And then he stepped back, and she drew in her head, and the car went on.

Well, she must have meant me. And there isn't anything strange in her not wanting me to go and stay with the Tarrants, because she naturally isn't keen on my being anywhere within ten miles of Uncle John. But why tell Arbuthnot about it? I'd seen him introduced to her about half an hour before, and it struck me as pretty good going.

I got Fay, and we drove home. I wished I had walked, because she began to play up like she does sometimes. I shouldn't want to flirt with Fay if there wasn't another woman on earth—and she might have the common intelligence to know that I wouldn't want to flirt with Peter's wife. She doesn't mean anything, of course, but it's jolly bad form, and she riled me till I told her so straight out. In a way I'm fond of her, like you are of a second or third cousin, and it annoys me to see her making an ass of herself.

It began with my saying she ought to drop this silly Miss Everitt business and call herself Mrs. Lymington. I said it wasn't fair. It isn't. It worries me to hear Corinna talking about Peter as if she were engaged to him. Of course I didn't mention Corinna—I just said it wasn't fair. And the silly goose made eyes at me and said,

"Because some one might fall in love with me? Is that what you mean?"

It wasn't in the least what I meant, but I let it go at that, and I supposed it encouraged her.

"If I hadn't been married to Peter——" she stopped there and put her head against my arm.

I said, "You *are* married to Peter."

"And if I weren't," she said—"if I'd been free all the time—would you have fallen in love with me?"

I said, "No, I shouldn't," and I said it pretty sharply.

"If I were free now——"

I took her by the shoulder and put her back in her own corner of the car.

"Drop it, Fay!" I said. "You don't mean anything, and you know it, and I know it, so why the devil do you do it? If you ask me, it's the rottenest of rotten bad form."

She flared out at me.

"I didn't ask you! I'm not asking you anything! I hate you!"

"Don't be an ass, Fay," I said.

Then she began to cry and said I was a brute.

XIX

September 21st—I'VE JUST BEEN READING OVER WHAT I wrote yesterday. The two points that matter are:

Who is employing me?

and

Why?

There are a lot of subsidiary ones. The most important of these seem to be:

1. Anna's connection with the affair.
2. Bobby Markham.
3. Fay.

I don't know what to think about Anna. If I hadn't lost my temper, I might have got something out of her. That's the worst of a temper—it always lets you down. I don't think she's the big noise in this affair.—I think she butted in. If I thought the money came from her, I'd chuck the whole show.

Bobby Markham—I can't make out whether it was he who interviewed me in the hut. Anna certainly gave me to understand that it was Bobby—but that's a good enough reason for its being some one else. Then there's the question of whether Bobby could have been in the hut to meet me after spending the evening with the Tarrants. I don't think so much of this point as I did, because I hadn't a watch, and though I think we were at the hut by eleven I may be mistaken. It oughtn't to take more than an hour from Putney to Linwood, but I was thinking of other things. I didn't notice how fast we were going, and I suspect the driver went out of the way on purpose. Then Isobel says Bobby didn't go away till about twenty past, after starting to say good-night at eleven. That's vague too. I can imagine time hanging a bit heavy whilst a fathead like Bobby was making pretty speeches. I suppose he could have got to the hut in ten minutes if he took the path through the woods.

All the same it sticks in my mind that it wasn't Bobby. I wonder if it was Arbuthnot. If Anna had never met Arbuthnot before, how did she get to the point of telling him to keep me away from the Tarrants, all in about half an hour? She spoke as if she was accustomed to giving him orders, too—I noticed that. She might have been speaking to the butler, and he took it the same way, as if it was a matter of course that she should fire orders at him out of a taxi. No, I couldn't believe that it was the first time they'd met. And if it wasn't, why go through the farce of an introduction, unless they particularly wanted me to think that they were strangers?

Well that's all I can get out of Bobby for the moment.

Then there's Fay. All the threads that connect Fay with this affair are as indefinite as the spider's threads that you get blown across your face on a dewy morning—you can't see them, and you can't find them, but you keep on feeling that they're there. Why should Fay want five hundred pounds just when five hundred pounds is being dangled in front of me? And then why should she afterwards go back on all that and swear she never said she was in a hole at all? And why did Isobel's letter disappear, and Z.10's first letter? And why did Fay cut her dance with me, just when cutting it obliged me to dance with Anna? It looks damned silly written down. Gossamer threads.

The post has just come in. Miss Willy has asked me to go

down to them next Tuesday. That's one letter. The other is a registered one with twenty five-pound notes in it and not a line of writing. If any one had told me a week ago that I should have a hundred pounds spread out in front of me on this table, it would have sounded like something out of Grimm's fairy tales. And if they'd gone on to say that all I wanted to do with it was to send it back, I should have told them that they were talking through the back of their neck. A week ago I didn't know where my next meal was coming from, or how long my last pair of boots would hold together. Now I've got into a kind of twisted fairy story in which bank-notes come tumbling out of letters like the diamonds and pearls which dropped from the mouth of the wretched child with the fairy godmother in Grimm. I remember, even in the nursery, thinking how beastly it must have been, and wondering whether she got any of her teeth broken on the diamonds.

I am writing to Miss Willy to say I won't come. And this is what I'm going to write to Z.10:

DEAR SIR,

I have just received £100 in five-pound notes. I suppose these are the funds spoken of in the note I received last night. [There are too many "received's" but I want to keep it stiff.] I should be glad to be given some work to do. I want to make it clear that I cannot continue to receive money which I have not earned. I was willing to accept a retaining fee for a reasonable time, but a sum of £100 does not come under that heading. I shall therefore return it, unless in the course of the next week I am satisfied that I have done, or am doing, something to earn such a salary.

Yours faithfully,
CARTHEW FAIRFAX.

XX

A Letter from Corinna Lee to Peter Lymington:

PETER HONEY, GO RIGHT OUT AND BUY YOURSELF A pair of yellow stockings. Did you know that meant being jealous? I didn't until Mrs. Bell, who is my cousin Car's landlady, told me. There's a girl in the same house—and isn't she a friend of yours, and why didn't you tell me about her? Her name is Fay Everitt, and she's pretty but very bad style, and she hates me like I hate cold water down the back of my neck, and I couldn't think why until Mrs. Bell said, "It's just her yellow stockings, Miss." Well, I thought she was color blind, and I said, "They're not yellow, Mrs. Bell, —they're taupe." And she laughed and laughed, and told me, "yellow stockings is just a way of saying folks is jealous, miss." She said Fay Everitt "wears them constant." I don't think she likes my being friends with my cousin Car.

Peter, he is a perfect lamb. So now you know why you've got to go out right away and buy yourself those yellow stockings. Isn't it a pity he's got a girl already?

Why didn't you tell me about her? I'm not wearing yellow stockings, because I love her too. She is an enchanting person called Isobel Tarrant, and she lives with a perfectly fierce aunt in a real old cottage with 1675 over the door. Why didn't you tell me about

Isobel? I can't think why you didn't fall in love with her. Perhaps you didn't know her—that would be a good reason. Or perhaps you didn't want to snatch her from Car. Or perhaps you are secretly in love with her all the time. Please tell me about this when you write. If there are any dark secrets in your past, I would like to know about them right away, and not find them out afterwards like they always do in books. I think I have used the wrong adjective. Isobel couldn't be a dark secret—she isn't that sort. But even if she's a bright secret, I would want to know about her.

I am going down to Linwood to stay. I love Linwood and my cousin John, but I am glad that Anna Lang is not my cousin. She is only Cousin John's wife's niece, and not my relation at all. Car says he is glad about this too. I love Car. But perhaps you needn't be very jealous—I have just mailed a letter to Poppa to tell him that if he thinks I'm forgetting you over here, he's just got to think again. I'd be very lonely without you if I didn't think a lot about how real nice it was going to be when I get back.

Do you think about me every day? I hope you do. Poppa said I wasn't to write you love letters whilst I was over here. He couldn't call this one a love letter, could he—not reasonably? But it kind of feels as if it was going to turn into one, so I should think I had better stop.

CORINNA

If I hadn't promised Poppa, I would send you my love and a lot of kisses.

Dear Peter, I send you my kind regards. I will tell Poppa I sent them.

XXI

ISOBEL TARRANT CAME DOWN THROUGH THE WOODS WALK-
ing slowly. In a few minutes she would be clear of the trees.
She walked more slowly still. The path was narrow, and on
either side of it were the straight black trunks of pine trees
frosted with gray-green lichen. It was a bright, clear morning. The sky above the pine trees was a very pale blue. The
patches of sunlight which flecked the path were a very pale
gold. It was still in the wood.

Isobel stood for a moment and let the stillness in. She had
wept until she could weep no more; but now the pain that
had made her weep had ceased. She felt as if her tears had
washed it away and left an empty place where it had been.
She shrank piteously from this emptiness. It was as if she
had had Car in her heart all these years, and as if now he
had gone and there was only an empty place. It would not
have been so hard to bear if she had not allowed herself to
hope. For three years she had not hoped. She had lived one
day at a time and kept her eyes from the future. And then all
at once the future had been irradiated with hope. Car was to
come to Linwood to meet his uncle—to step back into his
old place—to come back to them. She did not say he was
coming back to her, but the thought lay warm at her heart.
And then in a flash the radiance had gone and the dark
closed down. Car wouldn't come.

Isobel looked back to the moment at breakfast when Miss
Willy had opened his letter and announced that he wouldn't

come. It didn't hurt now, because nothing hurt any more; but in that moment it had hurt so much that she did not know how she had kept herself from crying out. It didn't hurt now, because nothing hurt any more; there was only an emptiness and blackness where the pain had been. And she must come down out of the woods, and go back to lunch and hear Miss Willy say all over again the things which she had said at breakfast, and would say again at tea.

The stillness of the woods was broken by the sound of footsteps. Isobel began to walk on at once and quickly. She had nothing that she could say to any one at this moment. She felt a sort of faint panic at the thought of voice and words echoing in this emptiness. But she had not heard the footsteps soon enough. Mr. Carthew had almost caught her up, and when she began to walk on, he called after her:

"Isobel—wait a minute! Where are you off to in such a hurry, young woman?"

He was about the last person she would have chosen to meet, but there was no help for it. When you have been properly brought up, certain things become automatic. Isobel turned at once and, turning, smiled with her usual sweetness. She did not consciously make an effort. She smiled and waited for Mr. Carthew.

"Well, where are you off to?" he said again.

"Home to lunch."

"Well, there's no hurry about that. Miss Willy's never been in time for a meal in her life—what? I can't think how she ever gets a cook. I know she doesn't keep 'em—she told me herself the other day she'd had thirteen since Christmas. And what beats me is, how does she get 'em—what? How does she get 'em? That's what I want to know. You wouldn't think there were so many cooks left in England—that is, you wouldn't if you listened to the twaddle every one talks about the servant question. And the moral of that is—don't listen to it. Least listened to, soonest ended—what? Did you ever hear that proverb before?"

Isobel went on smiling. Her lips felt a little stiff, but it easier than saying anything. You didn't really have to talk to

Mr. Carthew. He liked people who would listen whilst he told long stories about things which couldn't ever really have been very interesting to anybody, or said what he thought about the government and the condition of agriculture. He liked talking on these subjects to pretty young woman who did not answer back or have views of their own.

Isobel prepared herself to listen, but for once in a way he fell silent and walked beside her, flicking at the pine needles with his stick, his broad shoulders stooped, his weather-beaten face wrinkled and puckered, and his bushy eyebrows drawn together in a frown over the small, rather sunken gray eyes.

He looked sideways once or twice at Isobel, and just as she became aware of this, he stopped dead, cleared his throat, and said gruffly,

"I wanted to see you."

The trees were thinning out to the edge of the wood. A patch of sunlight touched Isobel's cheek.

"She's been crying," said Mr. Carthew to himself. "Bless my soul, she has!"

Isobel stepped back into the shade. She looked faintly startled. Her heart beat a little faster.

He cleared his throat again.

"About that nephew of mine——" he said, and saw the color spring into the pale oval of her face.

"About Car?" Why should any one want to speak to her about Car? Car wouldn't come—Car didn't want to come. Why should any one want to speak to her about Car?

"Car—yes, Car. I've only got one nephew, and that's been one too many. I suppose I may be thankful I never had a son, for a nephew has been as much trouble as I've wanted, and a bit more." He spoke as if he were working himself up to be angry, bringing out each short sentence with a kind of jerk that reminded Isobel of Dr. Monk's car starting up on a cold morning.

She did not say anything. What was there that she could say about Car to Car's uncle? "He doesn't care—he won't come." She couldn't say that.

"Well?" said Mr. Carthew explosively. "Well?"

"What is it, Mr. Carthew?"

"That nephew of mine. Have you been seeing him?"

"Yes," said Isobel, with her red flag flying.

"Ah, I thought so! Then you can tell me what I want to know. When did you see him last?"

"A day or two ago."

He looked at her sharply under his bushy brows.

"A day or two ago? What does that mean? That you don't remember—or that you don't choose to tell me? It's not my business—what? Well, if you can't tell me when you saw him, can you tell me where you saw him? Carrying a pair of sandwich boards—or fetching up taxis after the theater—what?"

Isobel's smiling ceased to be a convention. It became delightfully tinged with malice.

"Oh no, Mr. Carthew—it was at Leonardo's. I danced with him."

"And what's Leonardo's? You don't expect me to know the name of every disreputable fourth-rate dancing hall in London, do you?"

"Now you're being rude to me," said Isobel—"because I've been very nicely brought up and I don't go to fourth-rate dancing halls. Leonardo's is the latest place to dine and dance at. You know—the sort of place where a cup of coffee costs as much as a whole dinner does in one of those little Italian places in Soho."

"H'm!" said Mr. Carthew. He dug holes in the ground with his stick, making a vicious punch at each. "Car's come up in the world, then! The last I heard of him, he couldn't have risen to Soho. Splashing his money about, was he? Or sponging on a rich friend—what?"

A little vivid flame of anger burned suddenly in the cold empty places of Isobel's thought. She said, quickly and warmly,

"You know that's not true!"

"What was he doing there then?"

"I don't know."

"Pretty shabby—eh?"

The flame burned higher.

"No, he wasn't!"

Mr. Carthew punched another hole and gazed at it earnestly.

"Some one who saw him a while ago told me that he looked down and out." He prodded the hole with his stick. "Down and out—that's what he said—a friend of mine, old Beamish—not at all the sort of man to exaggerate. That's what he said to me in so many words. 'I saw that nephew of yours the other day,' he said, 'Car what's-his-name—Fairfax— and by Jove, he looks as if he's got down to his uppers,' he said. 'Looked as he wasn't getting enough to eat, by Jove.' That's the way he put it. Matter of fact sort of fellow, Beamish—didn't mean to be offensive—said he thought I ought to know."

"Yes," said Isobel, still with that warmth in her voice.

"How do you mean 'Yes'?"

"I think he was quite right—I think you ought to know."

"Oh, you do, do you? And what am I to believe? He says Car's down and out, and you say he's flourishing around dining and dancing at one of the most expensive places in London. What am I to believe?"

"I think his employer sent him there," said Isobel.

"Then he's got a job—what? Why didn't you tell me that at once?"

"Because that's all I know. He just told me that—he didn't tell me anything else."

"H'm!" said Mr. Carthew. "Well, he's coming to stay with you, isn't he, and I can ask him about it myself. Sounds fishy to me—very fishy. But I can ask him about it when he comes."

"He isn't coming," said Isobel in a low voice. It was as bitter to say it as if all those tears had not washed her clear of feeling.

"Not coming?" said Mr. Carthew sharply. "How do you mean 'not coming'? Your Aunt Willy told me herself she'd asked him down. A couple of days ago she told me she was going to ask him, and yesterday she told me she'd done it."

"Yes," said Isobel. "He isn't coming." Why did people make you say things that hurt so frightfully?

"Nonsense!" said Mr. Carthew very loudly. "If she asked him to come, he'd be bound to jump at the chance."

"Why?" said Isobel.

All at once she felt that she knew why Car wouldn't come. How could he come to his uncle's very door as if he were begging to be taken back? He couldn't—of course he couldn't. The relief was so great that it brought a mist to her eyes, and a lovely changing color to her cheek.

"Why?" said Mr. Carthew—"why? Because a lady's good enough to ask him. That's reason enough, isn't it?—or it would have been when I was a young fellow. I suppose it's no reason at all now that manners have gone out of fashion, and family feeling, and religion, and all the things that used to be expected of a man with a stake in the country. Dancing and enjoying themselves—that's all the present generation cares for!"

Isobel's heart gave a little leap. "He's disappointed. He cares. He wants to see Car again and make it up. He's angry because he's disappointed." Aloud she said:

"Why don't you ask him to come? He'd come if you asked him."

She was rather frightened as soon as she had said it. Suppose she had made him angry—he got angry rather easily. She might just have given him a push in the wrong direction.

His eyebrows were very bushy indeed. First he stared at her, and then he said explosively,

"I'm to ask him, am I—what? Go down on my knees to him and ask him to come back? Is that your idea, or it is his—what? Did he put you up to it?"

Isobel wasn't sure whether she would be telling the truth if she said "No." Car had certainly said "He'll have to tell me so," when she had declared that his uncle wanted to make it up. She blushed and said,

"Quarrels are such miserable things. Why shouldn't you ask him to come back? It—it would be so lovely if we could all be friends again"

"H'm!" said Mr. Carthew. "Did he tell you to say that?"

"No—of course he didn't. You know he's proud—you said so yourself. If he'd been doing well and making money, he'd have asked you to be friends again long ago—but he's been awfully, awfully poor. Don't you see he simply couldn't come back when it would look as if he were asking you to do something for him?''

Mr. Carthew planted his stick firmly behind him, put both hands on the crook, and leaned back against it.

"God bless my soul!" he said; and then, "You make him out a very fine, disinterested fellow, don't you, my dear— eh? Most young fellows wouldn't think so much about coming and asking an uncle to give them a helping hand. It's his damned pride and obstinacy, I tell you. I wanted him to marry and settle down, and he wouldn't—told me he'd no fancy for it. I've no patience with these young men of the present day—they've no sense of their obligations, no sense of responsibility. When a man's got a property coming to him, it's his duty to marry young. I married when I was twenty-three, and if I haven't got a son of my own, it's all the more reason why I should want to see Car's children— isn't it? Only, as I say, he set himself up against me, and the last thing he said to me—shall I tell you the last thing he said to me?''

"No, don't," said Isobel. "You ought to forget it. I expect you were both angry. Nobody means what they say when they're angry—you know they don't.''

Mr. Carthew stood bolt upright and brandished his stick in the air.

"He said, 'I don't care if I don't ever see you again, and Linwood may go to——' Well, I was brought up to consider a lady's ears—so we'll call it Jericho.''

Isobel looked at him with a sparkling challenge in her eyes. "And what had you just been saying to him?''

"God bless my soul, I forget.''

"Then don't you think you'd better forget what he said too?''

"H'm!" said Mr. Carthew. He turned abruptly and began to walk away. "I shall be late for lunch," he said, "Anna don't like my being late for lunch.''

XXII

M<small>R</small>. B<small>OBBY</small> M<small>ARKHAM</small> <small>OPENED THE DOOR OF THE HUT</small>
on Linwood Edge. A complete and dense blackness confronted
him.

The battery of his electric torch had given out, and at
eleven o'clock on a moonless, starless night it had been
dark enough coming here through the woods, but even to
eyes grown accustomed to this darkness the inside of the hut
presented an opaque and discouraging gloom.

Bobby Markham didn't really like the dark very much.
He found it afflicting to be asked to meet Anna at midnight in a lonely wood, and it may be said at once that
for no other human being would he have come. He had
hoped that she would have been here already. Comforting
thoughts of finding the hut pleasantly lit up had sustained
him. He opened the door, and the place was as black as
the pit.

Yet when he had advanced a step, and was wishing, not
for the first time, that he had a box of matches on him, he
thought that he heard something move. He stood still instantly, quite still, listening. Something ever so slightly
stirred in the black silence. A most unpleasant damp,
pringling feeling spread rapidly from the top of his head to
the tips of his fingers and toes. He grasped the defunct
torch. But, in his inmost mind, the thing that he was afraid
of was not a thing that could be bashed on the head or
struck down by a damp, heavy fist. The very ancient

menace of the terror that walks in darkness stirred, here, close at his side.

He stiffened, tried to draw breath, and felt the clammy air of the place stick in his throat. With paralyzing suddenness a round disk of brilliant light broke the dark. A beam sprang from it and just touched his face and his blinded, staring eyes. Then the torch dropped, and Anna's voice said,

"You're late."

He got hold of the table and stood there shaking. How beastly—how *beastly!* His heart was thudding. He felt for the chair and sat down.

Anna switched off the torch.

"We can talk in the dark," she said.

"Where's the lantern?"—he managed to say that.

"It's here. But we don't want it—there's always a chance of its attracting attention."

He persisted.

"Light it. I can't talk in the dark."

He heard the spurt of a match and saw, with a most extraordinary relief, the yellow tongue of flame, the match, the outline of the lantern with the white guttered candle inside it. The flame caught the wick, and he could see the four walls of the hut, and Anna drawing back her hand and blowing out the match. She was bare-headed, with long shining diamond earrings that made rainbows of the light, and a black Chinese shawl wrapping her from shoulder to ankle. It was worked all over with small silken flowers bright as jewels. Her bare arm emerged from the long black fringe that edged it.

In the light, Bobby was himself again at once—heavily good-natured and very much Anna Lang's adoring slave.

"Come—that's better!" he said.

"Is it?"

"Well, I like to look at you, you know. You look ripping in that shawl thing."

With the movement that she made it slipped a little, showing the curve of her shoulder very white against the black.

"You mustn't pay me compliments," she said. "That's not what I asked you to come here for."

Car Fairfax would have been moved to inward mirth by the sad dignity of her tone. Bobby Markham admired it very much; it made him feel that he must be on his very best behavior. When Anna looked away for a moment, he got out a silk handkerchief and dried his forehead, which was unbecomingly damp and shiny. Like most fat men he was exceedingly vain. He put the handkerchief away quickly as Anna turned back again.

"I asked you to meet me because there's something I want you to do for me," she said.

"Anything little Bobby can do," said Mr. Markham with an air of effusive sentiment which sat oddly on him. "As you know——"

She cut him short with a wave of the hand which he thought very graceful.

"Wait till you hear what it is."

"I wouldn't mind what it was as long as it pleased you."

Anna rested her chin upon her hand.

"I wonder whether you really mean that."

"Why, of course I do." Then, with a touch of caution, "That is, if it's anything I *can* do."

"It is something that you can do if you will."

He looked at her with a little sense of discomfort. There wasn't any one like Anna, and he was devoted to her; but he did sometimes wish that she could be just what she was, beautiful, romantic, exciting, and yet at the same time a little more comfortable. He would have liked to be talking to her by a decent, civilized fireside for instance; and if there was anything she wanted him to do, he would like her to tell him straight out, and not sit looking at him in that dark, mysterious, hinting sort of way.

"Well, little Bobby's willing," he said.

Anna leaned forward and whispered in his ear, and immediately the smoldering discomfort which had made him think yearningly of drawing-rooms and restaurants burst into a flame of apprehension. He drew back, got out his handkerchief again, used it this time under Anna's sustained gaze, and stammered,

"What for?"

"That's my affair," said Anna calmly.

"Not much it isn't—not when you want me to get it for you. Look here, Anna—for heaven's sake don't tell me you've started taking the damned stuff!"

The lantern-light shone on her pale composure.

"Would it be your affair if I had?"

She admired the tragic depth of her own voice. Car would have known that she was admiring it—that was why she hated him—but Bobby could be counted upon to be a fellow-admirer. He broke out into protest;

"For heaven's sake don't say such a thing! I'd go crazy! Of course it's my affair—everything that's got anything to do with you is my affair."

She shook her head slightly, and the diamonds swung at her ears.

"It's not for myself. Will you get it for me?"

Mr. Markham mopped his brow again. The palms of his hands were wet. He was wishing with great intensity that he had always kept on the humdrum side of the law.

"It's so damned dangerous," he said in a voice that was really like a groan. Then, as she looked scornfully at him, "I wish ten thousand times I'd never had anything to do with it."

"Yes," said Anna"—now that you've made your money out of it—I can understand that."

"I'm clearing out. I've told him so—I've told him I won't go on—and he said"—his voice dropped—"he's getting out of it himself. And a good job too—that's what I say. It's dangerous—it's a lot too dangerous. He said so—he said the police were sitting up and taking notice—he said they were out for blood, and he'd be hanged if he was going to let 'em have his." The sound of Mr. Markham's own voice had heartened him a good deal. He smiled a wide smile which showed a golden tooth upon either side, and concluded, "And little Bobby's just as keen on their not getting him."

"You're afraid," said Anna.

Mr. Markham acknowledged the compliment.

"Any one who wasn't a fool would be afraid. It'd mean a dashed long sentence. It's me for the shore before the ship goes down. And you take my advice——"

"I haven't asked for your advice—I've asked for your help. And if you won't give it——" She paused for a second—"then—*then* I'll go to some one who will."

She pushed back her chair and rose. The shawl fell back and showed her in diaphanous black, neck, shoulders and back all gleaming bare and white.

Mr. Markham leaned across the table.

"What a dashed hurry you're in! Look here, Anna—what do you want it for? I've got to know—*he'll* want to know."

"He's *not* to know. If I wanted him to know, I could ask him for it myself. You've got to get it for me without his knowing."

"Why do you want it? I can't get it like that. But if I could, I wouldn't—not without knowing what you want it for. It's too infernally dangerous."

She was gathering her shawl up slowly with one hand. The little bright flowers seemed to bloom as she moved them.

"It won't be dangerous at all. It——" She hesitated. "It—might be the very opposite."

"How do you mean—the very opposite?"

"I mean—you said they're out for some one's blood. Well, if they caught some one with the stuff on them——" She stopped, biting her lip, a dark colour in her cheek, her eyes brilliant and watchful.

Bobby Markham stared at her. He was wishing that he had never come.

"What do you mean?"

"Never mind."

Fear spurred Mr. Markham.

"I won't do a dashed thing unless you tell me what you mean—I'm hanged if I will!"

Anna smiled suddenly.

"Would it break your heart if Car Fairfax came to grief?"

Mr. Markham became incapable of words for a moment. Then he repeated those which he had just used:

"What do you mean?"

Anna was still smiling.

"I want the stuff for Car."

"Why?"

"Will you get it for me if I tell you?"

"I don't know," said Mr. Markham. "I can't get it—I told you I can't—and if I could—"

"You can get it if you like. Will you get it?"

"Tell me why you want it."

"I want it for Car Fairfax," said Anna in a warm, melting voice. "If they're looking for some one to send to prison, don't you think that Car would do nicely?"

"But he's not in the show at all."

"No," said Anna—"no. But if he were found with cocaine in his possession, all made up into neat packets for distribution, and if he wouldn't say how he'd come by it——"

Mr. Bobby Markham swore aloud and ran his hands through what remained of his hair.

"Anna, you're mad! What are you thinking of? Do you suppose for a moment that he'd hold his tongue? I tell you they're giving smashing sentences. They're out to stop the whole thing. It would come out that he got it from you. Do you suppose for a moment that he'd go to prison for you?"

"Oh, no," said Anna quite gently, "he wouldn't go to prison for me. He said so."

"Then what are you driving at? He'd give you away."

"Oh no," said Anna again. Her earrings dazzled in the light. "Oh no, Bobby, he wouldn't give me away, because he wouldn't know anything about me. He wouldn't say he'd had the stuff from me, because I shouldn't have given it to him. I'm not quite a fool, you know."

"You're not going to give it to him?"

"No."

"Then who is?"

"Isobel," said Anna sweetly.

A silence came down between them. Bobby Markham went on looking at her. At last he said,

"Isobel?"

"I think perhaps he might go to prison for Isobel. It would be interesting to see if he would."

Bobby Markham leaned back. For the moment he wanted to get farther away from Anna.

"Why have you got your knife into him like this? What's he done? Why can't you leave him alone? He hasn't done you any harm."

The words were hardly out before he regretted them. He had seen Anna in a fury once, and he had no wish to repeat the experience. The color went suddenly out of her face. Her eyes looked past him—big, black eyes, with something hot behind the blackness.

"Do you want me to answer that?"

He didn't—not now—not when she looked like that. He wanted to get back to the George and have a whisky and soda. But Anna had not waited for an answer to her question.

"I'll tell you what he's done if you like. He has insulted me in the worst way that a man can insult a woman. He wanted to marry me once, and when I wouldn't have him——" She choked and threw up a hand before her eyes. "Oh!" she said in a deep, gasping note. "Men can be brutes—brutes—brutes!"

The startled Mr. Markham turned plum-colored with embarrassment.

"Anna—hold on—what do you mean?"

The hand that had covered her eyes was thrown out towards him in a really fine dramatic gesture.

"Don't ask me—you're my friend—don't ask me any more." She turned away a little and stood drooping, with the shawl falling in a long straight line from her shoulder. "That is why my uncle quarreled with him. I didn't tell him *everything*. But I couldn't—couldn't go on seeing Car as if nothing had happened. Now Uncle John is beginning to hanker after him again—it's an old man's fancy, and I can't, can't bear it." She leaned across the table to him suddenly with outstretched hands. "Bobby, I can't bear it—I can't! You must help me! *Bobby*—don't you see that I can't bear it! And if he does go to prison for this, it's *just*, because he's never been punished for what he did to me."

Mr. Markham felt himself a good deal carried away.

"Look here, Anna—I say, don't upset yourself like that." He caught at her hand and held it. "Look here, if I do it——"

"You will? Oh, Bobby!"

"I didn't say I would—I said if——" He paused and imprinted a fervent kiss upon the hand which lay uppermost in his. It was cold and smooth—it was very cold. He let go of it almost involuntarily. As she drew back, he said, "What do you want to bring the girl into it for? You've not got your knife into her, have you?"

"Isobel?" said Anna.

"Yes."

There was a little pause. Anna's emotion had passed; she looked beautiful and cool and smiling again.

"Oh, no," she said.

"Then why bring her into it?"

"It won't hurt her. You've very chivalrous, Bobby. You needn't be afraid—Isobel won't come to any harm, because Car—Car will be chivalrous too. He won't give her away."

Mr. Markham salved his conscience with this. He had a conscience, but he had trained it to a certain degree of docility. It would demand satisfaction, to be sure, but it had learned to be very easily satisfied. He told himself that it was satisfied now. Anna's appeal had gone to his head and raised hopes which he had previously scarcely dared to entertain. Now, when he saw her withdrawing, cool and remote as a statue, he ventured beyond his prudence.

"Anna—" he said in an agitated voice, "if I do it——"

Instantly the statue came to life; the color rushed into the pale cheeks. She glowed and put her hands in his.

"You *will!*"

"If I do, will you—will you—let me take you out of it all?"

"Do you want to?" said Anna, looking at him.

"You know I do. I've made my pile. I got a lucky tip the

other day and made enough to clear right out of all this other business. I'll buy a place and settle down. You can have everything you want. I'm easy to live with—ask Cis. You wouldn't mind Cis living with us, would you—*Anna?*"

She drew away her hand very slowly, looking down, her eyes hidden, her long black lashes making startling contrast with the white of the eyelids and the rich blush of the cheeks.

"Anna—will you?"

"Will *you?*" said Anna.

"*If,*" said Mr. Bobby Markham with as much firmness as remained in him.

XXIII

Car Fairfax's Diary:

September 23rd—I HAVEN'T WRITTEN ANYTHING DOWN FOR days, because nothing special seems to have been happening—that is to say, nothing that has any bearing on this Z.10 business. I seem to have done nothing but run up against people I used to know, and they've all been very nice, and glad to see me and all that sort of thing. You don't meet people when you're crawling round looking for work in seedy clothes. It's been topping meeting people again. I'd forgotten what jolly good sorts most of them were.

Yesterday I took Corinna out. She's going down to Linwood some time this week. She talks a lot about Peter. I hate butting into other people's affairs, but I thought she ought to know that he was married. We were having tea at a quite sort of place she picked, so I thought I'd make a plunge and get it over. I'm afraid I did it very badly, but I don't see how you can break that sort of thing—besides I didn't want her to think that I thought there was anything to break. She'd just been saying that Poppa thought the world of Peter, only once he'd said a thing he didn't like to go back on it—"and of course I had said about a million times that I was just dying to go to Europe, so when he turned round and said I was to go, I couldn't very well say much about not wanting to—could I? He said that Peter and I weren't to write to each other, and I said 'Poppa *darling*, you just pinch yourself and come awake! You're about two hundred years out—this isn't the eighteenth century.' So he said we could write to each other as friends."

I got as hot as I've ever been in my life, and I said,

"You're a great friend of Peter's."

And she crinkled up the corners of her eyes and laughed like a child and said,

"I'm a great friend."

"And so am I." And there I stuck.

She stopped laughing—she's as sharp as a needle—and asked quickly,

"What are you trying to say, Car?"

I shoved myself along by main force. The only thing I could do for her was to get it out quickly.

"We're both his friends. Don't you think he ought to give out his marriage? Secrets are stupid things—don't you think so?" I went on because I was afraid to stop and I was afraid to look at her. Then when I had said "Don't you think so?" I couldn't think of anything else to say, so I stopped. Then I had to look.

She was sitting up quite straight, and rather puzzled.

"But we can't because of Poppa," she said. "Poppa won't let us be engaged till I get back. He doesn't say he will then, but I guess I'll make him." She laughed a little, but she kept looking at me.

It was perfectly horrible. I wanted her to tumble to it before she said anything like that. It was my fault—I ought to have been able to stop her. I was mad with Peter, and I could have kicked myself. I said,

"That's a joke—because Peter must have told you that he was married."

She sat there with her hands in her lap and her eyes wide open.

"It isn't a joke," she said in a little breathless voice.

I just forged ahead—I had to.

"Peter is married. He got married just before the smash. He was married before he met you."

She never took her eyes off my face. I wished she would move, but she didn't. Her voice didn't shake at all, but there was so little of it that I don't know how I heard what she was saying. I did her her say,

"Go on."

"Peter married Fay Everitt just before the smash."

I don't think she had been breathing. She began now to take a long breath. When she had filled her lungs, she gave a shiver and drew the back of her hand across her eyes. It was just like seeing some one wake up.

"Oh, how you frightened me!" she said.

"My dear——" I began, but she leaned over the table and took hold of my wrist.

"Don't be silly, Car—it's not true."

"Corinna——"

"Don't be silly! Of course it's not true."

"My dear——"

"Peter would have told me," she said, nodding earnestly and pinching my wrist.

I thought she was the pluckiest kid—but I won't write down what I thought about Peter.

I began to say "I'm afraid——" but she stopped me.

"*I*'m not. I'm not the least bit afraid—there's nothing to be afraid about. Let's get this right out into the light and have a look at it. Who told you all this?"

I looked back at her and tried to remember. She held my wrist tight.

"You weren't at the wedding, were you?" she said.

I never saw anything so confident as her eyes.

"No, I wasn't."

"You couldn't have been. Nobody was. There wasn't any wedding for you to be at. If fifty bishops all stood in a row and said they'd married Peter in Westminster Abbey, I shouldn't believe them!"

She let go of me and sat bolt upright again. She had the air of sitting in judgment. If I'd had anything on my conscience, I should have wanted to clear out. Cocksure wasn't the word for it.

"Now!" she said. "Did Peter tell you he was married?"

I was trying to think. I remember Peter and Fay going about together, and I remembered Peter saying "Look after Fay for me," when she and I went to see him off. No, I didn't—I remembered—

Corinna didn't give me time.

"Did he? Did he tell you himself? Or did *she* tell you?"

I remembered.

What I remembered was Fay telling me what Peter had said. It came back in the very tones of her voice—"Peter says you're to look after me for him. You will—won't you?" And then, "We're married. Didn't he tell you? We've been married a month, but it's a secret." And then she cried and said, "Don't tell him I told you—he'll be so angry—but I can't bear it all alone. You mustn't tell him, but you can say nice things about me when you write, to cheer him up."

"Did Peter tell you he was married?" said Corinna.

"No," I said.

"Who told you?"

"Fay did."

"And asked you not to tell Peter she'd told you."

"How do you know?"

"That's what I should have done if I'd been telling a lot of lies and didn't want to be found out."

I was appalled. It didn't seem possible—but then it didn't seem possible that Peter——

"Are you going on being afraid?" said Corinna in a little taunting voice.

I didn't say anything. I was remembering a heap of little things.

"Well?" said Corinna.

"We'll have to make sure," I said.

She gave a judicial nod.

"Right away. I'm going to cable Peter, and I'm going to see Fay Everitt just as fast as I can get to her. And I'm going to ask her where she was married, and if she puts up a bluff and *says* where, then we're going along to inspect that register, and if it's got Peter's name on it——" She paused.

"Well?" I said.

The color rose brightly in her cheeks.

"Well, then it'll be just the meanest kind of nightmare, and you can pinch me till I wake up, Car Fairfax."

XXIV

WHEN SHE HEARD THE KNOCK ON HER DOOR, FAY EVERITT turned slowly without the least suspicion that she was turning to meet a reckoning. She had spent a lazy afternoon—first a hot bath; then a little sleep; then a novel, chocolates, and some of those cigarettes which Car so unreasonably disapproved of. She was one of those people who could be desperately unhappy or desperately frightened at one moment, and the next forget, for the time at least, that there was anything to be unhappy about. She could come to the surface of her thoughts and move about there with, as it were, a thin sheet of ice between her and the things that moved darkly below. At any moment the ice might break. It was breaking now, though she did not know it.

She turned, blew a little puff of smoke into the already hazy air, and called,

"Come in!"

Even when the door opened and Car stood aside to let Corinna Lee pass him, her only feeling was one of sharp annoyance because he was not alone.

They came in, and Car shut the door. Corinna spoke at once. She had no intention of shaking hands with Fay. She stood a yard from the door, small, determined, purposeful, with round gray eyes that were very brightly aware. They took in the room with its green curtains—the bed, low and couch-like, with a green spread which was just out of key; the shabby carpet; the old chair, with one very new cushion, gold and green with a black spider embroidered on it; the mantelshelf, dominated by a large framed photograph of Peter. Peter's eyes in the photograph looked straight at Corinna.

She spoke at once in a little composed voice:

"I'm very pleased to find you in, Miss Everitt, because there's something I want to ask you. And I don't think I'll sit down, thank you"—this as Fay waved her towards a chair—"because it won't take you any time at all just to answer what I want to ask."

Fay stiffened. She was standing in the middle of the room with her book in her left hand and the right at her lips replacing her cigarette. She paused, stared, lifted her eyebrows at Car, and remarked,

"Americans are always in a hurry, I suppose."

"Well, I'm in a hurry," said Corinna briskly. "I'm in a hurry to know whether it is true that you say you are Mrs. Peter Lymington."

The book fell out of Fay's hand with a crash. She jerked round to face Car on Corinna's right.

"You told her! How dare you?" And then and there she stopped, choked down the anger that was carrying her out of her depth, and faced Corinna again. "I have never called myself Mrs. Peter Lymington!"

"Have you ever said you were married to him?" The

hand with the cigarette fell to Fay's side. "Did you tell Car Fairfax you were married to Peter?"

There was no answer.

Corinna did not move. Her small gray-gloved hands rested one on either side of the big lump of rose quartz which covered the catch of her gray lizard bag. Her small gray-shod feet were planted firmly. Her stern young gaze never left Fay's frightened face. It had been angry at first, but it was frightened now. The ice had broken and let her down amongst all those dark fears which sometimes came out at night and brought a reign of terror with them.

Corinna spoke again in the same clear voice:

"Did you tell Car Fairfax that you were married to Peter? Car says you did. Is he telling a lie?"

Fay looked at Car. For three years she had looked to him whenever there was anything unpleasant to be done. She looked to him now.

He came forward and put a hand on her arm.

"Haven't you got anything to say, Fay?"

She shook her head.

"You're not married to Peter?"

She shook it again.

"Why did you say you were?"

Fay moved back a step, freeing herself. She spoke for the first time since the questions had begun; and she spoke to Car, not to Corinna:

"Tell her to go away," she said only just above her breath.

"Well, I don't want to stay," said Corinna soberly. She turned and went out of the room without another word.

Car followed her down the stairs.

"Do you want a taxi?"

"No—I guess I'd like to walk."

"I must go back. This has got to be cleared right up."

She nodded, and on an impulse put her face up to be kissed.

He kissed the soft round cheek, and both of them felt a certain comfort. The kiss seemed to bring the pleasant ordered ways of family affection into sight again. He patted her shoulder, and she went out, her eyes not stern any longer but vaguely troubled. Why should any one tell stupid lies like that? Why should they?

Car went back. He was shocked, and he was beginning to be angry. He didn't understand what had happened, or why it had happened. He felt rather as if some one had struck him in the face; he would be angry as soon as he got over the first shock of surprise.

He found Fay just where he had left her, standing in the middle of the room staring at the door, waiting for him to come back. The end of her cigarette had scorched her thin green dress. A faint smell of burning crept through the smell of her cigarette.

Car was glad enough to have something to be angry about.

"Good Lord, Fay, what are you doing? You'll be on fire in a minute!"

She dropped the cigarette then, as she had dropped the book, just opening her fingers and letting it go.

"Now!" he said. "What's the meaning of this? What did you do it for?"

Fay began to cry. Quite gently and slowly the tears brimmed up in her eyes and began to trickle down her cheeks. It was an immense relief. Car was always sorry when she cried, and if he would only be sorry, it would be all right. The worst of being very frightened was that you couldn't always cry.

"What on earth did you do it for?" said Car in an angry, puzzled voice.

"You," said Fay with the tears running down her face.

Car made a violent movement.

"What are you talking about?"

"You," said Fay again.

He actually shook her a little then, lightly, and let go of her in a hurry because the impulse came on him to shake her harder, harder, harder.

"What are you talking about? What in heaven's name made you do such a thing? Were you engaged to Peter?"

She shook her head dumbly.

"Did he ever make love to you?"

She shook her head again.

"But, good heavens—are you mad? It's sheer raving lunacy! What was the good of telling me you and Peter were married—what was the point? It's so utterly crass!"

Fay shook her head again. She gathered her hands up under her chin. She stood there drooping, weeping, not saying a word.

Car felt a primitive desire to beat her. He took a hasty step back towards the door. It was beastly to be so strong and to want to beat people.

"Why did you do it?" he said in an exasperated voice.

Fay, seeing him recede, found her voice. She was still frightened, but there was a sort of delicious thrill about being frightened of Car. She didn't at all want him to go away. In a voice full of tears she said,

"I did it for you."

Car felt as if he had been struck again.

"For me? I suppose you're mad."

She shook her head.

He thought if she shook her head again, that he would probably throw something at her. He drove both hands deep into his pockets and glowered.

"Will you kindly explain—all right then, I'm going."

Fay sprang forward.

"Don't go, Car! I did it for you—I really did! I don't care twopence for Peter! He asked me to go out with him, and I went, because sometimes you were there too. It was the only way I could get to see you. And when the smash came and Peter went to the States, I thought I should never see you any more." The words came tumbling out half choked with sobs.

"That's enough," said Car. "Don't talk like that!"

He reached for the door handle, but she caught his arm with both hands.

"Car—listen! Don't be angry. It was for *you*. I thought I'd never see you again, and I was desperate. And I knew you'd look after me if you thought I was Peter's wife, so I said I was."

"Yes," said Car—"beautifully simple! I see. Let me go, Fay."

"Car!"

"You'd better let me go. I might"—he took a deep breath—"I might—hurt you." Then with a sudden jerk he had the door open, pulled free of her, and was gone.

She heard the front door slam so violently that the house shook. She put her hand on her own door and pushed it to. She was sobbing as she whirled round and ran to the hearth.

Peter's photograph looked down at her. She snatched it and flung it across the room. It struck the window-sill and fell with a tinkle of broken glass.

Fay began to laugh.

XXV

Car Fairfax's Diary:

September 23rd—I THINK FAY'S MAD. SHE'S SIMPLY BEEN lying all this time. She's no more married to Peter than Mrs. Bell is. She must be off her head, because it's the most absolutely pointless show. They weren't engaged—he didn't even make love to her—they just went about together a bit. And when he'd gone, I suppose she thought she was going to be at a bit of a loose end, so she said they were married.

She said she thought I'd look after her if she was Peter's wife. It's absolute lunacy.

Corinna and I went to see her. She gave the whole show away at once. After Corinna had gone, I lost my temper and came away too.

I've been looking through Peter's letters. He says things like, "You and Fay seem to be seeing quite a lot of each other," and, "Fay says you're looking after her." I can see now that he must have thought I was getting keen on Fay myself. Of course he'd think that, when I kept writing about how she looked and what she was doing. It makes me boil to think of the rot I've written to poor old Peter just because I thought he must be dying to know everything I could tell him about Fay. I used to think how grateful I should feel if any one would write to me and tell me all the little everyday things about Isobel, and then I used to fire away. Poor old Peter must have been bored stiff.

Well, I slammed out of Fay's room and out of the house, and went for a walk to get myself in hand. I've got a beastly temper.

On the way home I began to think about Fay. I'd been a bit brusque with her, and it worried me in case she got worked up to the point of doing something silly. She must be a bit mad, and it's no good going off the deep end because a crazy person does a crazy thing. I wasn't a bit keen on seeing her again, but I thought I'd better just blow in and make sure she was all right. After all, I've been looking after her for three years, so it's got to be more or less of a habit.

I knocked at the door, and nothing happened. It was getting darkish, because I'd been a good long way. I could hear Mrs. Bell striking a match to light the hall gas, but I couldn't hear anything from Fay's room. I got the most awful panic and fairly banged on the panel. And then I felt like a fool, because the door opened, and there was Fay, got up to the nines and all ready to go out. She'd drenched herself with scent, and she'd made up her face till she looked like one of those dummy figures they put clothes on in shop windows.

"Were you coming to see if I was dead?" she said.

I said, "Don't be an ass, Fay!" and she laughed.

"Have you come to console me for being divorced from Peter? Have you, Car?"

"I wish you'd talk sense, Fay," I said.

Well, that just seemed to set her off. You wouldn't have thought any one could talk such rot, even if they were balmy. I felt as if my temper might go again, so I thought it would give it a safety-valve if I put it across her a bit about the harm she might have done Peter, and the mischief she might have made by pretending to be married to him like that.

She jerked and flounced, and lit cigarettes and threw them about, like she does when she's annoyed. She kept trying to speak too, but I was determined to let her have it, so I just went on. When I stopped, she asked me if Corinna was going to marry Peter. It's extraordinary how women's minds work. I said I didn't know, but I hoped so.

"I don't mind if she marries *Peter*," she said. She edged up to me.

One of the things that has always annoyed me about Fay is the way she tries to flirt. It drives me wild. She does it because she thinks she can get round me that way. It's a most extraordinary thing that most women seem to think that they can get their own way by wriggling their shoulders and doing tricks with their eyelashes. I suppose it gets round some people. It makes me angry. Fay's most awfully bad about it.

"I shouldn't like her to marry *you*. Are you in love with her, Car?"

I said, "No, I'm not," and I scowled.

Fay did tricks with her eyelashes.

"No—it's Isobel you're in love with—isn't it? She's engaged to some one else. She's going to marry Giles Heron. He's awfully good-looking—much better looking that you, and much better off. She'll marry him, and what will you do then? Car, don't look like that. Oh—ooh—you frighten me! I only wanted to know. I don't believe you're in love with any one really. Are you? Are you in love with Isobel?"

"Yes, I am," I said, and I went out of the room, because, honestly, I felt as if I should murder her if I stayed there another second.

That's enough about that.

I wrote yesterday to Z.10 Smith to say I couldn't go on like this. Another fifty pounds dropped in by registered post this morning. I can't possibly take about a hundred pounds a week for doing nothing. I said if he'd really got a job for me to do, I'd like to know what it was and get down to it. I've thought till my head goes round, and I can't arrive at any possible reason why any one should throw money at me like this—which looks as if it might be a lunatic, because if you're mad, you *are* liable to do things without having any reason for doing them.

XXVI

September 24*th*—I WAS JUST WRITING ABOUT LUNATICS, when Mrs. Bell came up with a telegram. She disapproves most frightfully of telegrams.

"I don't know what things is coming to," she said. "Posts come in regular, and you do know where you are with them, but telegrafts I can't abide nor see any use in, because if it's bad news, you're bound to get it sooner or later, and the later the better."

"But supposing it's good news?" I said. I wasn't in a

hurry, because Z.10's the only person who wires to me now-a-days, and I've got past having heartthrobs over being told to ring him up at some unearthly place, or to be sure to send him back his last envelope, or something of that sort.

Mrs. Bell snorted.

"Nobody worries about sending you a telegraft when it's good news," she said. "If it's anything that's going to worry a pore soul into her grave, nobody don't grudge a shilling to send the bad news along. But if some one was to leave me a fortune, or something of that sort, it's my opinion the first I'd hear of it 'ud be on a post-card—and they wouldn't hurry themselves too much about that. And did you say there was any answer, sir? And I hope as it isn't bad news for you this time anyhow."

I said, "No, it wasn't bad news, and there isn't any answer."

Then she went away.

This is the telegram:

Meet me to-night ten-thirty far end crescent. Z.10.

Well, there it was. The crescent would be Olding Crescent.

Z.10's an odd creature. He has his queer moments of caution, like making me send back envelopes and not putting the name of the place in full—which is one of the things that make me wonder which side of the law he's on. I'm not going to quod for Mr. Z.10 Smith, so if that's his dream, he'd better wake up quick.

The telegram had been sent from the G.P.O., so I didn't get any help out of that. Telegrams aren't very helpful anyhow. A letter does give you something about a man—you can tell whether he got it straight off the bat, or whether he dawdled about, trying to make up his mind what he was going to say; and you can tell whether he was pretty well bucked with life or in rather a Weary-Willie frame of mind—but a wire doesn't give you any help.

I wondered what on earth he wanted, and whether he'd really got a job for me, and what sort of a job it was likely to be, and I wished that ten-thirty wasn't about seven hours away.

It came along at last. I got to the Olding Crescent about ten minutes before the time and walked along to the end of it. By the "far end" I supposed he meant the end that was farthest from Churt Row. I walked in the shadow of the wall where he and I had talked before. It was absolutely pitch-black under the trees. The other side of the road was just visible. There weren't many lamp-posts, only one every two hundred yards or so—a pretty poor allowance for a suburb.

I had the long brick wall of somebody's big garden on my left, and the trees on the other side of it hung over and made dense shadows. I felt my way along the wall. After about three hundred yards I came on a door. It was set flush with the wall, and it was locked. The wall went on and on. It seemed to me that there weren't going to be any houses on this side of the crescent at all. I thought I would cross the road and prospect, so I made for the next lamp-post.

All the lamps were on the other side. I was standing under the lamp looking about me, when a car with a rug over its bonnet went slowly past and came to a stand-still on the wrong side of the road under the trees. As it stopped, the lights went out. I heard the door open, but I didn't hear any one get out.

I stared into the dark, but I couldn't see a thing. Then I heard my name.

"Fairfax—is that you?"

It was Z.10 all right. I knew the sound of him at once. He has one of those dry, breathless and soundless sort of voices. You can do a very good imitation of it if you pitch your voice just above a whisper and see how far you can make it carry without putting any real life into it. It had struck me from the beginning that it wasn't at all a bad way of disguising one's voice. He called again, and I stepped out across the road.

The car was a saloon. I couldn't tell the make. The front door was open, and as soon as I got level with it he spoke again from the driver's seat.

"Get in—I want to talk to you."

I put one foot on the running-board and kept a hand on the door.

"Are you going out of town?"

He said "Why?" in rather a surprised sort of way.

"Well, last time—" I began. And then I realized I was making a break, because he took me up most uncommonly sharp.

"Last time? What do you mean by 'last time'?"

"Oh, nothing," I said—"nothing."

Really I wasn't sorry I'd made a slip of the tongue. I'd never felt sure how much Z.10 knew. He'd given me an appointment at the corner of Olding Crescent and Churt Row, and he'd written afterwards to say that he'd been prevented from keeping it. And some one else had kept it for him. Anna Lang had kept it. And Anna's account was that she'd overheard a conversation between two men whom she didn't know. One of them said that he had an appointment to meet me at his place—mentioning me by name— and that he wasn't going to keep it because he was putting me through some sort of test.

Speaking broadly, I should expect anything that Anna said to be untrue. She doesn't tell the truth if she can help it—I thinks she finds it dull. But on the other hand, bits of her story do fit in very well. So I couldn't make out whether Z.10 knew that Anna had met me or not, and I thought I should rather like to find out, because if Anna was in with Z.10, I was through.

"I think you must have meant something," he said, and from the sound of his voice he was leaning towards me.

"Well," I said, "last time—"

He interrupted me.

"Last time I met you at the corner. We walked up and down beside the wall and settled your salary."

"I didn't mean that time—I mean the time before."

"There was no time before."

"Oh yes, there was. You made an appointment to meet me at the corner at ten o'clock."

"And I did not come—I was prevented."

"Somebody came," I said.

I swear he was taken by surprise. He made some sort of a movement and drew his breath in quickly.

"What do you mean?"

"What I say—somebody met me."

"Somebody met you here?"

"Yes."

"How?"

"I don't know how. I thought perhaps you did."

He was silent for a moment. Then he said,

"Who met you, Mr. Fairfax?"

"A lady," I said.

"You don't know who she was?"

"Oh yes, I know; but if you don't, I can't very well tell you."

"A lady? A lady?"

I thought it was a blow to him. Then he seemed to pull himself together.

"What happened?" he said.

"She took me for a drive."

"She took you for a drive?" There was the extreme of surprise in his voice.

"For a nice country drive," I said.

"At ten o'clock at night?"

"From ten to eleven," I replied.

I could hear him beat on the wheel with an exasperated hand.

"Mr. Fairfax, you're not serious!"

"Oh, but I am."

"On your word of honor?"

"I'll take an affidavit if you like."

He said, "Well, well——" and made a clicking sound with his tongue against his teeth. Then he asked me point-blank "Who was this woman?"

I didn't say anything.

He hit the wheel again.

"Where did she take you?"

I thought I'd let fly at a venture. If he didn't know anything, I shouldn't be telling him anything; and if he knew already, there wouldn't be anything to tell.

"She took me to Linwood Edge," I said—and I'd have given a good deal to be able to see his face.

There was a complete and hollow silence. I could hear two branches rubbing against each other somewhere overhead where the trees crossed one another along the wall, and I could hear the sound of traffic on a main road a long way off. It's funny how town things and country things sound alike in the distance. That noise of cars and lorries and trams passing each other on a tarred road had just the sound of waves coming in on a pebble beach after a storm. I thought of that whilst I was waiting for him to speak. I had to wait a long time.

When he did speak, I could tell by his voice that he had turned away from me and was looking into the dark ahead of him. He said,

"Get in, Mr. Fairfax, and sit down. We shan't be driving down to Linwood to-night."

XXVII

I HESITATED FOR A MOMENT. THEN I GOT IN.

There was one curious thing about these talks with Z.10 Smith—I would go to ring him up or to meet him, feeling how damned fishy the whole thing was, but the minute I began to talk to him, the oddest interview seemed to be perfectly ordinary and respectable; before I had been talking to him for half a minute I felt as if I was being interviewed by my bank manager or my solicitor. I suppose it's partly something dry and prosaic about his voice, and partly the little jerky way he has of putting his pince-nez straight—but there it is, and it must be a tremendous asset to him if he's on the cross.

Well, I sat down and waited for him to begin. He'd got his glasses off, and I think he was polishing them—out of sheer habit, I suppose, for the place was nearly as dark as a shut room. I could just see the spokes of the wheel and his hands fidgeting to and fro, and once or twice his pince-nez caught the very little faint light there was. He finished polishing them and put them on. He was sitting well into his own corner facing me.

"So you want to throw up your job, Mr. Fairfax?" he began.

I said, "I can't throw up what I haven't got. If you give me a job, I'll do it; but I can't go on taking money which I'm not doing anything to earn."

"And yet," he said, "jobs aren't so easy to get. You've had some experience of that, I think."

I said, "Yes." I tried not to sound as depressed as I felt. I'd been too near the gutter to feel cheerful about giving up the best part of a hundred and fifty pounds and the promise of more to come.

"Well, perhaps you'll change your mind," he said. "We can talk first, and you can make your decision afterwards. Perhaps when you've heard what I've got to say—"

I wanted him to get on and say it, but he'd got his own elderly, fussy way of doing business. It was one of the things that made him seem so respectable. I couldn't help thinking that a sharp crook would have come to the point long ago—but perhaps that's what he wanted me to think. This sort of business makes one most frightfully suspicious. I was determined not to speak first. In the end he said about the last thing in the world that I could have expected:

"I believe you have an uncle, Mr. Fairfax."

It made me jump, because, naturally, I hadn't been

thinking about my uncle. I expect he thought me facetious because I came out with,

"Most people have."

He clicked with his tongue against his teeth in a reproving sort of way.

"Your uncle is Mr. John Carthew of Linwood?"

I made amends by saying "Yes," as soberly as I could.

"Now, Mr. Fairfax—why has your uncle not come to your assistance in the straits to which you have from time to time been reduced?"

"That," I said, "is his affair."

"Well—it might be said to concern you—yes, it might be said to concern you rather intimately. If Mr. Carthew did not assist you, it was not from lack of means to do so. He is, I believe, a man of large property and ample means."

"I believe so."

"What, in fact, would be correctly described as a wealthy man."

"I suppose so."

"Mr. Carthew is not married?"

"He is a widower."

"A childless widower?"

"Yes."

He moved slightly. I thought he leaned a little forward.

"You were, naturally, brought up to consider yourself his heir?"

I took a moment to think about this. It's very difficult to be sure just what one had thought about a thing like that.

I said, "I don't know—I don't think I thought about it very much—I don't really think that I thought about it at all—not before the smash anyhow."

"And after the smash?" he said.

"Well, then I knew for a dead cert that I was right off the map."

"Your uncle gave you to understand that he wouldn't do anything for you?"

I wondered what on earth he was driving at. It seemed to

me that we were working round to the Anna Lang business again. I couldn't see what it had got to do with him anyhow.

"My uncle and I had a quarrel," I said—"and that was the end of any prospects I might have had. I've never seen him nor heard from him since."

Mr. Smith leaned forward again. I could see his hand move on the wheel.

"Exactly. And you very naturally experienced some resentment?"

I didn't see what it had got to do with him if I had.

"That's my affair," I said.

"You're very cautious, Mr. Fairfax. But you can speak freely. Any young man of spirit must have felt resentment at being treated in the way that you were treated. I really think"—he leaned back again—"I really think that we may take your indignation and resentment for granted, and that being the case, we may proceed to my next point."

I nearly said, "Get on, you old stick-in-the-mud!" but his frightfully respectable manner kept me just politely attentive.

"Feelings of anger and resentment," he went on, "are, of themselves, of no practical use; but if you were accorded an opportunity of translating these very natural feelings into action, what, I wonder, would be your attitude?"

This was coming to the point with a vengeance. In his long-winded and respectable manner, Z.10 appeared to be "offering me the opportunity" of knocking my uncle on the head, or tipping him into a pond, or perhaps merely picking his pocket or what not. There was a beautiful rolling vagueness about "translating my very natural feelings of anger and resentment into action." I would have liked to draw him, but I didn't think it was decent. I wasn't going to discuss my uncle with him, and I was feeling a bit hot about his butting in on my family affairs, so I said pretty stiffly,

"I don't know what you mean."

He moved again.

"Don't you, Mr. Fairfax? Come, come—I think you do. I think you have had a pretty bad time of it during the last three years, and I think you must feel that you owe your uncle something of a grudge. Suppose you were offered an opportunity of getting some of your own back—would you not be inclined to entertain it?"

I thought this was pretty stiff. I wondered what he would go on to propose, and who was behind it. That is what I wondered most, so, by way of finding out, I asked him what he meant.

"You go too fast," he said. "We have, at present, your grudge against your uncle, and my proposal that you should be afforded an opportunity of realizing this grudge. Before we go any farther I should want a specific declaration of your willingness to proceed upon these lines."

I wanted to pick him up and throw him through the windscreen, the little rat; but I controlled myself.

I said bluntly, "Do you mean murder?" and I saw him jump.

"And if I did?" he said, breathing a bit quicker.

I had startled him out of some of his propriety anyhow. I couldn't hold on any longer.

"Why, you infernal little scallywag!" I roared, and before I'd got farther than that he had opened the door on the far side and slipped out.

I made after him, but it was too dark. His being so nippy took me by surprise. I called into the dark,

"Here you—Z.10! Where are you?"

I thought I heard something move. A moment later he called out,

"Here!"

The voice came from about twenty yards back. I made a dash for the place, but as I got there, I heard behind me the sound of the engine. Some one had started the car. I stopped and turned. The tail light was on, and the engine running. I began to run back, but as I came level with the rear wheels, the door slammed on the far side. The car was already moving, and whilst I was trying to make up my mind whether to have a shot at boarding it or just to let him go, it drew away and was out of reach.

I stood and watched it go. It was no good running. It was

no good looking either, for the matter of that, for the number plate had a bit of paper or something hanging down over it.

I saw the last of the tail light as the car turned into Churt Row.

XXVIII

I WAS WILD WITH MYSELF FOR HAVING MISSED SUCH A GOOD opportunity. I ought to have grabbed the little squirt and shaken the truth out of him. As it was, I'd about as much chance of finding him as one would have of picking a special drop of water out of the Thames. London is stiff with Smiths, and stiff with little men who wear pince-nez. Probably his real name was something quite different, and I hadn't one earthly chance of ever coming across him again. After what had just passed, he wasn't very likely to want to find me.

I stood there and cursed myself. Who would have thought the little blighter could have nipped out like that? Anyhow he'd got away, and I had to think what I'd better do next. I should have to send back the money. I hated that like poison. It's quite extraordinary how soon you get used to having money in your pocket again. I thought about going back to cadging for jobs and thinking myself lucky if I got a square meal once in three days or so. It was perfectly beastly.

Then I thought about my uncle. It seemed to me that he ought to know about Z.10; and yet for the life of me I didn't see how I was going to tell him. He'd probably think I was pitching him a cock-and-bull story, and at the very least he'd think I was trying to curry favor. It wasn't as if I'd got the number of the car, or a line of writing, or anything that I could show—it would be simply my unsupported word and a story that sounded like something out of the Arabian Nights. There was a distinct flavor of Baghdad about it— Adventure of the Poor Young Man and the Wicked Cadi sort of touch.

Well, I couldn't take root in Olding Crescent, so I shoved the whole thing into the back of my mind and started to walk in the direction of Churt Row.

I crossed to the lighted side of the crescent, and as I walked along, I kept looking over the way at the long black line of the wall with the trees hanging over it. That wall had a sort of fascination for me from the very beginning. I've always had a fancy for a wall, especially a high brick wall with a door going through it into a garden. Now, as I walked along, this wall began to have a most extraordinary attraction for me. I suppose it was because I didn't want to go on thinking about sending back the money and about my uncle. I wanted something else to think about—and there was the wall.

I began by wondering what the garden on the other side of it was like. And then I got on to the house, and from the house to the people who lived in it. By the time I got to the corner of Churt Row, the whole place, house, garden and wall, was fairly tugging at me.

I stood at the corner for a minute and looked along Churt Row. There wasn't a lighted window or any sign of a living thing. I looked back down Olding Crescent, and everything was dark.

The house behind the wall pulled harder, and what I wanted was any sort of an excuse for going to have a look at it. And all of a sudden the excuse burst on me like a Very light. I started to run back just as fast as I could go.

Why had Z.10 hit on this particular place to meet me? It was a very good place for his purpose—I doubted whether anything as dark and secluded could have been found without going a great deal farther afield. It was an admirable place. But how did he know about it? It wasn't the sort of place you would know about unless you lived there or thereabouts, and the first time he met me he had been on foot and I hadn't seen how he came. Suppose he had come out the door in the wall. Of course there were about ten million chances that he hadn't. But I didn't think about them; I clamped on to the chance that he had, and I went pelting down Olding Crescent looking for the way in.

The door in the wall was locked, but there must be a proper entrance somewhere—perhaps round the corner. If I was right, Z.10 could have driven along Churt Row, turned left, and left again, and come round to the entrance I was making for. If my Very light had only gone off at once, I could have made straight for the gate and watched him come home. By this time I was quite sure that he lived in the house behind the wall.

I found the entrance just at the corner. Olding Crescent runs into a biggish road with trees on either side of it. There was a big iron gate between brick pillars. The gate was open, and as I came on it, I saw the tail light of a car disappear along the drive. I wanted to shout, but I didn't. I ran after the car. There was a short drive, very dark, twisting through a high black shrubbery. I blundered into a holly bush and scratched myself, so I stopped running and felt my way instead.

A last twist brought the house into sight. The lower windows were lighted. I could see chinks and edges of light where the curtains let it through. It looked like a big house, with a portico sticking out and spanning the drive. There was a fanlight over the front door, very brightly lit. The car was standing under the portico. It had been turned and was facing the gate.

I hadn't thought what I was going to do, but it came to me in a flash. I marched up to the door and rang the bell. I had the sort of feeling that one gets sometimes—I felt absolutely sure of myself, and I didn't care a damn for any one.

The door opened almost at once. I think I'd expected to see a man-servant, but it was a pretty girl in a blue dress and a flimsy cap and apron, who looked as if she had walked out of a play. I had my piece all ready to say, and I said it.

"Does Mr. Smith live here?"

"No, sir," said the girl.

"What a nuisance!" I said. "I'm most awfully sorry to bother you, but I think I must have been misdirected, and looking for a Mr. Smith at this time of night is rather a hopeless sort of job."

"Yes, sir," she said.

"The other is I've forgotten the name of the people in the next house. I mean they said, 'It's next door to the So-and-So's,' and I've forgotten the So-and-So's name." She smiled and looked friendly, so I went on, "I suppose you can't help me? I'd know the name if I heard it. Who lives here?"

"Mr. Arbuthnot Markham, sir," she said.

I must have looked a prize ass. My jaw fell as if it had dropped about a yard. And just as I was trying to think of something to say, a door up at the end of the hall opened and I heard Anna Lang laugh.

I didn't dally. I said "Thanks ever so much," and I made tracks. I'd know Anna's laugh in a million. Anna and Arbuthnot Markham. . . . Oh, my hat!

I walked about a dozen yards for the look of the thing, and then I ran until I struck another holly bush—that beastly drive was full of them. It pulled me up, and I got behind some sort of cypress and did a bit of a think.

Anna and Arbuthnot Markham. . . . No wonder I'd had a feeling about the place. I suppose the car was waiting for her. It seemed pretty late for her to be visiting Arbuthnot anyway. Uncle John is strait-laced, and I wondered what he'd say if he knew. And then all the things I'd been keeping in the back of my mind came out with a rush. If Anna was behind this business, it had a very ugly look indeed. She had told me she'd forged my uncle's signature, and she'd told me she was in a blue funk about his finding out. On the top of this, Z.10 tried to induce me to—let us say, tip my uncle into a pond.

I had to put that away again. I couldn't think it out standing in a garden bed behind somebody else's cypresses. I felt as if it wanted concentration, and a wet towel round the head, and a good bit of midnight oil.

I came out on to the drive, and all of a sudden I thought what a mug I'd been. I ought to have had a look at the car before I marched up and rang the bell. I wondered if it was too late now. I went back, listening for the sound of the engine, but everything was quite still. The front door was shut. I could see the car plainly enough in the light that came through the fanlight. I wondered if there would be a chauffeur hanging about. I rather thought not, because in a house that size he'd get asked in.

I came up cautiously. There was no one in the car. Then I went round to the back of it and felt the number plate. There wasn't any paper over it now; but then I never expected there would be—he would have stopped somewhere along Churt Row and taken it off. I hadn't a match, or I'd have got the number—not that it really mattered very much. I had a shot at feeling for it, but the figures were not raised. I went round to the front again. There was a rug on the bonnet, a dark one. That 2ld me nothing—most rugs are dark, and all I had really noticed about Z.10's rug was that it was there.

I got round to the side away from the house and started to open the driver's door. I knew that if I sat in the car, I should have a very good idea whether it was the one I had sat in before; the feel of the seat, the angle of the windscreen, the set of the wheel, are the sort of things that register themselves in your mind. I had got the handle half turned, when the front door opened. I stood there like a fool, looking through the car at the brightly lighted hall and steps. Some one had switched on an outside light as well. It looked like a stage setting with the leading lady in the limelight.

Anna was the leading lady. She wore a gold dress and a gold and crimson shawl. I'll admit she looked handsome.

Arbuthnot Markham was just behind her, and she was talking to him over her shoulder. There didn't seem to be any servant about.

I didn't wait of course. I let go of the handle and got behind the nearest pillar. The portico ran right across the drive, with pillars along the edge of it. I got behind the middle pillar, and was glad to find it supplemented by some sort of creeper which almost doubled its width. I could hear their voices coming nearer, and then I heard the slam of the door.

I looked through the creeper and saw the shape of Anna's head against the light. She was in the driver's seat, so there wasn't any chauffeur. I hadn't time to wonder what had happened to Z.10, because I'd hardly seen Anna before Arbuthnot came round the back of the car. I just saw his white shirt-front, and then he turned away from me and leaned on the window by Anna.

It was a very uncomfortable position for me. Eavesdropping isn't much in my line. I hadn't the slightest interest in Anna's private affairs, but I didn't see my way out of the situation. If they were going to talk about their own concerns, I should feel like a cad. But if, by any chance, they were going to talk about Z.10, or my uncle, or me, I was bound to listen.

Well, first of all he said something so low that I didn't catch it; but I heard her say,

"I can't, Corinna Lee is staying. I'm not advertising this trip."

He said something again, and she laughed and said,

"You'll have to put up with it."

That sounds most frightfully ordinary, but it struck me no end. I've known Anna for about twenty-six years, and what struck me was this—she was speaking like an ordinary human being, not acting. It came over me that she felt, in some queer sort of way, at home with Arbuthnot; she didn't trouble to act for him.

I was so taken up with thinking this that I must have missed something, because all of a sudden he was saying,

"To-morrow?"

And she chipped in with, "Yes, to-morrow. I told you—it's his wedding day."

That brought me up sharp, because it brought us all back to Uncle John. He's tremendously keen on anniversaries, and his wedding-day is always kept with a lot of fuss—flowers in front of my aunt's portrait, and a queer sort of ceremonial, going through her letters, and her jewelry, and their wedding presents. I'd forgotten the exact date, but it came somewhere in this week.

Arbuthnot said, "You've made up your mind?"

She sounded vexed when she said, "Yes, of course I have. I don't know why I hesitated. He's for it." And she laughed again, a hard angry laugh.

I had never heard Anna talk like that in my life. It interested me very much. I wondered if it was Uncle John who was "for it," and exactly what that meant. And whilst I was wondering she started the car.

I heard two things more, and I'm hanged if I can make head or tail of them.

Anna said, just out of the blue as it were,

"They'll be sewn inside his coat."

And Arbuthnot Markham said,

"It's risky. Are you sure of her?"

Then she called out, "Good-night," and he said angrily, "You're in a deuce of a hurry!"

And that was all.

The car went away down the drive, and Arbuthnot went into the house and shut the door.

XXIX

September 25th—I WENT HOME AND WENT TO BED. I DIDN'T think I should sleep, but I was dog-tired and I pitched into sleep without knowing anything about it. One minute I was thinking I was going to lie awake for the rest of the night, and the next I was waking up into what I thought was a thunderstorm, but it was only Mrs. Bell banging on the door.

It wasn't till I was up and in the middle of shaving that I remembered I'd been having a dream about Isobel. It worried me, because I couldn't remember what I had dreamt. I kept on trying, and it wasn't any good.

As soon as I'd had breakfast, I did up all Z.10's money and went off the nearest post-office to buy a registered envelope and push it off. I kept three pounds as salary for the last week—I didn't think it was reasonable to leave myself without a penny at a moment's notice.

When I'd got rid of the stuff, I felt a good deal better. I think I'd really been afraid that something might argue me into keeping it. Of course I should have to do something about a job at once. Last night the prospects of my getting one had seemed particularly murky, but now I didn't think they looked so bad.

One of the people I had met a few days ago was Baron, whose young brother was at school with me. I'd never known the elder Baron particularly well, but he was very affable, and after I'd lunched with him and he'd told me all about Puggy and the job he'd got in Brazil, he said,

"You're fixed up, I suppose, or you might join him. You're just the sort of chap he's looking for."

Well, that was a big vague, but I thought I'd go and see Baron and ask what about it. Whatever happened, Z.10 had done me one good turn—he'd pushed me into going about and meeting people again. I'd got to the point where I'd run a mile if I thought I saw a pal.

I rang Baron up, and found he'd gone to Scotland, so I got his address and wrote to him. I also wrote to a man called Hartness, who had been very friendly, and who, I knew, had a lot of irons in the fire.

I went out and posted the letters.

When I came in, I met Fay on the stairs between her landing and mine. I hadn't time to wonder what had taken her upstairs, because she began to explain the minute she saw me:

"I've been up to your room. You needn't be frightened— there weren't any love-letters lying about. Car, you really oughtn't to glare like that—I haven't stolen anything."

She got as far as that, speaking in a sort of nervous rush, and then, to my surprise, she blushed, a real honest, unbecoming blush, and dashed past me into her own room.

Any other time, I suppose, I should have gone after her and asked her what she was playing at; but I was still angry. She had told me a lot of perfectly pointless lies and then tried to make out that it was something to do with me. I thought I'd cool down a bit before I had it out with her and told her what a little rotter she'd been.

I had hardly got to the top of the stairs when I heard Mrs. Bell calling me. She was halfway up the bottom flight, puffing and panting and waving an orange envelope.

I ran down, of course.

"Another of those there telegrafts! They'll be keeping a messenger special for you if it goes on like this," she said.

I wondered what on earth Z.10 could be wiring to me about. But the telegram wasn't from Z.10.

It was from Isobel.

It said, "Must see you. Very urgent indeed. Meet me Olding Crescent Putney eight-thirty to-night without fail. Isobel."

I stared and stared at the words. First they didn't seem to mean anything, and then they seemed to mean a great deal too much, and then they went blank and didn't mean anything at all.

I knew Mrs. Bell was talking, but I didn't hear a word she said.

Presently I said, "No, there isn't any answer," and I went upstairs to my room.

Fay's door was a little open as I passed, and I had a sort of feeling that she was watching me. I went up two steps at a time. I didn't feel in the least like talking to Fay.

I shut the door of my room and sat down at my table with the telegram spread out in front of me. The thing just took my breath away.

What did Isobel know about Olding Crescent?

Why did she want to see me urgently—very urgently?

And why eighty-thirty?

It would be quite dark—black dark under those overhanging trees.

Why did Isobel want me to meet her in the dark?

I sat there and tried to think of answers to these questions. What made it difficult was that when I thought about meeting Isobel, Isobel herself just swamped everything else. Trying to think about the other things was like trying to hear street noises outside when an organ is playing—you know the noises are there, but the music just floods over and through them and blots them out.

XXX

THE ANNIVERSARY OF MR. CARTHEW'S WEDDING-DAY began as it had begun for the last ten years or so. He came down to breakfast at a quarter past nine and was met by his wife's niece, Anna Lang, who offered him an affectionate embrace, and a bouquet of carnations and maidenhair, very tastefully arranged and all ready to put into a large silver loving cup which stood on the sideboard immediately below Mrs. Carthew's portrait.

Corinna Lee found the little ceremony "perfectly sweet." The flush on Mr. Carthew's cheek and the slight moisture in his blue eyes touched the romantic side of her nature to its very core. She watched appreciatively whilst the old gentleman himself put the flowers in water, thrusting them down rather awkwardly, so that some bright drops splashed up and trickled down the massive silver cup. When he stepped back and surveyed the portrait, she surveyed it too.

Mrs. Carthew had been painted in extreme youth. The portrait showed a girl of seventeen looking down at her new wedding-ring. Anna Lang was this girl's niece and name-sake, but she bore her no resemblance. Annie Carthew, who had been Annie Lang, was a thin, pale slip of a thing with big childishly blue eyes and a pretty, timid smile. It was very difficult to realize that she ought to be sitting here at the foot of the breakfast table, an old lady to Cousin John's old gentleman. She was just the picture of a girl, with a bunch of pink carnations stood up in front of her because it was her wedding-day.

Corinna found it touching but remote. It seemed odd to sit down to sausages and bacon, and to see Cousin John make a most excellent breakfast.

After breakfast the ceremonies of the day proceeded. Corinna's presence undoubtedly gave them a zest which they might otherwise have lacked. Mr. Carthew felt a good deal of pleasure in narrating the events of his wedding-day to some one who had never listened before to the story of how Annie Lang had walked to church. "It's only a step, and the village children had strewed the whole way with colored leaves from the hedges—the leaves turned early that year—and they stood in two rows for her to pass through them. They threw rose-leaves at her, and some of the red ones marked her dress, and the first thing that she said to me when she came out of church was, 'Oh, there's such a stain on my dress—and what *will* Mamma say!' And I said"—Mr. Carthew here thumped the table,—"I said, 'Your mother don't matter any more now, my dear. I'm the one that'll put you in the corner when you spoil your frocks.'" He leaned back laughing. "Her mother was very strict with all her children, but a very good mother for all that. Children were brought up in those days—they didn't just do what they liked."

"There must have been something kind of soothing about being brought up," said Corinna. "Now I've had the *hardest* kind of time bringing myself up and bringing Poppa up. I think the old times must have been real restful. What a pity we can't go back!"

Mr. Carthew gazed at her suspiciously. It was a fine warm morning. She was wearing a pale gray sleeveless frock. Her arms and neck looked as soft and white as milk; her gray eyes were as clear and innocent as a baby's; her small red upper lip just showed a glimpse of very white teeth.

"You don't want to go back. Nobody does. You like having your own way—don't you?"

"Don't you?" said Corinna.

"My own way? When you get to my age you don't expect to get your own way—and it wouldn't be any good if you did, because you wouldn't get it, my dear."

They were in the library. It was not a very studious-looking room. There was, to be sure, an old-fashioned roll-top desk, but the table at which he sat was strewn with picture papers and light novels. The walls gave more room to sporting prints than to bookshelves, and the chairs were less conducive to mental exercise than to sleep. Over the mantelpiece was another, and a later, portrait of Mrs. Carthew. It showed her tightly laced in black satin with a stiff fuzzy fringe under a hair-net. The small, pale features had a meek, obstinate expression. One felt that this was a lady who would say "Yes, John," and "No, John," and would then continue with meek pertinacity upon a predetermined way.

"It would have been rather fun to see them together," thought Corinna, whilst Mr. Carthew produced a large photograph album and proceeded to show her photographs of Annie as a child, with all her hair drawn back like the pictures of Alice in Wonderland, and a frilled apron and white stockings with colored stripes on them. There were also portraits of Annie's parents, culminating in a terrific one of Annie's mother in a Victorian widow's cap and a large black cashmere shawl. Corinna glanced from the photograph to Anna standing over by the far window. She was very like this handsome domineering old lady. She had the same fine, decided arch of the brow, the same abundant hair, the same dark eyes; and when she, too, was a grandmother, one could quite easily picture her with the same hooked nose, bitten-in lips, and air of authority.

Mr. Carthew passed to a water-color sketch of the church in which he had married Annie. It had been painted by Annie's younger sister Ellen. He began to tell her all about Ellen's deplorable marriage to a fellow of positively Socialist opinions.

Anna stood at the window and looked across to Linwood Edge. The sky was full of light. The trees showed no sign of turning. The scent of mignonette and heliotrope came in through the open window. The air was summer air, but she shivered a little as it touched her. She wasn't really seeing the trees, or the sky, or any outside thing at all; she was looking into her own mind and seeing just to what place she had brought herself—and Car.

It was a narrow, difficult place. If she took the next step forward, she could never go back any more. She had planned and schemed to bring herself to this place, but now that she had reached it, her heart beat and her senses shrank. She could still go back. Uncle John was showing photographs. He might go on showing them for half an hour. If he did, that would be half an hour's respite. But she couldn't count on it. At any moment he might look up and call to her, "Anna, where are my keys? Bless my soul, what have I done with my keys?" Even then it wouldn't be too late. There were things that she could say. If her imagination had not always been so ready to furnish her with things to say, she would not have come to this dark, difficult place.

She still had time, but it was slipping away. Every moment seemed to pass slowly, and each new moment might be the moment of decision. It hadn't ever been like this before. She couldn't remember any other time when she had stood with a space cleared before her and waited, not knowing for certain what she was going to do. She had always before been pushed—driven, without time to think, so that when she could think again it was too late to go back.

Sometimes it was fear that had driven her. She could not bear not to be praised and admired. The child, covering a fault with a quick lie, had grown into the woman who would ruin a man because he had slighted her.

She had not meant to ruin Car; she had only meant to force him into marrying her. Her wild accusation had not been premeditated. She had seen him look at Isobel, and had rushed from a passionate quarrel with him to his uncle, not caring what she said. Her reputation didn't matter. Nothing mattered except to damn Car in his uncle's eyes. Uncle John would make him marry her, or he would drive him from Linwood and from Isobel. After three years, she still did not know just why she had done it. Anger swept you away, and you did things, and then you couldn't go back. It had been like that ever since. She had said things that she had not meant to say, spoken aloud thoughts that she had played with—dangerously. She had acted, and been carried away by her own acting. But now she had come to a moment in which all the heat of anger, all the glamour and thrill of drama, were stripped away, and there was only fear left. If she went on, Car... She saw him in the dock, in prison. She saw him changed, coarsened, spoilt. She saw herself in the witness-box—a slim, black frock, a small, black hat, a pale profile, her emerald ring, her hands very white; Car looking at her; the judge's voice sentencing him.

The picture broke at the thrust of a stabbing pain. If she went back—she could still go back. Another picture rose up vivid and clear—Car at the chancel of Linwood church with Isobel's hand in his, and Car's voice saying "to have and to hold from this day forward." The pain stabbed again. Forward—the word stayed with her—Forward. She wasn't going back whatever happened. You couldn't really go back. She had been a fool to think of it. What? After all she had done and all she had made Bobby do? With all her plans ready and only one more step to take?

She lifted her head and saw the outer world again—the very blue sky, the green, smooth slopes running down to meet the trees, the sunshine flooding everything with gold. Her color was bright and steady as she turned at Mr. Carthew's call.

"Anna—where are my keys? I want to open the safe. Bless my soul, what have I done with them?"

XXXI

Mr. Carthew, having successfully conducted Corinna through a complete photographic record of his married life, had arrived at the next stage of the proceedings.

"People say one oughtn't to keep jewelry in the house, but I've had all my servants for years, and I trust them all just as I'd trust myself. And besides, a safe's a safe—what? No good having one if it won't keep a burglar out—that's what I say. Besides, I shouldn't like to think of my wife's things put away in a bank. Some of 'em were my mother's, and some of 'em were *her* mother's, and they've always been in this house, and they'll stay in it as long as I'm here myself."

"And no one wears them?" said Corinna. "Not ever?"

"No one's got the right to wear them," said Mr. Carthew gruffly. He dropped his voice, but he looked at Anna for a moment, and Corinna looked too; but Anna did not know that they were looking at her.

"I love seeing jewelry," said Corinna quickly. "Is there much?"

Mr. Carthew turned back the leaves of the album.

"She wore my mother's necklace to go to Court in—you can see it here. And the stars are what I gave her when we were married. But you can't see the Queen Anne bow, because it is on the other side of the bodice. Stupid of the photographer—what? But I'll show it to you."

"What is it?" asked Corinna.

"Aha! It's an heirloom. You're American—Americans like old things, don't they? It's a bow of diamonds—very fine stones—and a big emerald in the middle of it, with another one hanging down as a drop. Queen Anne gave it to my great-great-great-grandfather. And if you want to know why, I can't tell you, but it had something to do with some state secret—and if you ask me, I should say it was probably not anything very creditable, because there was a lot of dirty work going on, and the higher up you were, the more dishonest you were. So perhaps it's just as well we don't know any more about it. But it's a handsome piece of jewelry, and the emeralds are worth a lot of money. You shall see it for yourself. Now where are my keys? Anna—where are my keys? I'm going to open the safe."

Anna turned from the window and came down the room.

"Your keys, Uncle John? Haven't you got them?"

"Should I ask for 'em if I'd got 'em?"

Anna smiled.

"Well, you might. Aren't they in your pocket? Or—did you put them down under those albums?"

"Why should I do that?"

"I don't know." She smiled again, and found the keys under the corner of the largest photograph album.

Mr. Carthew took them, letting them swing and jingle.

"Pull down the blinds and put on the light," he said.

Corinna found it all very exciting. The library door was locked, the blinds pulled down, and all the electric lights put on. Then Mr. Carthew mounted three steps of a book-ladder, took down the portrait of Mrs. Carthew which hung above the mantel piece, stood it to one side of the black marble shelf, selected a key, and put it into a keyhole which hardly showed on the smooth, dark paneling.

"Good place for a safe—what?" he said, and Corinna clapped her hands. A square piece of the paneling opened like a door and showed a steel-lined cavity with three deep shelves.

It pleased Mr. Carthew enormously to have such an appreciative audience. He beckoned to Corinna to come nearer.

"And now for the Queen Anne bow! Why, bless my

soul—the case ought to be just here—just on the left of the bottom shelf! And I'll take my oath that's where I put it. Now what the deuce—I beg your pardon, my dear.'' His voice sharpened. ''Anna, come here! Where's that case! You saw me put it away. It's always in that left-hand bottom corner.''

Corinna's round eyes turned gravely from Cousin John, all flushed and stammering, to Anna. Anna was most extraordinarily pale. A moment ago she had had rather a bright color. It was all gone.

The ladder Mr. Carthew was using had three steps on either side. Anna mounted until she stood level with him. Corinna stared up at them both.

Anna said, ''It must be there.'' Her voice sounded as if she had been running.

''I tell you it's not there! And I tell you I put it there myself—what—you saw me!''

''It *must* be there,'' said Anna again. She leaned across him, looking into the safe. ''Uncle John—oh, what a fright you gave me! There it is!''

''Where? I don't see it.''

''There—on the right, by your hand—under the big, square case. Look!''

''And who put it there?'' said Mr. Carthew angrily. ''I'll swear it wasn't me. Who's been messing the things about? Who——''

He pulled out the case with a jerk. It was very rubbed and shabby and old; the leather, which had once been scarlet, was now a dim pinkish brown; the gold crown on the lid could only just be distinguished, a mere tarnished hint of royalty.

Mr. Carthew turned round, still grumbling.

''I suppose you'll say I'm losing my memory—but I never put it there, and that I'll swear to.''

Anna stepped down. She did not say a word. She kept her eyes on the table.

''Oh, do show it to us!'' said Corinna.

Mr. Carthew came down too. He opened the case, and the case was empty.

The library seemed to fill with silence. It was like water rushing into an empty place.

Mr. Carthew and Corinna both looked at what he had in his hand. The case had a satin lining, the white of which had turned to a yellowish brown. The outline of a loosely shaped bow was marked upon it, both by the dinting of the satin and by a deeper discoloration. Two brownish hollows marked the places of those emeralds which Mr. Carthew had described as worth a lot of money. From their size, he did not seem to have been guilty of overstatement.

Anna looked too, and then looked away.

Corinna spoke first. She said in a whisper,

"It's gone!"

And then, to her own surprise, her legs began to tremble so much that she looked round for a chair and sat down abruptly.

"What's it mean?" said Mr. Carthew in an odd, troubled voice.

Then, with sudden passion, "What's it mean? *Anna!*" The word came out with explosive force. Then, checking himself, he advanced to the table and put down the empty case.

As if his voice, speaking her name in that sharp peremptory way, had called her from the wings where like many another actress she had been standing dumb with stage-fright, Anna started, drew on that sense of drama which never left her for very long, and took up her part. It was the first step, the first plunge, that stopped one's breath and set one's heart thudding. She heard herself say, "It *must* be there," and approved the low shocked tone that contradicted the assertion.

It was she who rummaged in the safe, handing things down to Corinna until nothing more remained, whilst John Carthew stood half turned away, looking, still looking, at the empty case.

When the safe had been cleared, he roused himself and displayed a sudden energy. Everything was to be put back, the safe re-locked, the picture hung, the blinds drawn up.

When the sun was slanting in again, he slipped the case

into his pocket. He looked older. His sudden energy had failed. He leaned with one hand on the table.

"What are you going to do?" said Corinna, and Anna blessed her for the question. In another moment she would have had to ask it herself.

"Do?" said Mr. Carthew. "Do? The thing's an heirloom. It's got to be found." He straightened himself up as if his own loud voice had encouraged him. "What do we have police for? If we have got a Socialist government, we haven't got to the point where a burglar can break into my safe and take a family heirloom and get away with it—no, by jingo, we haven't, though that's where we're heading for! Thank God, I shan't be here to see it! Law and order'll last my time, and an heirloom's an heirloom. It don't belong to me—it belongs to all the Carthews—it belongs——" His voice had been dropping; now it ceased.

Corinna thrilled to the broken sentence. Was it Car's name that had broken it? Anna knew that it was, and a rising passion swept away her last qualm.

"You can't call in the police," she said in a hard, dogmatic tone.

Mr. Carthew stiffened at once.

"I can't—what? And why not?"

Corinna saw his angry flash, and remembered Car saying, "He's all right as long as you don't cross him. He likes his own way." Funny that Anna shouldn't have known better than to lay down the law to him like that, and to keep on doing it in the face of his rising anger.

"It will make such a talk."—Anna, pale and shrinking.

"And why the deuce should I care about that?"—Cousin John, the very image of the old squire who is just going to turn an erring daughter out into the snow.

"But, Uncle John, you can't!"

"And why can't I? And whose business is it except my own?"

"You mustn't!"

"Mustn't I—what?"—and a snort of wrath and the click of the telephone.

Corinna, standing back against the mantelpiece, a little abashed at this frank lapse into family manners, turned a pitying glance on Anna. Cousin John had just sworn—yes, really sworn at her. She received a shock, because, just for an instant as the angry man shouted into the telephone, a fleeting look changed Anna's shocked pallor into something else and Corinna thought that the something else was triumph.

XXXII

MISS WILLY TARRANT LIVED IN A DUMPY BRICK HOUSE exactly half-way down the village street. The original small casements of the two front rooms having been replaced by generous bow windows Miss Willy commanded a view of practically every front door in Linwood. She knew at once when Dr. Monk had been sent for to a case, or when the Vicar, to whom time meant nothing, was going to be late for church. She could follow him from a few feet within his own hall door all the way to the vestry, and if the vestry door had been left open, she would have been able to watch him robing. This from the dining-room.

The drawing-room afforded her a perfect view of the interior of the local grocery, a partial one of old Mrs. Hoylake's parlor, and, if she leaned out, an opportunity of seeing Linwood buy its Saturday joints from Mr. Brown the butcher.

Very little went on in Linwood about which Miss Willy did not know at least as much as the people immediately concerned. Sometimes it might be said that she knew a good deal more. She could certainly tell the Vicar just what was wrong with his sermons, and how to improve them; whilst she never met Dr. Monk without contending for the superior efficacy of some specific of her own. She had a finger in every pie, and a better way of baking it than the one which you had always thought quite good enough.

On the morning after Mr. Carthew's wedding-day anniversary Miss Willy was in her dining-room cleaning the cages inhabited respectively by a pink and gray parrot called Archibald, a pair of small, green parakeets, a very large and highly colored macaw, an invisible dormouse, and an elderly and partially bald, white rat. Whilst the cages were being cleaned, their tenants disported themselves about the room, with the exception of the dormouse, who remained obstinately in seclusion, although he should not have begun to think about hibernating for an least another month.

Miss Willy was so busy for once in a way that she did not observe the approach of Mrs. Hoylake's son Bert with the post. She heard the rat-tat too late to get to the door and detain him for news of his wife's sister Ellen, who had married a cousin of Mr. Carthew's second gardener and had just had twins. Miss Willy had the greatest possible contempt for Ellen's mother's views on the upbringing of babies, and she wanted to tell Bert Hoylake so, and to urge him on no account to allow his mother-in-law to give Ellen any advice about the twins. She might have caught him if Rollo, the raven, had not been immediately in front of the door. Rollo required careful handling and had to be coaxed away, by which time the only sign of Bert was the small parcel which he had pushed into the letter-box.

Miss Willy picked the parcel up and went back into the dining-room, where she was greeted by loud squawks of welcome from Archibald, who was climbing methodically up the left-hand curtain, and from the macaw, who was perched on the back of one of the dining-room chairs. She looked round anxiously for the rat, Augustus, because he was not very good at getting out of the way, and, if trodden on, was apt to retaliate. His teeth were still quite good.

When she had located him under the table, she opened

the parcel. It was small, about five inches by two, and it excited her curiosity very much. She had cut the string and was unfolding the brown paper, when the front door knocker fell twice with a sharp, clear rap.

Miss Willy looked out of the window, which commanded almost as good view of her own front door as of her neighbor's, and to her great delight saw Anna Lang standing on the step with her hand just raised to knock again.

Miss Willy tapped the window-pane sharply and screamed through the glass,

"Come in! Come in! Mabel's busy, and so am I—and Isobel's out."

Anna nodded and opened the door. Everything was going very nicely. She had watched Bert Hoylake deliver the parcel, and within the next half-hour the telegram should arrive. Isobel would certainly not leave Linwood House for at least an hour, since, after she and Corinna had stopped talking, Uncle John could be trusted to keep her for at least another half-hour. He liked Isobel. He liked her so much that nothing but the particular lie which Anna had told him would have prevented him from welcoming her as Car's wife with a good deal of pleasure. As a rule, Anna took care that his opportunities of talking to Isobel were strictly limited, but to-day he might make the most of them.

Anna opened the dining-room door, and was greeted by a chorus of shrieks and squawks through which Miss Willy could be heard screaming, first at her and then at the noisy parrot.

"Come in! Shut the door! *Shut the door!* Be quiet, Archibald!—*Archibald! Will* you be quiet! Shut that door, or Rollo will get out! Where is he? Rollo, where are you? Oh, come in—come *in!* And mind don't step on Augustus—he's somewhere about, but I don't know where."

Anna's color became noticeably less decorative. She had no affection for creatures, and on any other occasion she would have fled. She cast an anxious look about the room. Archibald always bit her if he could; but he had reached the curtain pole, where he stood clapping his wings and improvising a very fair imitation of a whining dog. The macaw really terrified her; but he appeared to be engaged in a careful toilet with one wing stretched out to its fullest extent and all his brilliant blue and yellow and crimson a-dazzle in the sun which shone straight into the room. Augustus made her feel sick, but as she looked about for him, she saw him run up Miss Willy's dress and come to rest upon her shoulder. Miss Willy said, "Did'ums, the bad boy?" and Anna hastily pulled the nearest chair to a safe distance and sat down. Rollo had gone under the table, and the parakeets were climbing ceaselessly over the outside of their cage.

"I hope you don't mind my coming when you're so busy," Anna began in a deprecating tone. "I know you are always busy in the morning, and so am I, but I thought I might just slip down for a minute whilst Isobel was talking to Corinna. I do so want to ask you about Lydia Pratt."

"Don't talk of her!" said Miss Willy with a snort. "A bad, ungrateful girl if there ever was one! We got her a good place between us, and she's leaving at the month because she's only allowed out once a week. I can't think what girls are coming to!"

On almost any other day Lydia Pratt's enormities would have taken at least half an hour to discuss, but on this particular morning Miss Willy had no intention of wasting time on Lydia. If Anna had not come to see her, she would within the hour have been on her way to see Anna, armed as likely as not with the same excuse. However that might be, Lydia Pratt had now definitely served her turn.

With Augustus sitting up on her shoulder industriously washing his whiskers, Miss Willy turned and faced her caller.

"Never mind Lydia," she said, "I've heard a most extraordinary rumor, and I want to know if it's true."

"What have you heard?" asked Anna quickly.

"That you've had a burglary. Anna—you don't say it's true—not really? I couldn't believe it!"

"But how did you hear? We haven't told any one. Uncle John——"

"You haven't told the police?"

"Not the local police. Uncle John rang up Scotland Yard."

"Who of course communicated with the local people—now didn't they?"

"Well—you won't repeat this, Miss Willy—we have had an inspector from Southerley to see us. Uncle John wasn't very pleased about it. I think he wishes now that he had waited—employed a private detective or—oh, don't take any notice of what I'm saying! It's all very, very distressing. Uncle John is quite ill. We don't want it talked about."

"Now what's the good of saying that? You want the widest possible publicity—then every one in the community is on the look out and can help you to catch your thief. You ought to have a description of whatever has been stolen circulated to all police stations, and pawnbrokers, and—and—people of that sort." She made a wide gesture with her hand which startled Augustus a good deal and made Cyril the macaw interrupt his toilet and fix her with a bright glassy stare.

"I believe that has been done," said Anna. "I wish—oh, I wish it hadn't!"

"Nonsense!" said Miss Willy. "The more publicity the better—you can't have too much."

"How did you hear about it?"

"Joskins brought the first rumor with the afternoon milk. I suppose he'd just been up to Linwood House."

"But the servants didn't know—we didn't tell them."

Miss Willy sniffed.

"Joskins knew. He said it was the Queen Anne bow that had gone. It is? Then he was right! Just that and nothing more. I'd have come up yesterday myself, only I had an old engagement to go out to tea at Wood End with Lady Silver, and she kept me and kept me to see her sister who was coming down by train, and in the end she never came, and I didn't get home till half-past seven, and the telephone has been out of order for two days—they'd only just got it right when Corinna rang Isobel up. It was most tantalizing, because of course I was simply dying to hear all about it.

Was the house broken into? Joskins said not, but Mrs. Hoylake told me that Annie's young man—not Brent, but the new one—his name is Mullins and he drives one of the vans of those big grocery people in Southerley—what's their name—Downings—well, he told Annie that his cousin, Ernest Mullins, who's in the police, told him that the Inspector told him in confidence that he shouldn't wonder if it was an inside job.''

Anna leaned back in her chair. The room swam for a moment. Suppose they thought—suppose they guessed. No—*no!* She dug her nails into the palm of her hand. It was Car who was going to be suspected—Car who *must* be suspected, now that things had gone so far. She was quite safe really. The jewel would be found on Car, and then Dr. Monk would remember that he had seen him in Linwood at midnight. What a blessing she had thought of Dr. Monk! He would remember quite a lot of useful things—Uncle John's sudden illness; her own agitation; the disturbed bureau; the keys lying where some one had flung them down. She recovered her self-possession.

''What's the matter?'' said Miss Willy.

''It's been—such a shock,'' she faltered. ''I—I can't bear to talk about it. Dear Miss Willy—you're so kind—you'll understand there are—*reasons* why I can't talk about it.''

''Not one of the servants?'' said Miss Willy breathlessly. ''Why, they've all been with you at least five years, except Gladys Brown, and her people are so respectable that I couldn't believe—though of course where young men are concerned you never can tell—only she's walking out with that particularly nice George Alton. Don't say it's Gladys!''

''Oh, no.''

''Though of course having been with you for years doesn't really prove anything, because my cousin Wilfred Earl's mother-in-law had a butler for sixteen years and never knew that she only got half the cigars that were down in her bill—but Wilfred assured me it was a fact. But of course cigars are one thing, and an heirloom is quite another pair of shoes. Was there anything else taken?''

Anna shook her head. The telegram ought to arrive soon—Bobby was to have sent it off half an hour ago. She looked at the half-opened parcel lying on the table against the parakeet's cage.

"Has any one been sending you a present?" she asked with the forced lightness of some one who must at any cost change the subject.

"No—I don't know—I haven't opened it—I don't know what it is." Miss Willy picked up the wrapping and turned it this way and that. "I can't make head or tail of the postmark, and I don't know the writing—though of course that's nothing to go by, because one's pen always sticks so on brown paper, and it simply ruins the nib. No—I can't think *who* it can be from."

"Why don't you open it?" suggested Anna.

"Well," said Miss Willy, "there's something fascinating about guessing. I always think I should have made a good detective—you may have noticed that I am very observant. The other day, when I was visiting Mrs. Pratt, I knew at once that Lydia was leaving Mrs. Greenway. I didn't wait for her to tell me. I walked in and sat down and said straight away, 'Now what's all this, Mrs. Pratt?' And she couldn't believe that some one hadn't told me. And I said to her, 'Well, they haven't—but when I see a letter from Lydia lying open in your work-box with things like "lots of good places" and "home Thursday week" staring me in the face, I can put two and two together without requiring any one to tell me that they make four. And if I'm to say what I think, Mrs. Pratt,' I said, 'Lydia is a bad, ungrateful girl, and she wants a good scolding, and not to be spoilt and made much of the way you've always done, and I only hope you won't live to regret it when it's too late—and then perhaps you'll remember that I warned you, Mrs. Pratt.' "

"Won't you open your parcel?" said Anna gently. The telegram might come at any minute now.

The wrapping had slipped to the floor whilst Miss Willy discoursed. It lay against the table leg. Rollo regarded it with a cocked head and inquisitive eye.

Miss Willy took up a small box in an inner wrapping of white paper. It was tied with string and sealed on either side with red sealing-wax. The impression on the wax had been made with a threepenny bit.

"How extraordinary!" said Miss Willy. She stared at the white paper and the name that was written there. "Car! It's addressed to Car—to Car Fairfax! How extraordinary!"

Under the table, Rollo extended a cautious claw, closed it on the corner of the fallen wrapper, and began with the help of his beak to drag it away. With an eye on the shelter afforded by the coal-scuttle and a fire-screen, he emerged on Anna's side of the table, saw her, squawked, and retreated, dropping the paper.

Anna stooped, picked it up deftly, and slipped it into her bag before Miss Willy had finished exclaiming,

"My dear Anna, isn't it a most extraordinary thing that any one should send a parcel for Car Fairfax here—to *me?* Why, I don't even know his address. Do you?"

"No, I don't. It's—it's been a complete separation."

Miss Willy looked up, brightly alert.

"Why, my dear? Why? I've always wanted to ask you that. I did ask John—and very rude he was, I consider. Whilst we're on the subject—what did Car do?"

Anna looked away. The hand she put to her cheek did not hide her evident distress.

"Don't ask me—*please*, Miss Willy. We try to forget about it."

Miss Willy tossed her head.

"If you ask me, John doesn't have to try very hard. He wants Car back, doesn't he? Well, I won't ask any questions if I'm not to be told anything, though I must say such an old friend——" She tossed her head again, and Augustus backed away until he over-balanced and fell scrambling to the floor.

Anna tucked her feet up on the rail of her chair. She had a horror of rats.

"There, Gussy—*there!*" Miss Willy's apology was rather perfunctory. She returned to the little white box. "What in the world am I to do with this, when I don't know where he is?"

"I thought you wrote to him the other day."

"Who told you that?" said Miss Willy sharply.

"You told me yourself. You said you were asking him to stay."

Miss Willy's florid color deepened unbecomingly. She was wearing a tight jumper of faded pink wool and an old red Cashmire skirt. Her hair was wild. At some time after getting up she had poked a pencil through it; it now stuck out at a rakish angle over her left ear. She wore about her neck a cerise ribbon tied in a bow, a thin steel chain holding a pair of scissors and small brass key, and another chain, of gold with an occasional pearl, from which depended a pair of tortoise shell-rimmed pince-nez. Her short, ugly fingers were covered to the knuckles with old-fashioned and very dirty rings.

"Yes, I asked him," she said angrily. "Isobel made me ask him. And all the thanks I got for it was a refusal."

"Then you've got his address?"

"Isobel has it," said Miss Willy—"or I suppose so. I never remember addresses myself."

Anna clenched her hand. How much longer was she to sit here and talk about Car? What was Bobby doing? Why didn't that telegram come?

"If John Carthew had taken my advice——" said Miss Willy.

The telephone bell rang a yard away in the window.

Miss Willy jerked around, took up the receiver, and stood with her back to the room. Over her head on the curtain pole Archibald imitated the bell and the click, and then proceeded to say "Hullo-ullo-ullo-ullo-*ullo!*" The sound pleased him; he pursued it through various keys.

"Ssh!" said Miss Willy. Then, to the telephone, "What did you say? . . . Yes, this is two-one-six. . . . Yes, I said so before—Archibald, *hush!* . . . Yes, I keep telling you I am. If you've got a telegram for me, will you kindly let me have it!"

Anna drew a breath of relief. Now that the telegram had

come, there could be no going back. It was curious how this thought kept recurring. She listened with strained attention whilst Miss Willy bickered with the exchange.

"My good woman, if you've got a telegram, let me have it! . . . No, I can't hear you. Kindly remember that you're three miles away and raise your voice a little—Archibald, *will* you be quiet!"

She turned at last, looking red and determined.

"Talk of the old gentleman! Here's Car wiring to Isobel to meet him in town this evening!"

Anna's heart jumped. If the telegram had really been from Car, she would hardly have felt her jealously flame up more fiercely.

Miss Willy had taken pencil and paper and was writing the message down, saying each word aloud as she wrote it:

"Meet—me—Olding—Crescent—Putney—eight-thirty—to-night—very—urgent—indeed—Car."

She jabbed her pencil down on the stop at the end and broke the point.

"Oh," said Anna, "you won't let her go?"

"Let?" said Miss Willy in a loud offended voice. "*Let?*"

"Isobel wouldn't go if you didn't want her to!" Anna was gently shocked. "Oh, Miss Willy—surely you won't let her go!"

"Isobel goes as she likes," said Miss Willy.

"Against your wishes?"

Miss Willy achieved a masterly change of position.

"And why should it be against my wishes?" she said. She came over to the dining-table and picked up the little white box. "As a matter of fact it will be very convenient. She can spend the night with Carrie, and she can give Car his packet. It will all fit in quite nicely, because Mrs. Messiter is coming down to stay with me for a couple of days, so I shan't be alone and Isobel can match my violet ribbon and get several other things I forgot last time I was in town." She turned the box this way and that. "Dear me, what an extraordinary thing! The writing is exactly like Isobel's."

Anna stood up. She stood and looked at the packet, with its red seal and Car's name on it in a hand carefully like Isobel's.

"Yes—isn't it? I wonder——" She broke off. "No, of course it couldn't be. You won't tell her I said that—will you?"

"Why should I?"

"No—of course you wouldn't. The whole thing's so strange—isn't it? I was just wondering—but it doesn't do with Isobel—does it? I think your way's much the best, really. Asking questions might just put her off telling you anything; but if you don't ask or make anything of it, she's sure to tell you all about it afterwards. I think it's very clever of you—but then you are very clever with Isobel—and with every one else too. I often wonder how you do it."

As she said the last word, a slight hissing sound disturbed the pleasant consciousness of having done a difficult job really well. She turned her head and saw the macaw a foot away. He must have slipped down from his chair back and approached with the greatest caution. He stood now on one leg, both wings extended, his head craned forward, his beak half open showing a horny tongue, and his round glittering eyes fixed maliciously upon her left ankle. A little more self-restraint and he would have achieved his object; but the hiss of triumph had escaped too soon.

As Anna turned, Miss Willy screamed and clapped her hands.

"Cyril! *Cyril!* Bad, wicked bird! *Anna!*"

Anna was already at the door, and the baffled Cyril retreated to his chair back with a scream of rage.

"I must go," said Anna breathlessly. She blew a kiss and slipped through the door. "Dear Miss Willy, good-by! I'll send Isobel back."

She shut the door.

Miss Willy gazed at Cyril with fond reproach.

"Mother's very, *very* worst boy!" she said.

Cyril screamed again.

XXXIII

(September 25th; BUT THE DIARY WAS NOT WRITTEN UP until later.)

Nothing happened all day until the evening. That is to say, I met Fay on the doorstep. I can't remember where I'd been, and it doesn't matter. I'm afraid I rather barged past her, because she seemed to want to stop and speak, and I was still angry. She had said some perfectly beastly things about Isobel which I haven't written down. I was trying to forget about them, but I hadn't got as far as passing the time of day with her just as if nothing had happened. Afterwards I felt as if I'd been rather a beast, because she was looking most awfully ill—white as a sheet, with black saucers under her eyes, and her hat was crooked. I don't think she was bothering about how she looked; and that's not a bit like Fay. I didn't think about any of this at the time, but it came back later on.

I walked down to Putney, and got to Olding Crescent at about a quarter to eight, just in case Isobel was early. Ever since her telegram came I had been racking my brains to think of any possible reason that would make her ask me to meet her like this, but I couldn't think of one. I was afraid she must be in trouble, but I couldn't think what sort of trouble it could possibly be. I kept going over all sorts of things in my mind.

It was a most awfully dark night. The whole sky was covered with the even darkness of clouds that are hanging so low that they seem to be a ceiling over your head. It wasn't raining, and it didn't rain; but there was the feeling of rain in the air. Every now and then the bushes, and the great sweeping branches of the trees overhead, moved and rustled in a sudden wind that was wet against one's face. The street-lamps gave hardly any light, and the shadow under the wall was as black as coal.

I walked up and down. I was going to see Isobel! Then I laughed, because I certainly shouldn't be able to see her unless I marched her up to one of the lamps and stood her there with her head well up facing it. And then I stopped laughing, because, of course, when you love any one very much, you don't just see them with your eyes.

I walked up and down for about three-quarters of an hour, but the time didn't seem at all long. Waiting for Isobel to come was like watching a wonderful tide of happiness rise. It seemed to come up all round me with bright, shining waves. I hadn't been so happy for years, and I couldn't help wondering whether she was happy too. I ought not to have let myself get into that state of mind. I thought of that afterwards, but at the time I just thought about Isobel.

And then she came. I must have been waiting for three-quarters of an hour, and no one had passed at all either coming or going. Olding Crescent is the loneliest place I have ever been in. There are houses all along one side of it, but no one ever seems to go into them or come out, and the windows do not let out a single spark of light. So when I heard a footstep, I was quite sure that it was the footstep I was waiting for.

She came from the direction of the main road, passed the lamp, and then stood hesitating. I could see her, and yet I couldn't. What I saw was a coat and skirt, and shoes and stocking, and a scarf, and a little close hat, all dark like the shadows of clothes. But I couldn't see Isobel herself, because she was a shadow too. I felt as if I should see her better if I didn't have to look at the shadows.

I came across the road, and she ran to me and slipped a hand through my arm.

"Car——" she said in a sweet, breathless voice, and we went back across the road into the black dark where the trees hung over the wall. Then—I don't know how it happened, but of course it must have been my fault—that shining tide of Isobel just carried me away. She was so near, and I could feel her trembling a little, and she pressed against me. And the thing I knew I had my arms round her and we were kissing each other.

I didn't feel as if it could be true. I never thought I should kiss Isobel really. I kissed her once in a dream, and it nearly killed me to wake up and know that it could never come true. I don't know how long we stood there without speaking. I had nothing to say, because I felt as if Isobel must know every thought I had, or ever could have.

She had put her arms round my neck, and after we had kissed she leaned her head against my shoulder and we stood like that, drowned fathoms deep in happiness. I didn't think about the past, or the future, or what we were going to do, or even why we were there. I've heard people talk about the world standing still, but now I know what they mean. The world stood still for us, and time went by.

I came very slowly back to realize what I had done. Then I said her name, and she said mine. I didn't know that my name could sound like that. It carried me off my feet again, but I made myself come back. I said,

"You mustn't."

And Isobel said, "Why?" and then, "Oh, foolish Car, don't you know——"

"We mustn't," I said. "I—I've no right. I'm—a brute. I didn't mean——"

Isobel said things I can't write down. She said she had been very unhappy. She said she wasn't engaged to Giles Heron. She said she had cared for me always. It didn't seem possible. I felt as if I had walked straight into a dream, and that presently I should wake up and find that it wasn't true. I said this to Isobel, and she said,

"Oh, Car darling, it's my dream too, and I don't think we shall ever wake up."

I don't know how long it was before I realized that it must be getting late. She hadn't told me why she had asked me to meet her, and it didn't seem to matter much; it was just one of the things that had got left behind when we went into the dream together.

I said, "It's getting late."

And she said, "It doesn't matter—I'm staying with Aunt Carrie."

And then she told me that they'd had a burglary at Linwood House, and that the Queen Anne bow had been taken. She said my uncle was dreadfully upset. And she went on to beg me to make up our quarrel. She said any one could see how much he wanted me back.

I told her what I had told her before, that I couldn't take the first step. I couldn't get her to understand about that— but he sent me away, and I think it's up to him to say if he wants me back.

"There's the little Manor House," said Isobel. She put her head against my shoulder. "Car, I've always wanted to live there. It—it would be heavenly."

I came out of the dream and shut the door behind me.

"My darling," I said, "the only house we shall ever have is a castle in the air. You oughtn't to have come here, and we ought not to have met—and the best thing you can do is to go back to Linwood and forget."

"After *this*?" said Isobel, and she kissed me.

I put her away.

"Yes, my darling," I said.

She laughed. She has such a pretty laugh, but it had a sad sound in it then.

"I'm not very clever at forgetting, Car."

"You must."

"I've tried for three years—no, that's not true—I've never tried to forget you, and I never shall. I'd rather be unhappy—I'd rather break my heart. But it won't break unless you forget *me*, or go away where I can't come. You mustn't do that again. My heart did nearly break three years ago when you went away without a word. It ached so dreadfully. Oh, Car, you won't make it ache that way again—will you?''

She was crying, and I had to comfort her. It broke my heart to think of all the times she had cried without any comfort.

In the end I had to promise not to disappear again. She said she could bear it if she knew where I was, and if we wrote to each other. When that was settled we both felt much happier, though I oughtn't to have promised, and I was worried about it afterwards. At the time I just banged my conscience on the head and told it to shut up.

And then I thought I'd better find out why she had asked me to meet her. I was just going to, when she said,

"What did you want to see me about?"

She would have seen how surprised I was if it hadn't been so dark.

I said, "*I?*" and then I laughed. "That's funny—that's what I was going to ask you."

"What do you mean?"

"I was going to ask why you wired me to meet you here. I've been racking my brains ever since I got the telegram, but I couldn't think of a reason."

"Car—stop!" she shook my arm. "What do you mean? I didn't wire to you—there wasn't time. I just came."

I began to have an odd, excited feeling.

"I think we're at cross purposes," I said. "Why did you come here?"

"Because you asked me to," she said.

This was news to me of course.

"Oh, I asked you? How did I ask you?"

"Car—what is it? I don't understand. You wired to me to meet you here. You said 'Very urgent.' I was spending the morning with Corinna, and I just got back in time to snatch some lunch and catch the two-forty at Bidwell. You know there's nothing after that till six unless one goes into Ledlington, and I wanted to leave my bag at Aunt Carrie's.

It was such a rush. Anna was with Miss Willy when the telegram came, but she forgot to tell me about it, so I had to hurry like anything.''

"You got a wire from me?" I said. I could hardly believe my ears.

"Yes, of course."

"And I got one from you," I said. "Is that of course too?"

She drew a very quick breath and pressed against me.

"No—no! Car—I didn't wire to you at all—I told you I didn't."

"Neither did I wire to you, Isobel."

"*Car*—oh—what does it mean?"

I felt her trembling.

"I don't know," I said, "I got a wire which was signed Isobel. It said, 'Must see you. Very urgent indeed. Meet me Olding Crescent Putney eight-thirty to-night.''

"I never sent it," said Isobel. "Miss Willy said a telegram had been telephoned through from Bidwell. She took it down as it came through. It said, 'Meet me Olding Crescent Putney eight-thirty to-night. Very urgent indeed. Car.' Didn't you send it?"

"No, I didn't."

"Then who—Oh, Car, I don't like it!"

I didn't like it either. It might be a practical joke, or it might be something else—I didn't quite know what. But all of a sudden I wanted Isobel to go almost as badly as I had wanted her to come. If she and I had been brought here to serve some one else's purpose—and that was what it began to look like—well, I wasn't for it, and the sooner I got her away the better.

I put my arm round her and began to walk her down the dark side of the road towards the main street. I don't know what it's called, but it's quite brightly lighted, and there are buses that ply over Putney Bridge. My idea was to put Isobel on to a bus and push her off to Mrs. Lester's, whilst I hung about a bit to see whether anything turned up.

Isobel was rather intractable about leaving me to it, but in the end she saw that I really meant what I said, and that if she stayed, I should only be thinking of her, and no earthly good as a sleuth.

We were waiting for a bus, when all of a sudden she dived into her bag and fished out a little white parcel.

"Here's another mysterious thing."

"What is it?"

"I don't know. It's for you."

She put it into my hand, and I read my own name on the white paper wrapping.

"Where did you get it?" I asked.

"Aunt Willy gave it to me just as I was starting."

"*Miss Willy?*"

"She said it came by post."

"This hasn't been through the post," I said.

Isobel turned her head and looked at me with wide, startled eyes. She opened her lips to speak but over her shoulder I saw the bus swing into sight, and I wasn't going to have her miss it for twenty mysterious packages. I slipped it into my pocket and stepped out into the road with my hand up.

XXXIV

WHEN THE BUS WAS OUT OF SIGHT, I WENT BACK INTO Olding Crescent, keeping on the dark side of the road. I couldn't make out in the least what sort of game this was; but it was clear enough that Isobel and I were being used as pawns in it, and I'd a fancy to see if I couldn't knock the board over and start a game of my own—and in that game I should be king, and Isobel would be queen.

I was a bit above myself, and no wonder. It was three years since I had dreamed that I should ever tell Isobel what I felt about her, and even three years ago I never got as far as thinking what it would feel like to hear her say the things she had said to me tonight. It didn't seem possible; but if it was possible, then everything I had ever hoped for or dreamed about was possible too. I wanted to sing and shout. I wanted to do something difficult and dangerous. I felt as if I could tackle anybody or anything. I suppose I as really quite drunk with happiness.

I walked as far as the door in the wall, and there I stopped. My idea, if I had one, had been to hand about for a bit and see whether anything happened. The door in the wall struck me as being the sort of place where things might begin to happen.

Well, I waited. Times goes slowly when you are waiting in the dark. That breath of rain had cleared off. The wind had dropped. It was dead still, with not a leaf moving. I thought I should hear a footstep a long way off, but no footstep came. It seemed to get darker and stiller every moment. The sky seemed to be pressing down on the top of my head, and the houses opposite were like a lot of dead things.

I slipped my hand into my pocket and touched the packet which Isobel had brought. And when I touched it, I wanted to know what as inside it, and I wanted to know it so badly that I couldn't wait another minute. I was tired of waiting there now—I wanted to do something.

I crossed over on a long slant and made for the nearest lamp. It was pretty dim and dull. I stood right under it and opened the packet. First there was a sheet of white note-paper, and then there was one of those long match-boxes, the sort that you buy full of vestas. I didn't some how think it was full of vestas now.

The box was full of little paper packets done up like powders from a chemist. One of them had fallen. I stooped down and picked it up. It had initials on it: A—J—

I put it back in the box and picked up another. This one had initials too, printed like the other: J—S—

The others were all the same. The only thing that was different was the initials. There were a dozen packages. I opened one of them, and there was a white powder in it. I shut it up again and put it back in the box.

I began to have the strongest feeling that there was something beastly about the whole thing. I thought of Fay and her yarn about the man Fosicker, who had got her to peddle drugs for him. I thought about Isobel getting a telegram from me, and me getting a telegram from Isobel, when neither of us had sent a telegram at all, and it came over me with a rush that I was being an absolutely prize mutt to hang around and wait for trouble. I felt a solid conviction that trouble was coming, and it seemed to me that if I didn't want it to hit me like a cartload of bricks, I'd better vamoose.

I went straight back across the road and chucked the match-box over the wall. And then I made tracks for home.

It was a good bit past ten when I got in. All the landings were dark, because Mrs. Bell turns out the gas at ten o'clock. She puts candles in the hall as a rule, but I couldn't find mine, so I supposed she'd forgotten I was out. I didn't bother, because I know the way so well, and I went as softly as I could, because if she hears you and comes up, it's ten to one you don't get away under twenty minutes—"Riotous living," and texts, and how her husband was always in bed at half-past nine, and what a steady young man her son was.

When I got up on to my landing, there was a light under my door. First I wondered whether I had left the gas on, and then I remembered going back from the top of the stairs to turn it out.

I walked up to the door and opened it.

Fay turned round to meet me with a scream. She had on a black dressing-gown and bright green pyjamas, and she had all my clothes out of the wardrobe and lying about in heaps. I felt pretty wild. They were all new clothes, and if there's a thing I hate, it's having my things messed about.

I said she screamed, but that's not quite correct. She turned round, and her mouth opened, but only a sort of a ghost of a scream came out of it. It was like watching some one scream in a film.

"What do you think you're doing?" I said pretty shortly. Fay caught at the table. She looked ghastly.

"Oh!" she said. "You've got it on!"

"Talk sense!" I said. "What are you doing in my room?"

She began to cry. She didn't make any noise about it; the tears just began to fall down her face, and her mouth kept moving as if she was trying to say something.

I came round the table and took her by the shoulder.

"Stop it!" I said. "You've no business here, and you know it. What are you doing with my clothes?"

She caught with both hands at the coat I was wearing. It was one of my new ones, a blue serge got out of the Z.10 money—Blake had made it rather well.

"I've been looking for it. I couldn't find it," she said in a whisper.

I thought she'd gone right off her head, because what she was saying didn't make sense. She kept on saying it, too: "I tried to find it—I did try—but you've got it on." I thought it was no good being angry if she wasn't right in her head, so I spoke as kindly as I could.

"Of course I've got it on! Now you buzz off to bed. It's most awfully late."

She gave a start when I said that.

"It's not too late—not yet. Take it off! I've got my scissors—I brought them. Quick, Car—quick!"

And then, I suppose, she saw my face and tumbled to what I was thinking. She let go of me, and I could see her pulling herself together. She didn't look mad, but she looked desperate.

"I've only got a minute to tell you, and you *must* believe me! The police will be here in a minute."

"The police!" I said.

I don't know why I believed it, but I did. I didn't think any more about her being mad. I suppose it was because she was so tremendously in earnest; and she was frightened, really frightened too.

"They're coming!" she said, and as she said it, there came the sound of heavy knocking on the front door.

A most dreadful look of fear passed over her face.

"Car—Car—*Car!*" she gasped.

I'm afraid I spoke roughly. I think I shook her.

"Look here—if you've got anything to say, say it!"

She spoke then in a whisper.

"It's the Queen Anne bow. It's sewn into the lining of your coat—the one you've got on!"

I said, "Nonsense!"

The knocking had stopped for a moment, but it began again. Fay went on speaking:

"I put it there—I sewed it in the coat you've got on. They'll find it and send you to prison. I did it because I was angry with you, and because of Isobel. If you'd spoken a kind word to me, I wouldn't have done it—but you didn't— and she said she'd get me sent to prison—"

I said, "What?"

Fay said, "She *did* say it—she *did!*"

"What are you talking about.? *Who* are you talking about?"

"Miss Lang. She hates you. What have you done to make her hate you like that? She knows all about what Fosicker made me do. She gave me the bow and told me to sew it into your coat. She said she'd get me sent to prison if I didn't—but I wouldn't have done it if you'd said a single kind word." She was crying all the time and twisting her fingers together. I didn't know she knew what she was saying.

I ran my hands over my coat, and sure enough there was something flat and hard between the lining and the hem.

Fay went on whispering and crying:

"I came up to take it out again—but you'd got the coat on. They'll send you to prison."

I saw the whole thing in a flash of light. It takes time to write about it, but the flash didn't seem to take any time at all. If the police found the Queen Anne bow sewn into the lining of my coat, I could only clear myself by accusing Fay. If I wanted to keep Fay out of it, I'd got to get away before the police broke in.

The banging on the front door was loud enough to wake

the dead. If it didn't wake Mrs. Bell in a minute or two, I imagined they would break in. I saw all that, and at the same moment I saw the trap-door which opens from my landing into the loft, and the ladder which Mrs. Bell kept in the corner of the attic.

I shook Fay really hard.

"Stop behaving like an idiot and help me! I'm going to get away through the loft. Pull yourself together!"

I didn't know whether she was going to be any use or not. If she wasn't, I was done. I got the ladder into position, and the trap-door open. Fay stood leaning against the door of my room, shivering and watching me. I climbed into the loft and called to her.

"Put the ladder back in the attic and shut the door! Put out the light in my room and shut that door too! Then go down to your own room and get into bed! Do you hear?"

She said "Yes"—or I thought she did—it was all mixed up with catching her breath and crying.

I couldn't afford to wait, because I could hear Mrs. Bell coming up the basement stairs, so I said "Look sharp!" and I shut down the trap-door and pulled an old tin box full of books over it.

The loft ran all across the middle of the house. There was a skylight at one end of it. I got it open and crawled out on to the wet, cold slope of the roof.

XXXV

I SHUT THE SKYLIGHT BEHIND ME. I WAS ON A STEEPISH slope which ran down to meet the next house. I slid down into the trough between the two houses. It was dark, but not quite dark. I could see the edge of the roof, and I could see above me the twin skylight to the one I had just come out of. It wasn't so easy to climb up as it had been to slide down, and when I got there, the window was bolted on the inside—at least I suppose it was bolted, for I couldn't get it to budge. I slid down again into the trough and went and looked over the edge. There was a nasty long drop to the street. The knocking had stopped. That meant that the police were in the house—talking to Mrs. Bell, perhaps searching my room, perhaps finding the ladder still propped against the trap-door.

I went to the back of the house and looked over there. If Fay had kept her head and put the ladder away, and if I hadn't been seen letting myself into the house, they might just go away after searching my room. There were too many ifs. They had probably had a man watching for me to come home. I couldn't risk staying where I was, and there was only one way of getting anywhere else, and that was over the ridge of the roof. I didn't like the idea a bit, but I liked it better than being caught with the Queen Anne bow on me.

I crawled to the ridge and slid down on the other side. Two more slopes, and two more skylights, and both of them bolted. I made up my mind to go on. If I found an open skylight, I might be able to get away; and if I didn't, I should at any rate be getting farther away from the police.

I didn't know how many roofs I crossed. I got pretty good at it, but it made me wild to think of the damage I was doing to my clothes. I should think I had put about a dozen houses behind me, when I made up my mind to take a breather and review the situation. I thought I should be quite safe, because I didn't see the police getting across those roof-tops without making a most almighty row, so I sat down in the gutter and took stock.

I was out of breath and dirty, wet about the hands, and slimy about the knees, but I was feeling a good deal bucked—I don't know why, but I was. I had no business to be bucked, with a stolen heirloom sewn into my coat and the police hot on my trail; but from the moment Isobel kissed me I didn't feel as if anything could ever hurt me again. I felt as if I could take anything on and make a success of it.

My head was most extraordinarily clear. I went over what Fay had said. Anna was behind this little trick with the Queen Anne bow. And then something hit me right between the eyes. The package—the package that Isobel had brought—the long matchbox with its little separate packets done up in white paper and initialed—where did that come in? I felt perfectly certain that it came in somewhere, and I thought I saw Anna behind that too.

My thoughts began to nose round that package like terriers round a rat-hole. I certainly smelt a rat. I thought I had done a pretty good piece of work when I chucked the match-box over the wall in Olding Crescent. All the things Fay had said about peddling cocaine came back to me. If those white paper packets contained cocaine, and information had been given to the police, I might have found myself pretty well up to my neck in the soup. *Because* if the information concerned unlawful drugs, they'd search me and they'd find not only a boxful of neat little packets of white powder, but also a valuable piece of stolen jewelry; and if the information concerned my uncle's stolen heirloom, they'd not only get that, but a dozen or so dollops of cocaine as well. And either way, I was for it; for if, on the one hand, I cleared myself by accusing Fay, who had planted me with the bow, I couldn't wouldn't and shouldn't in any conceivable circumstances involve Isobel by admitting that she'd ever been within a hundred miles of handling that beastly package of cocaine. I thanked Heaven for Fay's attack of conscience, and for my own feeling that a match boxful of mysterious packets was not the sort of thing to carry about.

I had got that all sorted out nice and clear, and I was just beginning to think that Fay had pulled herself together and done what she'd been told, when I heard a sort of smothered racket away behind me. I knew what it was too, without waiting to think. I'd done too much slipping and sliding on wet slates not to recognize the sound of other people doing the same thing. The police boot is a fine solid bit of furniture, but it doesn't lend itself to a stealthy approach. I thought I'd better be going.

I slithered up the slanting roof, using the skylight as a half-way house. I'd given up expecting to find anything open, but I just tried it for luck, and it came up in my hand and nearly sent me sprawling. I caught at the sill and saved myself, but it was touch and go whether I could stop the skylight from coming down with a bang on my knuckles. It was cold and slippery, and my hands were wet, but I managed to shift my grip, lift the light right up, and crawl through. The drop was only about four feet.

As I crouched on the attic floor and pulled the skylight down, I thought the police boots sounded nearer. I lost time looking for the bolt, and when I found it it wasn't any good. The wood of the jamb had cracked and taken the socket out of the true. Try as I would, I couldn't get the bolt to go home; and that, of course, was why I had been able to get in. I gave up trying and went groping through the attic, feeling for the trap.

That attic was cram full of stuff. I don't know why people put old baths and kitchen fenders up in a loft. I ran into a large birdcage, a marble slab, which I suppose was the top of a washstand, about a gross of curtain-rings, perfectly beastly to kneel on, and some frightfully dangerous wire-netting. The curtain-rings and the wire-netting were immediately over the trap, and I had to shift them before I could get it open.

I looked on to a dark landing. The stair ran down from it the opposite way to Mrs. Bell's stair, and the landing below was lighted. I could see the banisters like black ninepins against the yellow glow. I was most frightfully glad to see a light again.

There was, of course, no ladder. The drop was nothing in itself, but there's too much of me to drop any distance at all without making a noise; also I should have to leave the trap open behind me. It couldn't be helped, however. I took off my shoes, suspended them round my neck, hung by my hands, and dropped, I hoped, lightly.

Whilst I was putting my shoes on again, I thought I heard a noise on the roof, and as I stood up, I did hear some one raise the skylight in the attic above. There was a sound of voices. Some one shouted. I didn't wait to hear any more.

I made tracks down the stair, wondering all the time when somebody would put a head out of a door and scream. Nobody did. I passed the landing with a light on it and began to go down the next lot of stairs, but before I had taken a dozen steps there came a heavy banging on the front door.

Of course I knew exactly what had happened. The man who had been following me across the roofs had found the unbolted skylight and, I dare say, had taken a look inside; in which case he'd seen the open trap-door as well. He couldn't follow me, because I don't suppose that the law allows the police to break into a house, even in pursuit of a burglar, so he'd signaled from the roof to his pal below, and the pal was knocking at the front door. The minute any one came, there would be a request to search the house for a dangerous criminal; and with one man coming down from the skylight and another coming up from the hall, I would be fairly caught between two fires, unless I managed to get down into the basement before any one opened the door. Of course there might not be a way out of the basement.

I hadn't a chance to find out, because I hadn't taken two more steps down, before I could hear some one coming heavily up the basement stair. That did me in. I couldn't go on, because the next turn would bring me in sight of the front door. I went back on to the lighted landing.

Two closed doors faced me. I listened first at one and then at the other. There wasn't the slightest sound of any kind. I tried to see if there was a light on the other side, but I couldn't make anything of it.

The heavy steps below reached the hall. I heard a bolt drawn back and the rattle of a chain. Then voices—one very gruff, and the other a woman's voice, sleepy and cross. She kept saying things like "What did you say?" and "No, you can't see her—she's in bed." And then, "I didn't catch the half of that." And then "What did you say?" all over again.

I guessed her to be an old servant, fussy, opinionated, and rather deaf. She kept the door on the chain, and had the policeman fairly bellowing before I heard her say, "Well, I'll go and arst her." And at the same moment I saw the handle of the farther door begin to turn.

I've never moved so quickly in my life. Before that handle had finished turning, I had opened the other door and was over the threshold. I heard some one coming out of the next room, and I heard the servant coming up the stairs. I shut the door and turned to see where I was.

I was in a lighted bedroom, and on the other side of it there was an old lady sitting up in bed.

XXXVI

It was a perfectly frightful moment.

The room was full of solid comfort and very large Victorian mahogany furniture. There was a wardrobe that would have hidden half a dozen people comfortably; it took up all one side of the room. The bed and the fireplace were opposite. The bed was a big double one. The old lady was sitting up on one side of it with a great many pillows. She had a large fluffy woolly shawl round her shoulders, and a gray wig pushed crooked on her head. Across her knees was a newspaper, and a book or two. She had a writing-block in one hand and a pencil in the other. She didn't look up.

I advanced about three steps. There was a red carpet on the floor, and red curtains at the windows. The room was a double L-shaped one. From where I was now, I could see that both doors led into it. I had opened one at the exact moment that some one else had opened the other, with the result that I had come into the room as she went out, and neither of us had seen the other. I took another step forward.

The old lady spoke without looking up.

"A dark knight of Arthur's court—and the name ought to have nine letters and end with an 'S'," she said in a deep, strong voice.

I took one desperate look at the wardrobe, but it was hopeless to think of getting the door open without being seen or heard.

The old lady tapped her block with her pencil.

"Nine letters," she said. "A dark knight—a *dark* knight."

I was brought up on the *Morte d'Arthur*. I counted on my fingers to make sure. Then I said.

"Sir Palomides the Saracen."

I wondered if she was going to scream. I tried to look as little like a criminal as possible. I hoped that she had a grateful heart and would remember that I had given timely aid with her cross-word puzzle.

She didn't scream. I went on hoping. She wrote the word down quite calmly—at least she began to write it and then stopped and asked me how it was spelt, all without looking up. I wondered what on earth was happening in the house. I could hear footsteps on the stairs—formidable, earthshaking footsteps.

The old lady finished writing Palomides. Then she counted the letters on her fingers, just as I had done, and heaved a sort of satisfied sigh.

"Palomides it is," she said. Then she put down her pencil and looked up.

She had brown eyes, rather bulging, queer thick gray eyebrows, and a large fleshy nose. She looked at me with a bit of a frown.

"There wasn't the slightest occasion for you to come," she said.

I was so taken back that I nearly burst out laughing. If I could have thought of something to say, I'd have said it; because of course my voice was one of the things I was rather relying on to show her that I wasn't the low-class ruffian I probably looked after shinning up and down all those wet roofs.

"Not the slightest occasion," she repeated.

I thought her voice had slowed down and lost some of its ring. It struck me that she had seen the state of my knees. But she went on speaking.

"I told my niece there wasn't the slightest occasion to send for you. It was a momentary faintness, and I am feeling perfectly well again." Here she paused, frowned, took up a pair of spectacles which lay on the bed beside her, and putting them on, took a good long look at me.

I felt a most awful fool. When she spoke again, which she did after one of the longest minutes I have ever known, she was quite brisk. She said,

"You've had a busy day taking over from your uncle. I hope he'll enjoy his holiday. You *are* Dr. Wilmington's nephew, aren't you?"

"You know I'm not," I said, and waited for her to scream; but she only nodded her head.

"Speak the truth and shame the devil. I've seen you going up and down this street for the last three years. What do you want?"

She might well ask me that. It must have been nearly eleven o'clock, and I was in her bedroom.

I said, "Shelter," and heard a trample of feet go past the door at my back.

"What have you done?" she asked with a good deal of interest.

"*Nothing*." I wondered if she was going to believe me.

"Not murder?"

I laughed—I couldn't help it.

"H'm!" she said. Then, very quickly, "Get inside that wardrobe!"

I didn't wait to be told twice. The door was ajar, and I was inside and closing it in about half a second. If I hadn't been quick, I should have been caught, because the other door, round the bend of the L, had opened too.

The niece came fussing into the room. She fussed about half-way across it, and then stopped and said, in a voice that was bright on top and all shaky underneath,

"Well, dear Aunt, you must have wondered where I was."

"No," said the old lady. "No, not at all."

"Ellen wanted me for a moment," said the niece.

"Quite so," said the old lady. "My dear Fanny, how flushed you are! Ellen's conversation must have been very exciting—or was it the police?"

I could almost hear Fanny's jaw drop. She made a sort of bleating sound.

"Dear Aunt—"

"Oh, I know a policeman when I hear one—thumping up and down the stairs. What's the matter? Is any one murdered?"

"I don't know," said Fanny twittering. "They didn't say. They're looking for a man who got away over the roofs— from a house down the street—and they think he might be here, because our skylight wasn't bolted. They've been searching the house."

"I heard them," said the old lady very dryly. "Did they find him?"

"No, they didn't. And of course I wouldn't let them come in here, because, as I told them, you never leave the room, and I'd been here all the evening, and no one could possibly have come in without our seeing them, so of course there wasn't the slightest need to search this room. I kept telling them so."

"Dear me, Fanny," said the old lady, "you're very flustered about it all. I should have been delighted to see them, I'm sure. Have they gone?"

"No," said Fanny. "But I told them they couldn't see you and they had no right to bother you."

"Rubbish!" said the old lady. "Open the door!"

I hadn't quite shut the wardrobe, because I'd been afraid that Fanny would hear the click. I was standing behind the mahogany panel with a piece of fur tickling the back of my neck, and a silk dress hanging down over my left shoulder and rustling when I breathed. There was a strong smell of old clothes and lavender. I was thankful it wasn't napthalene, because napthalene always makes me sneeze. It would have rather torn it if I had sneezed just as the policeman was coming into the room. I should say by the sound of his voice that he was standing about a yard away from me, just inside the same door that I had come in by.

I wanted to laugh. He sounded so awfully stodgy and embarrassed and polite.

"Sorry to trouble you, ma'am."

And then the old lady, as sweet as honey:

"It's no trouble at all, constable."

"I understand you've been in this room all the time, ma'am."

"All the time," she said.

"And no one could come in without your seeing them, I take it?"

"Quite impossible," she said. "If you'll come over here by the bed, you will see for yourself."

I heard him cross the floor.

"And the other lady was here too?"

"Until she went down to see who was knocking us up so late."

I heard him come back again.

"Well, ma'am, I'm very sorry you've been troubled, but we've got to do our duty."

"It's most agreeable to feel that we are so well looked after," said the old lady. "Good-night, constable."

He said "Good-night" and shut the door. I could hear him speaking to the other man on the landing. Then one of them went upstairs and the other down. After a minute the front door shut. I began to wonder what was going to happen next.

Miss Fanny came back all in a flurry. I suppose she'd been seeing them off—or one of them; for I suspected that the second man had gone out by way of the skylight.

"You're not upset, dear Aunt? Now you are not to let it keep you awake. I'm sure I tried to prevent his coming in, but you mustn't let it excite you."

The old lady bit her head off.

"Don't be a fool, Fanny!" she said. "Or if that's too much to expect, don't be more of a fool than you can help! And if you want something to do, go and make me a cup of thin arrowroot. And remember it's got to simmer, so if you come back and say it's done in less than ten minutes, I shall know that it's not fit to drink."

I just caught a glimpse of Fanny as she went past my chink—a kind, limp, poking sort of woman with eyes like pale blue gooseberries, and light sandy hair that was turning gray. She had on the kind of clothes that make you feel that they must have been picked up secondhand a bit at a time. She stopped by the door. I could hear her fidgeting with the handle.

"I don't like leaving you."

"And why not?" said the old lady very short and sharp.

"You won't be nervous? You're sure? I don't think I ought to leave you."

"Am I to make my arrowroot myself?" said the old lady in an ominous voice. "I didn't ask you to think."

Fanny let go of the handle in a hurry. I heard her fuss away downstairs, and I opened my wardrobe door and came out.

The old lady wasn't looking at me. She had gone back to her cross-word.

"Seven," she said—"it must be seven letters. Now, what's a word with seven letters which means fine-drawn?"

"What about tenuous?" I said.

"Good!" she said. "Good—good—good! Yes—seven letters! That's broken the back of it! I shouldn't have slept a wink if I hadn't got the better of the thing."

She put down her pencil and beckoned to me.

"Come over here and tell me what you've been up to. Fanny's safe for ten minutes, and I want to know."

"I really haven't done anything," I said.

"Nobody ever has. What do they say you've done?"

"I'm not quite sure."

"Then why did you run away?"

"Because it was the best thing to do." I thought this sounded rather bad, so I went on in a hurry: "I really haven't done anything, but I mightn't be able to clear myself."

"Because of some one else?" she said.

I nodded.

"A woman, I suppose? And you're in love with her? Is that it?"

I felt myself getting red; but it was because I was angry, not because I was embarrassed.

"No, it's not," I said.

"Then why don't you clear yourself?"

I didn't answer that, and she saw I wasn't going to. She took up her pencil again and tapped with it on the writing-block.

"Well, well—what are you going to do next?"

I didn't know. There would probably still be a man in the street, and I didn't suppose they'd finished searching the roofs yet.

"Your best way is to wait till Fanny comes up with my arrowroot. Then you can get out into the yard and over the wall into the back garden of one of the houses in Ely Street. If you go out of the front door, you may just walk into a trap."

"I say—you're most frightfully good!" I said.

"I hope the Recording Angel thinks so," she said. Then she put out her hand and beckoned to me.

I came close up to the bed.

"What's your name?" she asked, looking up at me under her queer thick eyebrows.

"Carthew Fairfax."

"Do they call you all that?"

"No—Car."

"Is your mother alive?"

"No."

"Grandmother? Aunts?"

"No."

"I thought not. Have you got a sweetheart?"

The thought of Isobel came over me like the sun shining suddenly on a dark day.

I said, "Yes."

"Will you tell me her name?"

"Isobel."

She laughed in a queer sort of way.

"Mine is Ginevra Cambodia Stubbs. That's funny enough for a cross-word—isn't it? Well, if things turn out all right for you, will you come and see me some day?"

I said, "I'd like to." I tried to thank her, but she stopped me.

"I live entirely surrounded by old women. My doctor's the worst of them—what Ellen calls 'a proper old maid.' She's one herself, so she ought to know. So is Fanny. They're all kind, they're all fussy, and they all bore me to death. I like young men, and as I've no sons, and no grandsons, I never see one. I've watched you from the window going up and down—I told you that, didn't I?" She stopped, picked up her pencil, and tapped on the block. "If I don't do crosswords, I should get as soft in the head as Fanny. Now you ought to be going. You'd better go down to the next landing and wait in the drawing-room till you hear Fanny come up with the arrowroot. You can get into the yard through the scullery. There's a box of matches on the mantelpiece, if you haven't got any. You'd better not turn on the electric light, because Ellen sleeps in the basement."

She shook hands with me, and I did my best to thank her, but I don't think I made a very good job of it. I liked her most awfully, and I hope she knew how grateful I was.

XXXVII

I took the matches and went down to the next landing, which had two doors at right angles to one another just like the one above; they both opened into the drawing-room. I'd hardly got safely in before I heard Fanny coming upstairs. She must have hurried like mad over making the arrowroot.

As soon as I heard the old lady's door shut, I came out of the drawing-room and went down the stairs. There was no light below the bedroom landing, but I didn't want to strike a match unless I was obliged to. The house was on the same plan as Mrs. Bell's, so I thought I could manage.

I crawled down the basement stairs, because of course I realized that Ellen would most likely not have gone to sleep again yet. I wasn't quite clear about the kitchen, and the scullery, and her room; but Fanny had left the kitchen door ajar and I saw the glow of the fire, which was a stroke of luck I couldn't have reckoned on. .

The scullery had an outer door with heavy bolts, the sort that were simply bound to make a row if I tried to shoot them back. I decided that it would be much safer to get out of the kitchen window.

Well, I slid back the catch, pushed up the window, and was half-way out, when I heard a sort of flapping sound. I recognized it at once, because I'd noticed when she went upstairs that Fanny had on slippers which flapped on every step. I pulled my other leg up, but before I could drop into the yard the kitchen door opened with a push, and there stood Fanny with a waggling candle in her hand and her mouth open all ready to scream. I ought to have cut and run, but like an ass I tried to stop her.

"Miss Fanny——" I began, and then she screamed. It was the most ineffectual scream I had ever heard. I think she was too frightened to put any breath into it. "I say—don't do that! Mrs. Stubbs knows I'm here."

She screamed again and let the candle fall with a clatter. I think some of the hot wax must have got her on the instep, because her third scream was much louder.

"For the Lord's sake——" I said, but before I could say any more, the light went on in the passage and an amazing fat old thing in yards and yards of white night-gown rushed up to Fanny and caught her by the arm.

"Where is he, the nasty toad?" she cried, and began to let off screams like a steam siren.

I got out on the sill, banged down the window, and dropped.

The yard was one of the sort that has given up pretending to be a garden. I ran into a dust-bin and a clothes-line before I got to the wall at the bottom. I shinned up it, ran along as far as I dared, and dropped into the garden of one of the houses facing on Ely Road. They are rather better houses than the ones in our street. Some of them really have gardens. This one had. There were trees against the wall, and I'm afraid I trod right in the middle of a bed of geraniums; there was an aromatic smell from the plants I broke.

My idea was to lurk in the bushes until I saw what was going to happen. I couldn't hear Ellen screaming any longer, but that probably only meant that she was using her breath to call in the police and tell them all about it.

There were some lilac bushes close up against the house. Lilac makes a very good screen. When I got to the bushes, I wasn't more than a couple of yards from the house. There was a window on the ground floor. I couldn't help thinking how convenient it would be if I could walk through the house and out into Ely Road. I suppose this made me go up to the window to have a look at it.

I wasn't expecting anything—it was just an idle impulse; but, to my extreme surprise, the bottom part of the window was open. It seemed an impossible bit of luck. I thought I must be mistaken. I put out my hand to feel, and touched thick curtains drawn together behind the open sash.

Well, I wasn't wasting any luck. This was a lot better than lurking in a lilac bush, so I pulled myself up over the sill and stepped down into the room.

I was still straightening myself up and wondering who on earth had left the window open, when the curtains were parted and some one said "*Darling*" and threw both arms round my neck. It was so frightfully sudden I couldn't possibly have stopped her. The voice sounded quite young, and the arms were soft. I didn't know if I said anything, or whether she just found out when she kissed me. Anyhow, she gave a sort of stifled shriek, began to push me away, and then slipped right down on the floor in a faint.

It was simply frightfully embarrassing, I couldn't very well go off and leave her fainting, but I certainly couldn't afford to dally. I picked her up, felt round for a chair, put her into it, and then hunted about until I found the electric light switch.

The light went on and showed the room. It was the little third room you sometimes get on the ground floor in a London house. It looked like a girl's sitting-room, rather pretty-pretty, with lots of photographs and nick-nacks. The girl was beginning to catch her breath and open her eyes. They were the large, rolling, pale-blue sort, and she had fair fluffy hair and rather good ankles. She was dressed for going out, all except her hat, which was on the floor. I don't know why girls always throw their hats on the floor, but they do. There were two suit-cases next to the hat.

I thought it would be perfectly awful if she began to scream, so I weighed in at once:

"Please don't be frightened—I'm not a burglar."

"I thought you were Tom," she said.

"Did you?"

"Of c-course I did. And you're n-not!" She sounded as if she thought it was my fault that I wasn't Tom.

"I'm awfully sorry," I said.

She put her head on one side and listened, and she said "Ssh!" though I wasn't making any noise. After she'd listened again for a minute she whispered,

"Did you hear anything?"

I shook my head.

She was sitting up and quivering with fright. She said, "Are you s-sure?"

I nodded.

"If he w-wakes, we're d-done for."

I really never have seen a girl look so frightened. It wasn't about me, which was something to the good. I was only some one she could shiver at and say "Ssh!" to. I said, "Who is he?"

She said "Ssh!" again; and then, "My f-father. T-Tom and I are running away."

"Well—why don't you run?" I asked.

She said "Ssh!" every time I spoke, though I didn't make a bit more noise than she did. It was most awfully annoying, and I could have shaken her. I thought I had better go before I lost my temper, so I said in a frightfully polite whisper,

"Can I get out of the front door—or would a window be better?"

She said "Ssh!" and made reproachful eyes.

"You're not g-going to *leave* me?"

I thought that was the limit. I said,

"Suppose your father wakes up and finds me here?"

"I'd rather he f-found you than T-Tom."

"Where *is* Tom?" I asked.

And just as I said it, there was a scrambling noise at the window and Tom fell into the room. He made about twice as much noise as I had done, but she didn't say "Ssh!" to him. She jumped up and said "Darling!" and flung her arms around his neck just like she had done to me. I thought she might have managed to think out something different, but she was evidently a creature of routine. I felt sorry for Tom, because I could see he'd got years and years of being called "Darling" stretching before him, and I thought that after the first few thousand times he'd get bored, especially if she always said it in exactly the same way. The time she said it to me and the time she said it to him were as much alike as if you'd been playing the same gramophone record over twice.

She said it again, and Tom glared at me over her shoulder. He was a dark, stocky fellow about my own age. He looked at me as if I'd been murdering her.

"Who's this?" he growled.

"I d-don't know," said the girl.

"I want to get out into Ely Road," said I.

Tom unhooked his young woman and put her behind him.

"What are you doing here?"

"Wasting my time," I said.

"He came in through the w-window," said the girl. "He f-frightened me d-dreadfully, and I c-couldn't scream because of F-father."

I thought I'd never heard anything so mean in my life.

"Did he hurt you?" said Tom.

"No, I didn't," I said. "Don't be a fool! I want to get into Ely Road. And you want to elope—don't you? She said you did. Hadn't we better all get on with it, instead of doing our best to wake the house?"

That fetched her, and she said "Ssh!" again. And just as she said it, there was a loud thud overhead. It might have been a piece of furniture falling, or it might have been a heavy man getting out of bed in a hurry. I didn't wait to see, nor did Tom. I had started for the door, and as I went through it, he shoved a suit-case at me and I clamped on to it.

The hall door was not bolted—I suppose the girl had seen to that. I got it open, and Tom and the girl and I all went tumbling down the steps. I don't know which of us banged the door. It made an awful noise, and through the noise I could hear a military voice of the first magnitude roaring for "Maisie!"

Tom had a suit-case and I had a suit-case, and Tom had Maisie as well. She was simply dithering with fright, and we hadn't gone half a dozen yards before she wonked and said she was going to faint. She was the sort of girl who'd have done it too.

"My car's at the corner," said Tom. "Maisie—*darling!*"

The door we had banged behind us had been violently wrenched open. I looked over my shoulder and saw a large man in purple and yellow pyjamas come hurtling down the steps. He had red hair and a red face, and a considerable command of language.

Tom and I each put an arm round Maisie's waist and ran her along. He had left his engine running like a sensible fellow, so we didn't have to waste time at the corner. He put Maisie on the front seat beside him, and the suit-cases and myself at the back. The car was a Morris saloon. I looked out through the back window and saw the red-haired man in the loud pyjamas getting small by degrees and beautifully less. I couldn't imagine why he should be upset about losing Maisie. It was Tom I was sorry for, poor chap.

I don't think he knew I was there until I poked him in the back. He was steering with one hand and cuddling that limp rabbit of a girl with the other. I suppose he looked at the road sometimes, but I didn't see him do it, and the sort of baby language he kept talking to her was an eye-opener to me. I thought if he was going to smash up the car, I would rather get out, so I spoke to him.

He jumped about a foot into the air and just missed the last tram from Tooting, or somewhere like that. He ran on out of range of what the conductor had to say about it, and then pulled up.

"Oh, it's you?" he said.

I said, "Yes. Thanks awfully for the lift," and I opened the door and got out.

"One minute," he said. "You—er—helped us get off— so I won't ask you what you were doing in the house."

I laughed.

"Just passing through," I said. "Here to-day and gone to-morrow."

"I'm not asking what you were doing—I only want to say

that I'm taking Maisie—Miss Sharpe—I'm taking her straight
to my grandmother. I've had a license ready for a fortnight,
and we're going to be married to-morrow."

He was a decent sort, so I didn't laugh. I said,

"All the best to you both—and thanks again for the lift."

Then I stood and watched his tail light dwindle to a red
spark, whilst I made up my mind what I was going to do next.

XXXVIII

I SET OUT TO WALK TO PUTNEY. IT TOOK THE BEST PART
of an hour, so I had plenty of time to think. I hadn't any
plan when I got out of Tom's car, but one came to me as I
stood and watched him drive away. The more I thought about
it, the more I felt sure that I must go back to Olding Crescent
and recover the package I had thrown over the wall. For all I
knew, the thing might have my name on it somewhere, or
some one might turn up who had seen it in Isobel's possession.
I simply couldn't afford to leave it lying about.

Some one was taking a good deal of trouble to compro-
mise me. There was the Queen Anne bow, and those beastly
little packets of white powder. . . . Whoever it was believed
in having two strings to her bow. I said *"her* bow" to
myself, because I hadn't the slightest doubt that I was up
against some of Anna's work—Fay had as good as told me
so. I couldn't think why she should hate me enough to play
that sort of game, and I couldn't imagine how she had got in
touch with Fay. She had met her at Corinna's party; but you
don't go up to just any stray girl you've met once in a
restaurant and say "Look here, come and join me in a

criminal conspiracy,'' or words to that effect. Of course
Anna's got a mind like a Surrey-side melodrama, but even
she would draw the line at that.

Olding Crescent was darker than ever when I got back to
it. The darkness was full of Isobel. I went to the place
where we had stood together, and I could almost feel her in
my arms again. It came over me that she was mine and I was
hers, and there wasn't anything in the world that was strong
enough to keep us apart. I knew that just as certainly as I knew
black from white, and light from darkness. There was nothing
emotional about the feeling; it was comfortable, and steady,
and immensely strong. It made everything quite easy.

The first thing that I had to do was to get over on to the
other side of the wall. It was too high to climb. I tried the
door, just as a chance, but it was locked. There was nothing
for it but to go round by the drive. The difficulty would be
to locate the right place. I had to remember just what I had
done. I had gone over to the lamp to examine the package,
and when I had decided that it wasn't the sort of thing to
carry around, I had walked across the road and chucked it
over the wall.

I went back to the lamp, repeated my actions as nearly as
I could, and threw over a white handkerchief. It had my
name on it, so I tore the corner out first. Then I went down
to the end of the crescent and in at the gate.

I struck off to the left at once, keeping along the wall. I
had counted my own paces, so I thought I ought to be able
to hit off the right place without much trouble. I was
counting again as I groped my way along. I hadn't much
attention to spare, but what I had kept worrying round the
open gate through which I had just come. It seemed so
incongruous to have a ten-foot wall all round your garden,
and a *chevaux de frise* on top of that, and then leave your
gate open all night. It had been open the first time I came,
but that wasn't so late. It was well past midnight now.

The bit of my mind that was counting paces stopped,
because it had reached the number which it had set out to
reach. The other bit gave a sort of jump. The gate had been

open before to let a car drive in and out. Perhaps it was open now for the same reason—perhaps for the same car.

I put that away to think about presently and started to look for my handkerchief. I realized at once that I wasn't going to be able to find anything without a light. The trees grew just inside the wall, and there was a double line of them, and a bank of evergreens beyond that again. Even at midday it must have been dark; and now, on a cloudy midnight, the place was as black as the inside of a coal mine. I only knew that the trees and bushes were there because I kept on running into them.

I got out Mrs. Stubbs' match-box and struck a light. The spurt of the match sounded horribly loud. It was like hearing it through a megaphone. I felt as if the people in the dead houses on the other side of the Crescent must hear it too. The little yellow flame burned straight up in the still air. I saw the underside of branches, black hummocks of bushes, and the wall, like the side of a house. The match burnt my finger and went out. I lit another, sheltering it with my hand. I couldn't see my handkerchief anywhere. I struck six matches before I saw it, caught up on a low, thin branch just over my head.

It took me ten minutes to find the package, because it had pitched a good deal farther in and lay between two evergreen bushes. I had just picked it up, when I heard some one coming through the bushes, moving slowly and cautiously.

I moved too. I don't know if he heard me, but I couldn't just stand there and let him walk into me. I got about half a dozen paces and dived as noiselessly as I could into the shrubbery. The ground was soft and newly forked. The shrubs grew close together, and were well above my head.

I stood still, with an aromatic smell of bruised cypress all round me, and waited to see what was going to happen next.

What did happen was rather startling. The beam of an electric torch cut the dark. It was as sudden as a lightning flash. The beam moved rapidly, up, down, sideways, and came to rest in a bar of light right across the bushes where I was standing. It was on a level with my shoulders. I could see a black tracery of cypress against it like seaweed.

There as a gap by my head. I bent a little, looked back along the beam, and saw the black bulk of a biggish man. He was holding the torch up. I could just see his white shirt-front. I guessed it was Arbuthnot Markham.

I'd got as far as that, when he turned the light and it went straight into my eyes. I had just time to shut them. Eyes catch the light worse than anything. If I'd had them open, he'd have spotted me for certain. As it was, I hoped for the best. The gap was a very little one.

The light flickered away again and turned in the opposite direction. I opened my eyes, and saw it pick out the bricks and moss on the wall. At that moment I heard some one call Arbuthnot Markham's name:

"Arbuthnot! Arbuthnot!" And then again, "Arbuthnot!"

It was Anna's voice.

I wasn't really surprised. I had come back here to get the package, but I think I had had an idea all the time that I might run across Arbuthnot and Anna. There was the business of the telegrams. Isobel had had a bogus telegram asking her to meet me, and I had had another asking me to meet her, in Olding Crescent. In the back of my mind I was pretty sure that Anna had sent both of them; and if she had, it seemed likely that she would be somewhere around. The only thing was, it was now getting on for four hours since I had met Isobel. It seemed a bit late for Anna to be wandering round Arbuthnot's garden with him. However, that was her affair; it certainly wasn't mine.

Arbuthnot turned with the torch in his hand.

"I told you not to come."

I liked the way he said it. I'd often wanted to put Anna in her place. It did me good to hear the rasp in his voice.

She came rustling through the bushes.

"I didn't come till you turned the torch on. Did you see anything?"

"No."

"This is where I saw the light."

"Imagination!" said Arbuthnot.

"It wasn't. Some one struck a match."

I was glad to hear her say "*a* match," because I suppose first and last I had struck about three dozen. I gave myself marks for not having chucked them about. If she'd only seen one match struck——

He was speaking:

"You've got too much imagination. There's no one here."

"Some one struck a match." She sounded positive and obstinate.

He began to flick the light to and fro. Then he walked past me. I could hear him moving towards the drive, and after a moment coming back again.

"There's no one about. You've got the jumps." Then, in a different tone, "Well, if you're going, you ought to go."

"I'm going," said Anna.

"Damned nonsense, I call it," said Arbuthnot Markham. "Why can't you stay here and have done with it?"

"Because I haven't finished my work."

He threw back his head and laughed.

"You're damn funny when you talk in that high-falutin' way! Come off it, my dear!"

"I don't know what you mean." Anna had the pathetic stop out.

"Oh yes, you do—and it doesn't go down with me. You're a very pretty woman, but that's no reason why you should talk like a fool."

My heart warmed to Arbuthnot. Anna knuckled down to him in the most astonishing way. She said, in quite an ordinary human voice, that it was getting late and she thought she ought to go.

Arbuthnot laughed again.

"You might as well stay here to-night as come away with me to-morrow," he said.

Anna took him up with a sharp cry.

"To-morrow?"

"That's what I said."

"I can't."

"I'm afraid you must, my dear."

"Why? What has happened?"

There was a pause. I wanted to hear the answer as badly as Anna did. What *had* happened?

"I'm leaving to-morrow instead of next week," said Arbuthnot.

Anna gave a sort of gasp.

"Why?"

"My affair, my dear."

She said, "Isn't it mine too?" in a melting sort of voice.

Arbuthnot didn't melt. He said,

"You can come, or you can stay behind."

"Don't you *care* which I do?"

"Oh, I'd rather you came. You'd find it more comfortable than traveling by yourself later on."

"Do you think I'd come later on?"

"Oh, you'd come all right."

She gave a little gasp—anger, I thought, but I wasn't sure; it may have been fright. I could see she was afraid of him.

I could hear him make a sudden movement. I think he took hold of her by the shoulders.

"Now look here, Anna! You've got to drop all this play-acting. I've let you alone because it seemed to amuse you, and it didn't hurt me. Now my plans are changed, and you've got to drop it."

"What do you mean? Oh! You're hurting me!"

"No, I'm not. I mean you've got to drop all this revenge business. It isn't pretty, and it doesn't amuse me any more."

She gave an angry laugh at that.

"If I drop it, it's because it's *done*," she said.

"Oh, it's done, is it? What a fool you are, Anna!"

Something in the easy sarcasm of his tone must have startled her.

"What do you mean?" she said in a new breathless voice.

"What I say."

"*Arbuthnot*—tell me what you mean!"

"I'm going to. I'd like it to be a warning to you. Perhaps you'll think of it next time you try to go behind my back."

"I—didn't."

"Oh yes, you did—you tried to square Bobby to get you some dope, so that you could plant it on that unlucky devil Fairfax."

"Bobby—*promised*——"

"Bobby's got himself into a nasty mess." Arbuthnot's voice hardened. "What the silly fool wanted to touch this dope business for, I don't know. Fosicker got him into it, and I've had to get him out of it."

"Oh!" said Anna.

Arbuthnot went on in a cold anger.

"You played it pretty low down on Bobby, promising to marry him."

"Oh—I didn't!"

"Bobby thought you did. Now do you really suppose I'd let him do anything so risky as plant Fairfax with dope that any detective would trace back through you as easily as falling off a log? Not much, my dear!"

I could hear Anna twist herself free and stamp her foot.

"Well then, he did!" she said. "He did it. Do you hear? He got it for me. I told him to get it, and he got it. And by this time Car Fairfax has been arrested with it on him, and no one will ever trace it back to me, because it didn't come to him from me. It came to him from Isobel—Isobel— *Isobel*, do you hear? And Car would go to prison a dozen times before he would give Isobel away." She stopped, panting.

She was working herself up into one of her rages. When Anna is in a rage, she tells the truth. It's almost the only time she does, so I was listening with a good deal of interest.

"What do you say to that?" she said, and stamped her foot.

He said, in a cold, amused sort of way,

"Well, if you've made a fool of yourself, you've made fools of the police to keep you company."

"What do you mean?"

He laughed.

"Don't be afraid—I'm going to tell you. It's much too good a joke to keep to myself. Bobby sent you what you asked for, did he?"

"Yes, he did."

"Neat little packets of white powder—neat little packets of cocaine?"

"Yes," said Anna defiantly.

"Cocaine—*nix!*" said Arbuthnot Markham. "Common salt, my dear—common or garden salt."

XXXIX

Anna repeated the word in a perfectly flat tone:

"Salt——" she said. Then quite suddenly her voice broke and choked. I had heard that happen before in one of her rages. She had tried to scream, and not been able to get out more than a ha'porth of sound. It was beastly to listen to, and it meant she was fairly off and would only stop raging when she hadn't the strength to go on.

Arbuthnot took her by the shoulders again and shook her—at least that was what it sounded like. When he stopped, she stood catching her breath and whispering,

"You hurt me! You hurt me!"

"I meant to. I've no time for hysterics. You'd better be getting home if you won't stay here. Pack what you want, and meet me at Croydon Aerodrome at three. We're flying to Paris."

"You hurt me!" she said, half sobbing.

"No, I didn't. But I will if there's any more nonsense. Don't forget to bring your passport."

"Has Bobby gone to Paris?" said Anna.

"Never you mind where Bobby's gone. The less you know about it, the better. You've been playing with fire, and it'll do you good to sit still and twiddle your fingers for a bit. If Fosicker's arrested, you may find yourself in a hotter place than you care for."

I was getting most awfully interested, because I'd had an ideal all along that Fosicker and Arbuthnot were the same person. I was listening as hard as I could, when quite suddenly, just as he said "arrested," I wanted to sneeze. I pinched the bridge of my nose and did everything else I'd ever heard of, but for about a minute I just hung on the edge of a crash. Then I downed the beast, and began to listen again. You can't listen when you're hanging on to the tail of a sneeze and wondering every moment if the thing isn't going to get loose and do you in.

I heard Anna say in a quite a loud, surprised voice,

"*Fosicker?* But you are Fosicker!'"

I forgot all about the sneeze. For once in a way Anna and I were twin hearts that beat as one, because that was just what I had been thinking.

"*What?*" said Arbuthnot Markham in a voice that sounded as if he'd had all the breath knocked out of him.

Anna whispered the name she had just said.

"Fosicker—I've always known—you were—Fosicker."

"Are you crazy?" he said.

"No, I'm not."

"You thought I was *Fosicker?* Why?"

"I thought you were. I think—you *are*."

"I'm sorry to disappoint you. Did you really think you'd married a dope king? However, unless you want a husband in jail, I'm the better bargain. If Fosicker didn't manage to get clear to-day, he'll be arrested to-morrow. Personally I hope he got clear, because of Bobby—otherwise I'd be very pleased to see him go down for a five years' stretch. Anyway the game was up—and that, my dear, was why I put a spoke in your wheel. There's going to be a slump in dope.''

"How do you know," said Anna, "if you're not— Fosicker?'' Her voice seemed to fade a bit when she got to the name. I thought she was frightened to say it.

"Drop it!'' he said. "Fosicker's bolted. I wasn't in with him, and I don't care a hang what happens to him. Bobby told me all I know, and that's not much. He came to me to get him out of the scrape. And now you'll go home.''

They began to move away. I could hear her saying something, and I could hear him shutting her up. And then I couldn't hear them any more.

I'd have a very interesting time listening, but I was most awfully glad when they were gone. I'd had a bit of cypress tickling my left ear, and I didn't dare scratch it, to say nothing of having been stuck in one position for about ten minutes without being able to move. It felt much longer than ten minutes, but I expect it was about that.

I stretched myself and stamped my feet, and felt my neck to see if there were really spiders or caterpillars crawling on it. There weren't any.

I came out of the bushes and made my way to the gate. I'd got plenty to think about. The thing that stuck out on top was Anna being married to Arbuthnot Markham. I thought that was pretty good news for the family, but a bit rough on him. I didn't like the man, but if I had to choose between five years' penal servitude and being married to Anna, they'd find me beating at the prison gates and begging them to let me in. I'll say this, Arbuthnot seemed to have her pretty well in hand. It was an eye-opener to me the way she knuckled down to him.

I began to sort out what I'd heard. I wondered if Arbuthnot had been telling the truth about the packet I'd come to retrieve. If it contained nothing worse than salt, there didn't seem to be much point in my taking it away with me.

I got it out, opened one of the little packages, picked up a grain or two, and tasted it rather gingerly. Salt it was— decent, honest salt. It came over me how funny it was, and I backed up against the wall and shook with laughter, all by myself in the dark. Anna's great melodramatic revenge and silly-idiot hatred, her lies, her intrigues, and her bogus telegrams, all fizzling out like this!

I took up the nice little harmless dollops of salt, and I as just going to empty them out, when I thought of something better. I put them back in their box, rummaged out a pencil, and wrote as well as I could in the dark, "A. Markham Esq."; and under that, "A Present for a Good Boy." I sucked the pencil to make it as black as possible, and hoped the result would be legible.

I'd just got it done, when Anna's car came down the drive. The lights dazzled for a moment, and then were gone. It struck me it was a pity I couldn't get her to give me a lift, when she was going to Linwood and so was I.

I went up the drive. There were no lights showing in the house. I came under the portico, mounted the steps, and pushed Arbuthnot's present into the letterbox. I wondered what he would make of it.

I laughed again, and ran back along the drive to the gate. But when I got there, I stood still, because I hadn't thought what I was going to do next. The laughter went out of me like the air from a pricked balloon. One minute I was as pleased as Punch and full of laughter and the spirit of adventure, and the next I was flat and cold and tired.

And right into the middle of that flat, cold moment there came two things, very suddenly. The first was a torch turned full in my face, with a policeman behind it. And the second was the recollection of the Queen Anne bow.

I had forgotten all about it.

The torch hit my face, and the idea hit my mind, one after the other—right—left—bang! Between them I lost my head. Instead of saying "Good evening, constable," and behaving as if I'd every right to be there I was, I gave the whole show away by taking to my heels and bolting up Olding Crescent.

I heard the policeman's whistle go behind me, and I thought I'd never heard such a beastly row in my life; it sounded as if it would wake the dead. But it didn't wake those dark houses on the other side. They stayed in their black silence; not a blind moved, not a window opened, not a spark of light showed in the whole grim crescent.

I kept in under the trees. After the first start I took it fairly easy. I used to be able to touch two minutes for the half mile, so I wasn't really worrying about any policeman. I aimed at getting round the corner and cutting up the first side road. The minute I began to run, I felt quite happy and confident again.

It's rather odd how you can think of two things at once. I had my eye on the corner of Churt Row, and my ears cocked for the sound of the bobby behind me; and at the same time I was most awfully taken up with the question of whether Arbuthnot Markham was, or wasn't, Fosicker. I can't think why I should have bothered about it, but I did. All the time that I was running, I was trying to make up my mind.

First of all I thought he was speaking the truth. And then I wondered why he had talked about Fosicker at all, out there in a dark shrubbery with at least the possibility that some one might be near enough to overhear what he was saying. Anna had seen a match struck, and he had come out with a torch to see who was there, and on the top of that he had gone out of his way to talk about not being Fosicker. All at once it came to me that the beam from his torch had struck through a gap in my cypress bush and hit me in the face. It was quite a little gap, and I thought he hadn't seen me; but now I wondered whether he had.

I didn't think all this in words; it just came in my mind, like a picture comes in water. And then something broke the whole thing up, as you break a reflection when you pitch a stone into the middle of it. The policeman behind me blew his whistle again—he was a long way behind—and just round the corner of Churt Row another whistle answered it, and, blip round the corner, there came policeman number two, running for all he was worth.

I stopped bothering about Arbuthnot Markham. The second policeman was only about thirty yards away. I thought about tackling him low; but if he managed to get a grip of me anywhere, the other man would have time to come up. I only had a second to make up my mind. Just ahead the trees hung so low that they would only just clear me. I ran up close to the wall and felt above my head for a sizeable branch. As luck would have it, my hands closed on a limb as thick as my wrist. I pulled on it and brought a larger branch within reach, and, scuffling, scraping and sliding, I went up the wall.

I was nearly up, when I remembered the *chevaux de frise* on the top. It was a perfect beast to negotiate, but the tree stood my friend and saw me through. I got hold of a higher branch, swung myself over, and dropped.

Just as I let go, two torches flashed up their light from below, and two hearty police voices shouted to me to come down out of it. I came down with a thud—but not on their side of the wall.

It was good soft falling—leaf-mold a foot deep—and I was up in a moment. I didn't think they'd try to climb the wall. I shouldn't have liked to take it on myself in a heavy tunic, or in cold blood. They'd have to go back to the gate, and my idea was to cut across the garden, climb the wall anywhere I could, and get away. I didn't know, of course, whether there was a road on the other side of the garden, or the grounds of a house; but it didn't really matter.

I pushed through the shrubbery, got out on to a lawn, and started to run across it. Away from the trees it wasn't so dark. There was no actual light; but the sky wasn't black, and the trees were, so I could get my direction. All at once something was right in front of me. I put out my hands just in time to save myself from running headlong into a holly hedge. As it was, I got scratched.

My luck seemed to have broken down—for I defy any one to climb a holly hedge. I had to decide which way I would go. If I followed the hedge to the left, it might run along between me and the wall as far as the corner of Churt Row or farther, in which case I should be dished. I couldn't risk it. I turned to the right and ran along the hedge in the direction of the house—at least that's the way I figured it out.

I ran for a bit, and then slowed to a walk and listened. I could hear some one tramping about down in the direction of the gate, and I could see an occasional flash from his torch. I thought there was only one man looking for me, which meant that the other was up the Crescent or watching the gate. I was getting my wind back nicely, but I was worried about my clothes. I felt pretty sure I must be horribly begrimed, and I knew I was bleeding from a scratch on the hand, and that my right trouser leg was torn below the knee. I was going to be a fairly conspicuous object whenever I emerged into the light.

The holly hedge ran on to the end of the lawn. My feet left the grass and scrunched on gravel. The hedge went on on my left. It came to a stop about twenty yards farther, at the entrance of a stable yard. There was an open arch, and then I was on cobble-stones old enough to be worn almost smooth. I couldn't see anything in front of me, but there was the feeling of a closed-in space, and a smell of petrol.

I stood still, because something told me to stand still. And then, without any warning, the headlight of a car sent two brilliant shafts across my path.

XL

I STOOD JUST WHERE I WAS. THE NEARER OF THE TWO dazzling lanes of light was about four yards away. I could see shadows round all the cobble-stones on the farther side of the yard; the shadows were as black as spilled ink. I could see the lanes of light, but I couldn't see the car from whose headlights they sprang. I couldn't see it, because the wide, dark screen of the open garage door cut off my view.

As soon as I saw that, I moved as silently as I could, until I was standing right against the open door and behind it. Then I had another look.

I had altered my position for the worse as far as seeing anything was concerned. The door made a right angle with the front of the garage. I stood behind the edge of it, and didn't dare put my head round to see what was on the other side. All I could see was the bright misty dazzle and a lot of cobble-stones, with a dim impression of the wall and the arch through which I had come.

On the other side of the door some one was trying to start up the car, and when the self-starter had buzzed and failed for the third time, I heard him swear vigorously, and I recognized Arbuthnot Markham.

I don't like a man who swears at his horse or his car. The thing he is swearing about is pretty nearly always his own fault. The way Arbuthnot took it out of his battery made me put him down as a pig-headed ass, but after a bit he got out and cranked her by hand. When he had got her running, he walked across the yard and came back with a suit-case in his hand. That made me sit up and take notice. He'd pressed Anna to stay and made an appointment to meet her at Croydon Aerodrome at three next day, and here he was, starting up his car and ramming suit-cases into it in the deuce of a hurry at somewhere about one in the morning. If it was one, it was to-day that he was going to meet Anna; but I wanted to know why he should be pushing off about ten hours too soon.

He opened the back door on the farther side, threw the suit-case in, and went back again across the yard. By this time I knew what I wanted. I wanted a lift down the drive and out of the gate past the police. I had to think quickly and take a bit of a risk.

As soon as I saw the headlight strike his back, I nipped round the garage door and got behind the car, opening the door on that side as I passed. The garage was in darkness, and it was a hundred to one against his noticing anything unless he came round that side—and I had to risk something.

He came tramping back, threw something heavy into the car, and slammed the door on it. Then he got in on the near side himself and slipped across into the driver's seat.

As he put her into gear, I came round and got in by the door I had left open. I timed it so that my weight came on the running-board as she moved off. You can't make thirteen stone feel like a feather, but I did my best, and he never turned his head.

I crawled in about an inch at a time. The suit-cases were on the seat, which was all to the good, because I badly wanted the floor for myself. I left the door flapping, and as we passed the arch and swung out to take the corner, he heard it, swore, reached back, and banged it to. I began to feel rather pleased with myself.

We went softly down the drive, and then, at the gate, checked suddenly. I couldn't see anything because I was lying particularly low with a rug over me; but I could hear Arbuthnot getting out, and I guessed that the police in an access of zeal had shut the gate. I heard it creak, and then I heard voices. I couldn't hear what they said, and I didn't need to. The constable was telling Arbuthnot how he'd chased a dangerous criminal over his garden wall; and Arbuthnot was telling the constable to go to blazes—at least that's what I thought at the time, but after a minute Arbuthnot got in again, still talking, and to my amazement he was being as polite as pie.

"And you'll keep a watch on the house?" he said. "I've some valuable pictures I shouldn't like to lose." And after that it was, "Good-night, constable," and all the compliments of the season.

We came slowly out of the gate and turned up the Crescent. I heard Arbuthnot whistle through his teeth, and as I looked out from under my rug, I saw him take out his handkerchief and mop his brow.

I came to the conclusion that he wasn't in a frame of

mind to meet the police without getting a nasty jar, and I wondered all over again whether he wasn't Fosicker after all.

We ran along Churt Row and turned out of it to the left. Presently we were on a main road. After a bit I got cautiously on my knees and took a look out of the window. I didn't want to get carried out of my way—and my way lay in the direction of Linwood. I wondered if he was making for Croydon. If he was, I had better see about getting out.

I threw off the rug, got up, and said,

"Thanks very much for the lift. I think I'll get off here."

I must say I admired his nerve. He swerved about six inches, and it was a minute before he said anything. He slowed down, drew in to the side of the road, and stopped. Then he said,

"What the devil are you doing in my car?"

I got out and stood by his window. It was open. I could see him like a big smudge of shadow leaning forward over the wheel.

"Do you want to call in the police?" I said.

It was a stupid bit of bluff, but I made pretty sure he'd be as anxious to keep clear of them as I was.

"Fairfax?" he asked; and then, "They are looking for you in my garden, aren't they? As far as I am concerned, they can go on looking. Do you mind telling me why you were striking matches there about half an hour ago? It was you, wasn't it?"

I said, "Yes."

"And how much of our conversation did you overhear when Anna and I came out to look for you?"

"Oh—some."

"Enough to congratulate me?"

"On your marriage?" I said.

He laughed.

"Where were you? In the bushes?"

"I was nicely placed for listening in," I said.

He moved round to face me.

"You're going to Linwood, I suppose? Will you give

Anna a message for me? I don't particularly want to wire or ring up.''

"Well?" I was waiting for the message.

"Give it to her when she's by herself." He had an easy, commanding manner. "Tell her she'll have to cross alone after all—I'm going on. Tell her some one will meet her. That's all."

He turned to the wheel. Then suddenly he jerked his head back over his shoulder.

"Anna's got it in for you. I suppose you know that?"

I said it was beginning to dawn on me.

"Did you ever hear of a thing called the Queen Anne bow?" he asked.

I laughed.

"To the best of my belief, I've got it sewn into the hem of my coat at this moment," I said.

"Oh, you know?" He seemed surprised.

"Yes, I know. That is why I'm going to Linwood."

He waited for a moment. Then he laughed too.

"All right—that's all—I thought I'd just let you know. You'll give Anna my message?"

I said, "Yes." Then I watched him drive away.

I walked on to the nearest lamp. I was considering what I was going to do. I had enough money to go to an hotel, but I wondered whether they would take me in, grimy, disheveled, torn, and without a stick of baggage. I thought a railway hotel would be my best chance. I stood under the lamp and dived for my wallet, just to make sure how much money I had.

My wallet was gone.

XLI

Dr. Monk was having a most uncomfortable quarter of an hour. He sat on one side of the library table and looked across it at his old friend Mr. Carthew, who was not looking at him in at all a friendly manner. At the end of the table stood Anna Lang, one arm resting on the back of the chair from which she had just risen. She was very pale. The other arm hung at her side, the hand white and ringless.

Mr. Carthew thumped the table.

"What cock-and-bull story is this?" he said in a loud, intemperate voice.

"My dear Carthew——"

"I asked you a question, Monk."

"I can only say——" Dr. Monk was not allowed to say it.

"And I want an answer!" said Mr. Carthew, and thumped again.

Anna Lang stood quite still. She was looking down at the table edge.

"If you will allow me to speak——" said Dr. Monk with some offense.

Mr. Carthew pushed back his chair and flung himself into the corner of it.

"Oh, speak—speak—*speak!* Let's have the whole thing out and have done with it!"

"It was on the evening of September the seventeenth," said Dr. Monk, frowning. "Miss Lang rang me up and told me you'd given her a fright—she said she'd found you unconscious on the floor—she seemed to think you'd had a shock. She asked me to come up and have a look at you. I came along at once, and in the street just outside Turner's I saw Car Fairfax.''

Mr. Carthew snorted.

"In the dark?" he said.

"*Really,* Carthew! He was holding a torch for a man who was doing something to his car. Just as I passed, the man reached up for the torch, and as he took it, the light shone in Car's face.''

"Go on," said Mr. Carthew combatively.

"I came up here. Miss Lang told me that you didn't remember anything at all about your attack.''

Mr. Carthew snorted again.

"I didn't remember anything about it because I never had it!''

Anna went on looking at the edge of the table. Her black lashes lay without moving upon the pale, even skin of her cheek.

Dr. Monk, leaning a little forward upon the arms of his chair, cleared his throat and went on:

"I found you sleeping comfortably"—Mr. Carthew gave a loud, angry laugh—"but Miss Lang was in a state of considerable distress. She had found the library window open. I came in here with her to see whether anything had been taken.''

"Well?" said Mr. Carthew explosively.

Dr. Monk turned in his chair and pointed past Anna at the tall bureau which stood between the windows.

"That top drawer was open. Some one had been rummaging in it—the papers had all been turned about, and your check-book was lying across the top of them, open.''

"Is that all?"

"No," said Dr. Monk. "No—not quite. I pulled down the flap of the bureau, and some one had been making hay there too—everything had been turned out of the pigeon-holes, and your keys were lying straggling on the top of the pile.''

Mr. Carthew got very red in the face.

"And why wasn't I told all this before, pray?"

Dr. Monk looked uncomfortably at Anna. She spoke for the first time, in a low, colorless voice.

"I said I would tell you." She paused, then repeated, "I told Dr. Monk that I would tell you."

"I thought Miss Lang had told you," said Dr. Monk. He hesitated a little. "I didn't think that I should refer to what might be a—a—well, a painful family matter."

"Painful!" said Mr. Carthew angrily. "Family!"—more angrily still—"Upon my word, Monk—a painful family matter! What put it into your head that there was anything painful—what? Or that it concerned my family? I say what put such a thing into your head?"

Dr. Monk sat back in his chair. He had said his say, and was glad to get it over. He saw no reason for holding anything back now.

"Miss Lang's distress," he said. "When I mentioned having seen her cousin, she was—er—very much affected. It was impossible not to notice it, impossible not to draw one's conclusions—especially when she begged me not to tell any one that I had seen Car Fairfax."

Mr. Carthew turned towards Anna, rapping sharply on the table.

"Why was that? Why did you ask him that?"

"I don't know," said Anna in a whisper.

"You did ask Monk not to tell any one he had seen Car?"

"Yes."

"Why? You must know why you did it! Come—out with it—what!"

Anna drew a long sighing breath. It seemed to send a tremor over her from head to foot.

"I was afraid."

"What were you afraid of? Of Car?" He laughed harshly. "You won't ask me to believe that, I hope?"

"Not of him—*for* him," said Anna.

"Good Lord! Can't you speak up?" A mounting exasperation big fair to choke his utterance.

With a sudden tragic gesture Anna hid her face in her hands.

"Oh!" she said. Her breath caught on a sob. "I was—afraid—afraid—he——" Her voice stopped.

"Out with it!" said Mr. Carthew. "Say what you were afraid of and have done with it—what!"

"I *can't*," said Anna, only just audibly.

Dr. Monk looked reproachfully across the table. Very affecting, this distress. Young scamp in a scrape. Lovely, tender-hearted girl. Old playfellow. Very distressing and affecting.

Mr. Carthew restrained himself, moderated his voice, and controlled a strong desire to take his niece by the shoulders and shake her.

"What were you afraid of?"

Anna shrank, but made no sound.

"You thought Car was a thief? Car Fairfax—your cousin—my nephew—a thief—what? You let Dr. Monk think so? You want to make me believe that he stole the Queen Anne bow? What, I say—what?"

Anna's hands dropped from her face. Her face was wet.

Then she heard a sound from behind the heavy leather screen that masked the door. The door was opening—some one was coming in. She turned blindly to the window.

William came in with a note. She heard her uncle say,

"What's this—what? I'm busy." And then, with an exclamation, "No, not in here—the study!"

William's footsteps retreated. She heard Mr. Carthew jerk himself up.

"I'll say good morning, Monk. I've got business waiting for me, and you'd better be getting along—what? Leave her to find her tongue."

He went out, taking Dr. Monk with him.

A faint wonder as to what was happening crept into her mind and disturbed it. She stood looking out, her thought clearing momentarily. She had felt a real fear under her uncle's battering questions. A sense of having come to an end was upon her. Anna Lang was dead. She would never live here again. She would never see Car again. It was all over. Everything would go on without her after this. They would not remember her, or be troubled by anything that she had done. Car would not remember her when he had married Isobel. She couldn't touch him, really. Burning up from the depths of her, came the desire to reach him, touch him, hurt him—force him to remember her. Like cold drops of this burning, fell the thought, "I shall never see him again."

She heard the door open behind her, and turned from the window.

Car Fairfax was coming into the room.

XLII

Car Fairfax's diary:

WHEN I FOUND MY MONEY WAS GONE, THERE WAS ONLY one thing to do, and that was to get away from streets and paving-stones and houses, and find somewhere to lie down for an hour.

I was pretty well all in when I reached what I was looking for, a heathery common with clumps of trees here and there. It had kept dry, thank goodness; the damp in the air which had made the roofs wet and slippery a few hours ago had gone. The heather was dry enough. I flung myself down on it and fell into a deep pit of sleep. I didn't dream and I didn't move, for I woke in the very same position in which I had thrown myself down.

I opened my eyes and sat up feeling stiff, dirty, and ragingly hungry. I must have slept for a good many hours, for by the sun it was getting on for ten o'clock.

There was a sun shining over low mist. Some of the

heather was still in bloom, the rest burnt red and brown. There were birches here and there, and young pines lifting out of the mist. The sky overhead was a very jolly pale blue. I glanced at my wrist watch. It was ten minutes to ten.

I did my best to clean myself up. My suit was in a frightful state. Besides the tear I knew about, there was another on the outside of my left sleeve. My hands looked as if I'd been cleaning a chimney with them. I found all that the drought had left of a pond, and got the worst of the grime off my face and hands. Then I had to find out where I was and get to Linwood.

I got there at eleven, and walked up to the front door feeling a good deal like a tramp. I wondered who would answer the bell. I was most awfully pleased when I saw William, because of course every one in the house might have changed for all I knew.

William hadn't changed a bit—same red hair, same freckles, same crooked nose. He seemed most awfully pleased to see me.

I had looked at my watch just before I rang the bell, and I thought that if it was eleven o'clock, I had better give Anna her message from Arbuthnot Markham before I did anything else, because she'd probably be catching the twelve-fifteen, so I asked for her.

He said she was in the library, and then put in,

"Mr. Carthew's just gone into the study, sir. Shall I tell him you're here?"

I said, "No, wait a minute. I want to see Miss Anna first." And then I crossed the hall and opened the library door.

Anna was over by the window. I got the impression that she had turned round in a hurry, and I'm sure I was the last person in the world she was expecting to see. She looked as if she had been crying.

I shut the door behind me and walked over to her.

"Good morning, Anna," I said.

She didn't say anything for a moment. She looked at me. I think she was trying to register shock, or something of that sort—or perhaps, for once in a way, she wasn't trying.

Come to think of it, it really must have been a bit of a shock to see me walk in like that, when she'd been picturing me safely put away in a nice quiet police cell.

"How did you get here?" she said at last.

"On my feet," I answered; and then, "I've got a message for you."

"*You* have?"

"Yes—from your husband."

She walked past me when I said that, until she came to Uncle John's chair with the high carved back. She took hold of it and leaned there.

I went on giving her the message:

"He told me to tell you you'd have to cross alone. He's gone on. He said some one would meet you. That's all."

I didn't want to stop there and talk to her, so I turned round and began to walk to the door. I hadn't gone a yard before she called me back.

"Is that all you've got to say to me?"

"Yes, that's all of it—he didn't tell me anything more. I've given you his message."

She didn't ask how he had come to tell me that. She stood holding the chair and looking at me across it. She had a bright color in her cheeks, a very bright color. I wished myself well out of the affair.

"A *message!*" she said in a deep, scornful sort of way. "Haven't you anything to say to me from yourself?"

"I don't know that I have, Anna," I said.

"*Nothing?*"

"Or too much," I said.

She pushed the chair away from her.

"Say it then!" she said violently.

I shrugged my shoulders.

"Why should I? You'd better be thinking about catching your train."

"There's time for that," said Anna—"and there's time for us to talk."

I looked at my watch.

"Not so very much, if you're going to leave Croydon at

three." I didn't say it to provoke her. She hadn't even got her hat on, and I thought she'd better not miss that train.

She took offense of course. I don't know why, because she couldn't really think I should have anything to say which she would enjoy hearing.

"Yes," she said, "I'm leaving Croydon at three. I'm going out of England, and I'm going out of your life. But before I go——"

My temper was getting up, and I cut in.

"For heaven's sake, Anna," I said, "put on your hat and go to your husband! And cut out all this futile film stuff!"

"Oh, I'm futile?" said Anna. "Futile! That's what you think of me, is it? I suppose I was futile when I turned you out of here? Futile? I had only to say a word to Uncle John and out you went—out of his house, out of his will, out of his thoughts—out of sight, out of mind. I did that! Was that futile?"

"Don't you think it was?" I said.

She laughed.

"I picked you up, and I threw you away! No—I haven't done. I'm going, you know—but before I go I want you to know just how *futile* I've been. You got quite a decent job when you went away from here—didn't you? Did you ever wonder why you didn't keep it—and why you didn't keep the next job, which wasn't quite such a good one—and the next—and the next—and the next?"

I had often wondered, but I wasn't going to say so.

"You needn't wonder any longer. I drove you out of every job you had. When it comes from a man's own family that he is—unreliable——" She paused. I wondered if she was frightened, for she drew back from me and put the table between us. "I drove you out of here—I drove you out of every job you had! And when I've driven you to prison— shall I still be—*futile?*"

I hadn't meant too let her make me angry, but the blood began to sing in my ears. I was on one side of the table, and she on the other. Neither of us had heard the door open. The screen masked it. Neither of us saw my uncle and some one else come into the room. Neither of us saw or heard anything but our own anger, until all at once I saw Anna's face change and I felt my uncle's hand on my shoulder and heard him say in his very loudest voice,

"What's all this—what? What's all this, I say?"

XLIII

I MOVED ROUND AND FACED HIM. I MOVED SLOWLY, BECAUSE the whole thing was such a surprise and my mind seemed to have stuck. I couldn't get it to work on this being my uncle's hand on my shoulder. I had a sort of dazed feeling which was probably due to my not having had anything to eat.

After a moment I began to get there. Uncle John was clapping me on the back and saying things in a loud angry voice; but the anger wasn't for me, it was for Anna.

"I heard what you said—what? You're very clever at persuading people, but you can't persuade me out of what I've heard with my own ears—what? You can't do that—not if you were twice as clever as you think you are! I heard what you said to him! Do you hear that—what? I heard you with my own ears, and how you have the face to stand there and look at me, I don't know!"

Anna was doing just what he said. She stood there, and she looked at him. The tips of her fingers just touched the table. I saw a picture once of the arrest of a Nihilist—I think it was called *The Order of Arrest*. I saw it when I was about then, and it made a great impression on me. There was a girl standing behind a table, just touching it. She had big dark eyes, and she was staring out of the picture as if she was looking at something dreadful. Anna was standing and looking just like that. I suppose it was wrong of me, but I couldn't help wondering whether she remembered the picture too. She didn't say anything; she just looked.

My uncle turned to me.

"She was trying to make me believe you'd taken the Queen Anne bow. We've had a burglary, and it's gone. She was trying to make me believe you'd taken it."

"It's sewn into the corner of my coat," I said.

He let go of me and stood back. It must have been a bit of a shock. If I hadn't been feeling so stupid, I might have broken it a bit more gently. He looked at me, and he looked at Anna, and Anna laughed.

My uncle thumped the table.

"And who put it there?" he said.

I didn't answer him. I went over to the bureau and picked up a penknife. I thought it was time the Queen Anne bow was back in its safe. I cut a stitch, pulled the thread and broke it. The bow was pushed right down into the hem. I took it out and laid it on the table by my uncle's hand. The setting was tarnished, and the diamonds looked dull, but the two big emeralds were like burning green water.

Anna's eyes went to them and stayed there. I expect she was thinking they would suit her. I don't know whether it went through her mind that she wouldn't ever wear them now.

"Who put it in your coat?" said my uncle. Then, when I didn't answer, he got angry and banged again. "You don't sew, do you—what? Some one put it there, and I want to know who!"

Anna laughed and stepped back from the table.

"You are very chivalrous all of a sudden, Car! Don't you know who sewed the bow in your coat?"

I said, "Yes. Don't you want to catch that train of yours, Anna?"

"Train?" said my uncle. "What train? Where's she going?"

The door opened, and William came in. He was trying to look as if he didn't know that there was something up. I felt sorry for him—it's his ambition to be the perfect butler, but he hasn't got a butler's face.

"The car's at the door, miss," he said. Then he tried not to look at us and went out again, fairly boiling with curiosity.

Anna saw her chance of a good exit and took it.

"I'm going to my *husband*," she said in her best tragedy voice.

My uncle's jaw dropped about half a foot.

"Your *what?*"

"My husband," said Anna. "I was married to Arbuthnot Markham a fortnight ago."

My uncle got very red in the face. He began to speak, stopped, and got redder still.

Anna looked at us both, very loftily.

"Good-by," she said, and she began to move towards the door; but she had only got half-way, when she stopped.

She looked round at me, and I thought she was going to say something, but she didn't. She went quickly out of the room and shut the door.

My uncle stared after her, angry and confused.

"Bless my soul! Married?" he said. "What? *Married? What's all this?*" He jerked his shoulders back as if he was throwing something off. "Well, I wish him joy of her!"

It was whilst he was speaking that I saw there was some one else in the room. I very nearly jumped, because there was a sort of effect of his having appeared out of nothing. As a matter of fact, as soon as I had time to think, I realized that he had come in with my uncle. I hadn't seen him, because he had been standing behind me. But Anna must have seen him. It struck me afterwards that that was why she didn't say whatever it was she was going to say before she went out of the room.

Well, I looked at him and pulled myself together. He was a little man with thin, neat hair, sharpish gray eyes, and the sort of nose that is made for a pince-nez. The pince-nez sat neatly on the nose. He wore a natty gent's suiting, and he took a very small size in black boots. I had never seen him before, but I knew him at once.

He put up his hand and fiddled with his pince-nez, and he said,

"Good morning, Mr. Fairfax."

It was Z.10 Smith.

It was such a relief that I felt as if a ton of bricks had been suddenly lifted off me. The beastliest part of the whole beastly nightmare I had been wandering about in was the perfectly damnable idea that Z.10 was acting for Anna. I had never been able quite to shake it off. Z.10 here, with my uncle, meant something quite different. This all went through my head very quickly.

I said, "Good morning, Mr. Smith," and my uncle stopped staring after Anna and slapped me on the back.

"Well," he said—"well? So you recognize him—what? What did you think? Did you guess he came from—me what?"

"No, I didn't," I said. I was feeling a bit angry. "I wish I had!" I said.

My uncle broke into a shout of laughter.

"You weren't meant to! No, no—not a bit of it! His name's really Smith, you know—Smith and Wilkins, Enquiry Agents."

He took me by the arm and walked me away to the other side of the room, dropping his voice till I could hardly hear what he said.

"Worried about you—began to think Anna'd been bamboozling me—found her out in a lie or two—makes you wonder whether it isn't all lies—what?" He gripped my arm. "I missed you, my boy. We've both got tempers—runs in the family—said a lot of things that didn't make it easy to climb down, both of us—what?"

I looked round and saw Z.10 vanishing discreetly. I heard the door close behind him. I don't think my uncle noticed. He went on, still holding me tight and mumbling between embarrassment and discretion:

"Thought I'd find out how you were getting on—couldn't

do it myself—got him instead—Smith—Perkins recommended him—very efficient—what?—discreet—confidential—had to take him into my confidence a good deal—about Anna—what?"

"She knew," I said.

"Yes—Smith said so—said she butted in—sent that fellow Markham ferreting round—kept the appointment Smith had made with you——" He broke into a half laugh and slapped my shoulder. "He saw her carry you off, and didn't know what to make of it, by Jove!"

"How did she know?" I asked.

"Listened when I was telephoning. You don't think of things like that—not with your own family—but that's what she must have done—eavesdropped—opened letters too, I shouldn't wonder!" He made a sound of disgust. "Who's this fellow she's married? He'll be sorry for himself before he's through—what?"

"Or she will," I said.

My uncle looked up hopefully.

"What? Is he that sort? I hope he is—I hope he is!"

Then he let go of me and stepped back.

"You don't bear me a grudge, do you—what? I didn't think you did—not when you spoke about me."

"When I spoke about you?"

He got very red.

"Perhaps it wasn't altogether fair—not playing the game—what? But I wouldn't have held it up against you if you'd grumbled a bit."

I hadn't the slightest idea what he was driving at.

He turned plum-color.

"The other night!" he said explosively. "Damn it! What was I to do—what? I wanted to see you—couldn't think of any other way—wanted to know—what you felt about me—got my pride as well as you, you know."

My mind was a complete blank. I suppose I looked as puzzled as I felt.

He made a sound like "Tch-h!" and blew out his cheeks.

"Back of the car," he said—"what? The other night—
Olding Crescent—what?"

I got there suddenly.

"You were in the back of the car the other night when I
was talking to Z.10 Smith in Olding Crescent?"

He nodded and looked past me.

"What made you hit on Olding Crescent?" I said, partly
to relieve his embarrassment, and partly because I wanted to
know. I couldn't remember just what I had said about him to
Z.10, and I thought we'd better get off the subject.

He seemed relieved at my question.

"Good place—what? Lonely place—dark—no traffic—
what?"

"What made you hit on it?"

He burst out laughing.

"Anna put me on to it—dined there with that Markham
fellow, and I came down from my club and picked her up,
and I thought to myself it was as lonely a place as you'd
find within ten miles of town." He stopped laughing rather
suddenly. "She's gone—and a good riddance. And now
she's gone, you—you'll come back home—won't you, my
boy? The place wants looking after. Jenkins can't keep up
with it. He want to go and live with his married daughter in
London. There's no accounting for tastes—what?"

I supposed he was offering me the agent's job, but he
hadn't said so. I thought it wasn't any good beating about
the bush, so I asked him straight out.

"What do you think?" he said. "I want you back. And
there's the job if you'll take it—and the little Manor House
by and by if you want to get married."

I thought about Isobel. She had always wanted to live
there, and I had said—I had said—that the only house we
should ever have was a castle in the air. Things danced in
front of my eyes, and I suppose I must have looked queer,
for my uncle took me by the arm.

"Here—hold up!" he said. "What's the matter?"

I said, "It's—very good of you."

He said, "Nonsense! Nonsense!" Then he let go of me

and blew his nose violently. "You ought to have let me know. When Smith told me—" He blew his nose. "Such straits—no idea—you ought to have let me know—what? Damn proud young pup!" He blew his nose again.

I heard the door open, and walked away to the window, because I wasn't just feeling like confronting William. It wasn't William.

It was Isobel.

My uncle turned round with a grunt.

"I'm busy," he said; and then he saw who it was and went to meet her.

She didn't see me. I was up by the window, and the curtain screened me. She was looking so beautifully happy that I wondered what had happened. She took both my uncle's hands and said,

"Don't be busy for just a minute, Mr. Carthew, because I've come on purpose to tell you that Car and I are engaged."

And then she kissed him—at least that's what it looked like to me. She says he kissed her.

My uncle turned round and roared at the top of his voice,

"What? What? What's all this? Car—I say—what? Engaged? Bless my soul! Come and kiss her yourself! What?"

I came.

XLIV

Corinna Lee to Peter Lymington:

PETER DARLING,

A great many things have been happening. When

you get to the end of this letter you will know why I am calling you "darling." If you don't like it, you had better cable right away, the same as you did about not being married to that Fay creature. First of all, you needn't get all puffed up about her being in love with you, because she never thought about you at all. She was just head over ears in love with Car Fairfax, and she said she was married to you so as to keep him right there looking after her, which he wouldn't have done if he hadn't thought you wanted him to. Crazy—isn't it?

Peter honey, everything has come right. Isn't it just perfectly splendid? It all happened so quick I'm still taking long breaths and pinching myself to see if I'm awake. Cousin John and Car are friends again. Anna Lang has run away with a dreadful man called Arbuthnot Markham. And Car is going to marry Isobel, and I am going to marry you. So now you know why you are "Peter Darling."

You see, Car got engaged to Isobel, so I couldn't have him. And then I got your letter, and it did sound as if you were just rather fond of me, and then I felt terribly homesick and kind of alone in the world, so I sent Poppa a cable—a real long cable—and I'm not going to tell you what I said. And Poppa cabled back—and I'm not going to tell you what he said either, but we're engaged.

I hope you will like being engaged. Isobel and Car are perfectly sweet together. He looks at her as if she was the sun and the moon and the stars and everything beautiful you can think of. I don't suppose you'd want to look that way at me. If you would there will be just time for you to write and tell me about it. Car and Isobel are getting married at the end of October and as soon as the wedding is over I am coming home. I was just going to write "I am coming home to you," but then I thought I wouldn't, because you don't know about being engaged to me yet. Of course you will know it by the time you get this far—so perhaps I'll say it after all.

Peter darling, I'm coming home to you.

Your

CORINNA

The End